FLAVIA'S SECRET

Spirited, young scribe Flavia hopes for freedom. She and her fellow slaves in Aquae Sulis (modern Bath) have served the Lady Valeria for many years, but their mistress' death brings a threat to Flavia's dream: her new master Marcus Brucetus, a charismatic, widowed officer toughened in the forest of Germania. Flavia finds him overwhelmingly attractive but she is aware of the danger. To save her life and those of her 'family' she has forged a note from her mistress. If her deception is discovered, all the slaves may die.

FLAVIA'S SECRET

Flavia's Secret

by

Lindsay Townsend

Magna Large Print Books
Long Preston, North Yorkshire,
BD23 4ND, England.

British Library Cataloguing in Publication Data.

Townsend, Lindsay
    Flavia's secret.

    A catalogue record of this book is
    available from the British Library

    ISBN   978-0-7505-3657-8

First published in Great Britain in 2008 by
www.BookStrand.com

Cover illustration © Nik Keevil by arrangement with
Arcangel Images

The moral right of the author has been asserted

Published in Large Print 2013 by arrangement with
Lindsay Quicke

Magna Large Print is an imprint of Library Magna Books Ltd.

Printed and bound in Great Britain by
T.J. (International) Ltd., Cornwall, PL28 8RW

To Alan, with love

Chapter 1

Britannia, 206 A. D.

Flavia was sweeping leaves when he came out of the villa. Carrying a brazier, he strolled down the steps and passed the frosted lavender bushes with that loose-limbed stride of his, looking as if he owned the place. Which he did, she conceded. Marcus Brucetus now owned the villa and everyone inside it.

She clutched the broom close and darted behind one of the columns fringing the square courtyard and its central open space, whispering, 'Please.'

Please do not see me, she meant. She wanted him to leave, to be an absentee landlord of this small estate in provincial Britannia. It would be safer for everyone if he left. He had been watching her at the funeral, scrutinizing her with thoughtful dark eyes. She hoped he had forgotten her since then.

She risked peeping round the column. He had set the brazier in the middle of the courtyard, beside the ivy-clad statue of the god Pan, and was coaxing the fire into leaping tongues of flame. In the red glow of dawn and the orange glare of the brazier, she could

11

see him plainly: tall and long legged, his simple dark red tunic showing off muscular shoulders. Above tanned, lean features his short, dark brown hair looked as tough and straight as a boar's pelt. He was a tribune, off-duty and no longer in armor, but still a soldier and a Roman, one of the conquerors of her country.

'Come here, Flavia,' he said quietly, without raising his head.

Disconcerted at being discovered and more so by his remembering her name, Flavia stepped out of the shadows of the peristyle and approached, her rag-shod feet soundless on the icy gravel path.

'Gaius said that I would find you out here.'

Another shock, she thought. He spoke her language perfectly. Satisfied with the fire, he looked her up and down, studying her flyaway hair and wiry figure, her baggy, patched dress of undyed wool, one of the cook's cast offs. She gasped as he took the broom from her.

'I ask you again – is sweeping not Sulinus' job? He is the gardener.'

'He's chopping wood,' Flavia stammered, ashamed and alarmed at having missed Marcus Brucetus' first question. She was conscious of his height and strength, both in stark contrast to the frail, elderly bodies of the male household slaves.

'Sweeping is one of your tasks?'

12

Flavia nodded. 'When Lady Valeria was alive, she wanted the courtyard kept tidy. We are a small household, sir. My mistress preferred to live quietly, with a few close attendants.'

'Four ageing slaves and you,' Brucetus corrected, 'My adopted mother's female scribe.' He shook his head, tossing the broom casually from hand to hand. 'Valeria never liked a man to tell her anything, and she always did pick the unusual over the conventional.'

Ignoring his amusement at her expense, Flavia fought down panic. *Surely this Roman would not be so cruel as to sell the older servants? Surely he would not separate Gaius from his Agrippina, or Sulinus from Livia?* She swallowed the rising knot in her throat. 'We are all loyal, sir, and we know what the house needs to run smoothly.'

'Indeed.' Looking into Flavia's bright gray eyes, he smiled and gave the broom back to her. 'Be at peace. I don't throw servants out into the streets to starve: loyalty cuts both ways. When you know me, you will see this.'

'Sir?' Flavia felt confused by this unexpected candor. She knew that she, more than any of the household, should be wary of this Marcus Brucetus, but she could also still feel the warmth of his hand on the broom handle. Over the crackle of the brazier fire, she could hear his steady breathing. 'Thank you,' she murmured, and turned to go.

13

'Wait,' he commanded. 'I have some questions. Now that the official mourning period is over, it is time.'

Flavia's heart began to race, but she did not think she had betrayed herself until Marcus said firmly, 'Don't stand there shivering. Warm yourself by the brazier. That is why it is out here, so we can talk in private.'

Flavia took a sideways step towards the glowing charcoal. She was trembling, but not from the cold. She was afraid of what he might ask.

'How old are you?'

'Almost eighteen, sir.'

His black eyebrows came together in a frown, swiftly replaced by a grin. 'Don't try to fool me, Flavia. You are young enough to be playing with dolls, a spry little thing like yourself.'

Flavia said nothing. If he underrated her, so much the better. *Above all, let him not ask too many questions about the death of her beloved mistress.* She tightened her grip on the broom and wished herself far away.

'No indignant denial? Maybe you are almost eighteen.' Marcus stretched a hand towards her, giving a grunt of amusement as Flavia stiffened. 'You are almost as skittish as my horse. You have a leaf in your hair – see?' He plucked a copper beech leaf from one of her blonde plaits, his thumb pushing her soft fringe away from her forehead. 'Such smooth

14

skin,' he murmured. 'You could make a fortune in the great bath-house in this city, selling your secrets for that skin.' He flicked the leaf onto the brazier. 'How long have you lived in Aquae Sulis?'

'All my life.'

'With the Lady Valeria?'

'No, sir. She was the second person – this is the second household in which I have served.'

'Were your parents free?'

'No,' Flavia whispered. 'They were not.'

She tried to lower her head but, quick as she was, Marcus was too fast, catching her chin in his hand. She stared into his dark blue eyes, hating herself for the tide of color that she could feel sweeping up her face.

He watched her a moment. 'Truly, you Celts are a proud people and you, little Flavia, you are so stubborn you will not even admit your condition. I can acknowledge the vagaries of fate that make us as we are when our situations might easily be reversed, but mark this–' He lightly shook her head and then released her. 'You are mine now.'

'Do you think I don't know?' Horrified at her own free way of speaking, Flavia clamped her jaws so sharply together that her head seemed to ring. It was instead the sounds of the metal-workers' shops beginning another day's work, she realized. Around her, hidden by the walls of the town villa, Aquae Sulis was

15

stirring into life.

'I shall let that go, but be careful.' Marcus hooked his thumbs into his tunic belt and leaned back against the marble statue of Pan. 'Do you remember them, your father and mother?'

'A little.' Flavia was unsure what to make of this man. One second he was looming over her, threatening, the next patient, rippling the fingers of one hand to invite her to talk. She was reluctant to share her memories with a Roman, but knew she must say something. 'My mother had a beautiful singing voice. My father was very quick.'

'Like you.'

Again, he had surprised her. In the silence that fell between them, Flavia heard a young street trader in one of the alleyways begin his piping cry, 'Sweet chestnuts, freshly roasted!' She could hear the rumble of hand-carts and smell the aroma of freshly baked bread. All were signs of her city waking up. A day her mistress, the formidable yet generous Lady Valeria, would not see.

Trying not to think of the old lady, Flavia looked up as Sulinus wandered past, dressed in his swathe of ragged cloaks – as many as the gardener could find in this frosty weather. A dark head blocked her view, a face in profile, gleaming in the red winter morning light like a cast of bronze, although no statue had such watchful eyes.

16

'Have you people no proper clothes?' Marcus muttered, a question Flavia knew she did not have to answer. She found herself watching his mouth: there was a small ragged scar close to his lower lip. His forearms carried several scars, the results of sword cuts in many skirmishes. A warrior, her senses warned, but even so, she was unprepared for his next question.

'And where is your sweetheart in this city? An apprentice cobbler, perhaps? Or do you prefer someone with softer hands, another scribe like yourself? A desk man!'

'Follow me!' he barked, and strode along the gravel path, his sandaled feet stamping through ice puddles.

Flavia scrambled to keep pace with him. Whatever happened, she did not want him taking his ill temper out on Gaius or Agrippina or any of the others. These were all the family she had and she was determined no harm would come to them. No harm, especially, from what she had done.

'No.' Marcus ducked under the peristyle and then stopped, slapping one hand against the nearest column. He turned back to face her, his face rigid with distaste. *Memories of Germania do no good here,* he thought. He stepped out into the courtyard again and smiled at her, with his eyes more than his mouth. 'We were speaking of your past, not mine.' He took her free hand in his, running his fingertips over her palm. 'These hands have held more than a pen. What else do you do here?' And before Flavia could answer, 'Let us walk in the air. The house is still hers to me – Lady Valeria's. I am not surprised that you miss her.'

'Every day,' Flavia admitted. 'She was a good lady.'

'An honorable woman and a shrewd judge of character. I enjoyed our correspondence.' He gave her a searching look. 'Did you write her letters?'

'Not all,' Flavia said quickly. Her mistress had been writing or dictating letters to Marcus for the last four years, ever since the Lady Valeria had met the tribune on her single trip to Rome. Flavia had no idea why her mistress had made him her heir, but they regularly corresponded, especially in the last year after Marcus' military career brought him to Britannia, to the northern city of Eboracum.

Flavia had never seen the tribune until he rode down from the north in response to her own letter to him, informing him of the Lady Valeria's sudden death. Now that she had met him, Flavia only knew that he made her uneasy in all kinds of ways.

They had returned to the brazier and the statue. Flavia leaned her broom against the statue and began to tease away a strand of ivy from the squat marble figure. Marcus had not yet released her other hand. She was wary of that and of having to look at him.

'The letters I received from your lady – yours was the rounder hand?'

'Yes, sir,' Flavia agreed, wishing that she did not blush so easily. They were coming to dangerous ground again, and she said nothing more.

'Could either of your parents write?'

'No, sir.'

'So you didn't learn it from them.' Marcus lowered his head towards hers. 'From your first master, perhaps?'

Flavia shook her head. 'I was very young, then.'

Marcus' fingers tightened around hers, almost a comforting gesture, and then he let her go. 'How old were you when you were separated from your mother and father?'

Flavia stole a glance at him, but his face was unreadable. 'We were not separated. I lost them – when I was eight.' Her voice faltered.

Marcus crouched beside the statue so that he was looking up at her. 'Go on,' he said quietly.

'There was a fire in the slave quarters. My father got out, but he went back for my mother and the roof fell in on them both. I was told this. I was not there. I was with the daughter of the first mistress, walking with her by the river. I had been ordered to play with her.'

Marcus saw the change come over the

19

small blonde slave. When he had first seen her, standing so grave and quiet beside the cremation pyre at the funeral of the Lady Valeria, she had reminded him, piercingly, of little Aurelia, his own daughter. Flavia had the same delicate appearance, the same golden tumble of hair, even down to the way it tended to curl by her ears. In these things she might have been a mirror of Aurelia, who was now dead. Little Aurelia and her mother both dead of fever in the wilderness of Germania, five years ago.

The memory had almost overwhelmed him a moment ago, but he should not take out his grief on Flavia. He had thought her a soft house slave, as insubstantial as a water spirit, but her hands were toughened with years of work and she had endured loss. He could hear it in her voice.

'They sold me soon after the fire. Perhaps they were afraid I would sicken and die. Everything was an effort to me. I could hardly run, much less play.'

She would run well, Marcus thought. Her body – the little he could see under that patched gray shift – looked straight. Skinny, one part of his mind said, but then he had surprised himself by asking about her sweetheart. A crass inquiry. Marcus scowled and listened to the rest of her story.

'I was sold when I was eight years old and the Lady Valeria bought me. She gave me a home, a new family. She taught me to read and write. I owe everything to her,' Flavia said simply.

He could hear her honesty, and something more. The girl was hiding something. Then he shrugged. Although his father owned slaves, this was the first time he had done so for himself and only because of Valeria's inheritance. He felt uncomfortable with the whole business of slave ownership, especially a girl as young and pretty as this. *What poor wretch of a slave did not have secrets?* 'Tell me your duties,' he ordered.

'I was my lady's scribe and personal maid,' Flavia answered crisply.

'In place of the foolish woman who used to style her hair? Yes, I remember Valeria scribbling something to that effect on one of her letters.' Marcus Brucetus smiled at Flavia's stare. 'So you will do the same for me?'

Flavia ripped another strand of ivy from the statue. 'If that is your wish.' She whirled about and dropped the ivy onto the brazier so that her back was to Marcus Brucetus.

'Even your neck goes red when you blush,' was his smug response, a remark that made Flavia long to use her broom on him. Surprised at her vehemence, she tended the fire, glad to be doing something. He chuckled, rising to his feet. 'You are not used to dealing with men, are you?'

'I talk to Gaius and Sulinus every day,'

21

Flavia shot back, a reply that made him laugh out loud.

'Indeed! But I see that Valeria was right. How did she describe you?'

Behind her, Flavia could hear Marcus Brucetus tapping his face with his fingers. She clenched her teeth, part of her angry that her mistress had mentioned her, part of her alarmed. If the Lady Valeria had regularly added more than her signature to her letters before sealing them, what else had she told Marcus Brucetus?

Please do not let harm come to the others, Flavia prayed. If she had done wrong, only she should pay.

Marcus Brucetus cleared his throat. '*A nettlesome little thing. May need watching.* Valeria was a shrewd old bird, would you not say?' Flavia remembered the Lady Valeria walking in this courtyard only a few weeks earlier, in a sunny day in late summer, when the roses were in bloom. Her mistress, who had once been as straight as a spear, had been forced to lean on Flavia's arm and use a stick. She had complained vigorously.

'Look at me, shriveled like an old fig!' Lady Valeria had pinched one of her arms and then continued, 'I used to stride around this garden and now I shuffle. Don't you dare help me on these steps, girl! I want to do it myself.'

She had been an independent woman, the

widow of a Roman knight. Her mother had been a British princess and Lady Valeria, tall and handsome in her youth, had become a learned and decisive woman. With her iron gray hair in its severe, old-fashioned bun, her plain green gowns, her penetrating brown eyes and her restless curiosity, Lady Valeria had displayed another kind of Celtic pride. She had fought the infirmities of age.

'I've buried a husband and a daughter. I've endured the worst,' she often told Flavia. 'Let it all come! These aching limbs and failing eyes. When I become too bored I shall end it. Now that I have adopted Marcus Brucetus, he can perform the funeral rites.'

Flavia never liked to hear her mistress speak in this way, but in the end Lady Valeria, proud Romano-British matron, had chosen a Roman death. Leaving her papers all in order and dressing in her richest gown and in her best jewels, Valeria had told her attendants to leave her alone in her study for the evening. There she had taken a draught of poison in a glass of her favorite wine and died, sitting in her wicker chair, her head supported comfortably by cushions. Flavia had found her the next morning.

Remembering, Flavia shuddered. She had not cried since Lady Valeria died and she did not weep now, but every night since then she had come awake in the middle of darkness with the question, *Why?* on her lips.

'It is a pity,' Marcus Brucetus remarked.

Restored to the present by his voice, Flavia blinked and turned to face him. Strangely, his presence tempered her grief, if only because she had to be wary of him. 'What is, sir?' she asked.

'Your lady. My adoptive mother.' Marcus Brucetus pointed a long bronzed arm towards the great bath house and shrine of Aquae Sulis, the heart of the city. 'I wrote often to her of the virtues of the hot springs of this city, but no doubt she continued to bathe no more than her usual twice a week.'

'She did,' Flavia agreed faintly. Lady Valeria had considered more than two baths a week to be wallowing in luxury, a sign of moral weakness.

'But the winters were always hard for her,' Marcus Brucetus said. 'She never complained, but I could tell.'

'Often in the darkest months she would speak of making her final journey to join her husband Petronius,' Flavia found herself admitting.

'Now she has done so – and we are the losers.' Frowning, Marcus Brucetus watched a raven floating over the thatched and tiled roofs of the villas and shops. With a curse, he turned and strode over to the nearest of the four strips of garden that bordered the courtyard's central marble statue. He snatched up a handful of earth, returned to the brazier

24

and threw the frozen soil over the fire, instantly extinguishing the flames.

'Don't worry, I will carry this back into the house myself, later,' he said wryly, catching Flavia's anxious glance at the large, heavy bronze brazier. 'We have said enough here and I have something to show you.'

He moved off, beckoning her to accompany him.

Flavia's spirits sank further when Marcus Brucetus led them straight through the villa to the small cozy room Lady Valeria had chosen to be her study. Closing the door, drawing the door curtain across, Marcus sat at her desk on the simple stool that Flavia had used in this room. Someone, possibly Marcus himself, had moved the wicker chair in which her mistress had died to the darkest corner of the room, a small mercy for which she was deeply grateful.

There were no windows, but Marcus Brucetus lit an oil lamp, placing it on one end of the desk. He picked a stylus from the desk, then put it aside.

'You found her here,' he said, reaching for a jug and a cup, both of red Samian ware, both new to this house.

'I did.' As he poured a cupful of wine, Flavia wondered if she should have offered to serve him.

Across the desk, he stared back at her, his

dark blue eyes bright with amusement. 'I can do many things for myself. Often I prefer to. Now are you going to sit down so we can talk comfortably?'

Flavia looked hastily about the room. Aside from the wicker chair, which she would not use, there was only the blue and gold couch set against one of the plain plastered walls and the wolf skin rug in front of the desk. Lady Valeria had never permitted any of her servants, even Gaius who had been with her for twenty years, to sit on the couch.

She began to make an excuse. 'Cook will be expecting me to go with her to market for the shopping.'

'Cook can take someone else with her today, but never mind. If you want to stand, you can.' Marcus took a drink of wine and resumed. 'You also found Lady Valeria's final letter?'

Flavia felt as if her throat was closing up, but she managed to say clearly enough, 'Yes.'

Marcus studied his cup a moment. 'I know this is difficult for you, Flavia, but I am trying to be clear in my own mind that my adoptive mother passed away peacefully.'

'Oh, she did, sir,' Flavia said. 'Her face, it was so calm.' She stopped as Marcus held up a hand.

'There were no signs of disturbance in this

26

room, no signs of a struggle?'

Flavia shook her head. 'What are you saying?' she whispered.

'Nothing.' Marcus drained his cup and rose to his feet. 'I suppose I cannot quite believe that she has gone. Wait here a moment.' He walked past her and out of the room.

Once she was alone, Flavia put her face in her hands and tried to take a deep breath. She knew that in the end, Lady Valeria had chosen her own path, a path which she would never take because her secret Christian faith forbade it. Although her mistress had never questioned her about her beliefs, Flavia guessed that the Lady Valeria had known that her young female scribe had been distressed each time she spoke of choosing death and so, in a final kindness, Lady Valeria had acted without telling her.

That was what Flavia believed, which was why she had done what she had. Finding her mistress sitting peacefully at her desk, looking as if she had fallen asleep, Flavia had written a final message as if from Lady Valeria, faithfully copying the hand of her mistress. She had done this because only two days earlier Gaius had rushed in from the market, deeply distressed by a rumor going around Aquae Sulis that a nobleman had died in Rome in suspicious circumstances and that his entire household of slaves had been put to death.

'They were all crucified!' Gaius had shouted in the kitchen, his usually carefully combed-over hair falling into his staring eyes and his wrinkled, homely face bleached with distress. 'Even the children!' When she had embraced him to comfort him, Flavia had felt the old slave trembling.

That remembered horror had remained with her, a goad and a warning that she must continue to be careful. Marcus Brucetus was a soldier, used to dealing in death. If he decided that he did not trust Lady Valeria's servants, might he not be tempted to make a clean sweep of them?

He was coming back; she could hear his quick firm tread on the floor tiles outside the study. Flavia let her hands drop by her sides and checked her appearance in the faintly distorting reflection of the metal tray which held the Samian wine jug. A pair of wide bright eyes, flushed forehead, cheekbones, and chin and trembling full mouth flashed into view before she stepped back onto the rug and straightened, ready to face him.

'Read this.' He thrust a piece of papyrus at her.

She knew what it would be, but even braced for the shock, Flavia felt herself begin to sway. She blinked and her own writing swam back into view, her hand faking the Lady Valeria's spare, spindly scrawl. A hasty letter, written in panic and in fear of the pos-

28

sible consequences should any kind of suspicion fall on the household.

'Read it aloud,' Marcus commanded, standing in front of her.

'To my adopted son and heir, Marcus Brucetus, greetings–'

'Get on with it,' he growled.

Flavia skipped the rest of the opening. The papyrus shook slightly in her hand as she read on. 'I am sorry if what I've done here causes you any grief, but you should know that it is no hardship for me to leave this painful life. I have chosen my own end willingly, secure in the knowledge that I will be reunited in the hereafter with my beloved husband Petronius.'

'Stop.' Marcus cupped her chin in his hand and raised her face. 'Why did she not free Gaius or Agrippina?' His voice was soft, but the planes of his face were unyielding. 'Would that not have been a final generous act?'

'I don't know why!' Flavia tried to tear herself free, but even as his grip fell from her chin, Marcus clamped his arms around her middle.

'No, you don't.' He gave her a shake and, as Flavia's hands automatically came up to fend off possible blows, he dragged her against himself, trapping her arms against his chest.

'Is that what you believe, Flavia? That your mistress was not thinking when she acted?'

His arms were tight around her and, just for

a moment in his arms, Flavia experienced a sense of peace that she had never known before. In that second she spoke her heart. 'It was unlike her to forget loyal service, but then in the end she may not have had much time.'

Flavia closed her eyes, seeing Lady Valeria in the wicker chair, her eyes closed, one hand lying flat on her desk as if stretching for her stylus. That was what must have happened. That was why her mistress had left no note.

'How did she come by the poison?'

At the sound of Marcus' voice, Flavia started, suddenly becoming aware of him again, making her even more conscious of the gulf between them, free and not. He could do virtually what he liked to her, to any of the others, and nothing would stop him, least of all Roman law or morality.

'I don't know,' she stammered, looking up into his eyes. She wanted to plead for the others, but in the end it was the grave intensity of his face that made her add purely for his peace of mind, 'The day before she died, Lady Valeria went out alone to the baths. There was a healer there, an apothecary she knew well.'

'You think she bought the hemlock from him?'

Flavia nodded, afraid to speak in case she broke down. For the hundredth time, she wished Lady Valeria had not done it.

'If only she had spoken,' she murmured. 'I used to massage her with oils – she told me that they helped, that they eased the pain.' She could not go on.

'I will talk to this apothecary.' Marcus was staring at her again, his eyes as brilliant as a falcon's above his aquiline nose. 'You have eased my mind, Flavia.'

'I have?'

'Indeed. In some ways, at least.' His mouth quivered with suppressed amusement, but even as Flavia sagged slightly against him relieved that he was not angry, Marcus lowered his head.

For an instant, she was actually convinced that he was going to kiss her, but instead he gave her hair a quick tug. 'Are you listening?'

What else would I be doing? Flavia thought, but she stopped herself from saying it. She was still locked into his arms. 'May I sit down?' she asked, despising herself for asking, but wanting to be away from this disturbing man who remained a danger to her and to the rest of the household.

Marcus lowered his arms. 'There is your usual seat.'

Flavia walked stiffly round the desk and sat on the stool, her head high as she stared at him.

'Comfortable?' he asked, in mock solicitude.

'Perfectly, thank you,' Flavia answered,

31

determined to show nothing, although her hands tingled with the desire to strike back.

'Good! I like my people to be comfortable.' Marcus began to pace across the wolf-skin rug, crossing the room from side to side.

'You are listening?' he asked a second time.

'Yes, sir.' Flavia found herself becoming apprehensive again. Her new master's next words did nothing to dispel her sense of foreboding.

'Then, I admit it, Flavia: I am puzzled. I find it curious that in the last letter I received from her, Valeria told me that she was looking forward to meeting me during the mid-winter holiday of the Saturnalia! Why should she say that, and then do what she did?'

Marcus stopped pacing, giving her a long, considering look, his black lashes and brows sooty in the flickering light of the oil lamp. 'You didn't know this? You didn't write that letter?'

'No!' Flavia was too shocked to be polite. 'You know I did not!'

'Yes, the differences in the hand-writing; I had forgotten those for the moment.' A glib answer that convinced Flavia he had done no such thing. As she stared back at him, Marcus began to explain.

'Lady Valeria was looking forward to meeting me in Aquae Sulis. She seemed keen to discuss a recent imperial appointment with me; that of Lucius Maximus as a decurion, with a duty to collect taxes. For some reason, my adoptive mother disliked Lucius Maximus. She called him – what was it? "A traitor to the living and the dead, a grave robber, an unholy fellow. Not the sort of man anyone should make responsible for taxes in a city like this." Yet Lucius Maximus is related to her through marriage: he is a Roman, one of the lady's own class. So I do not understand.'

Marcus raised and spread his hands. 'Do you understand it?'

'I have never heard of Lucius Maximus,' Flavia answered at once. 'Is he a friend of yours?'

The instant she spoke, she regretted the easy jibe, while at the same time being astonished at the words coming out of her mouth. She had never spoken this way to Lady Valeria, never so ... freely? Risking a glance at Marcus, she saw him become dangerously still, the dark stubble on his chin defining his clenched jaw. Flavia's hands bunched into fists on her lap, then realizing what she was doing, she jumped to her feet, the stool scraping on the floor tiles.

'Don't think that because the desk is between us, I cannot reach you,' he growled. He leaned over the papers and writing tablets and pinched out the lamp. 'For your information, I do not know Lucius Maximus,

33

but I have arranged to meet him at the baths this afternoon. You will be there as my scribe.'

His darkly handsome face took on a wicked look. 'Perhaps you can massage me? Use some of the soothing oils you used on the Lady Valeria.'

Grinning, he turned and strolled from the room.

Chapter 2

Marcus spent the rest of the morning in the tablinium, an airy dining room with cheerful red and yellow walls. Here, Lady Valeria had received guests and those seeking her help or favor and Marcus did the same, opening the door and gate leading out into the street so that people would know the master of the house was at home.

As she hurried across the frosted court-yard-garden to the kitchen, Flavia spotted several people hovering in the street, waiting to be admitted. One, a tall, gaunt Celt in a threadbare cloak, she recognized as the freedman-manager of the farm Lady Valeria had owned, a place Flavia had never seen and which now belonged to Marcus Brucetus.

She sped along a dark corridor to the kitchen at the back of the house, where she and the other slaves did most of their indoor work and where Gaius and Agrippina slept, snug beside the fireplace. Flavia slept in another room, a tiny, windowless chamber with a sloping roof, damp in winter and sweltering in summer.

Ducking into this room, Flavia caught up her spindle. It seemed that she spent every spare moment in spinning the thread needed to patch clothes. She walked into the kitchen, finding the other servants seated around the big central table. They stopped talking the instant she appeared.

'What?' Flavia asked, irritated afresh at Marcus. Usually this kitchen was a place of easy banter, but with his coming everyone was tense. She glanced at the wary faces in turn: bandy-legged old Gaius with his fine-boned features and wispy red hair and moustache; his Egyptian born wife Agrippina, with her firm, round body and nimble cook's fingers; the sallow gardener Sulinus, squat and weather-beaten, wearing his boots and hat even indoors and lastly, his partner Livia with her lank brown hair and tired eyes. This winter, like her old mistress, Livia had withered. Flavia crossed the room and laid a gentle hand on her shoulder.

'Are your teeth hurting again?' she asked, seeing how Livia hid her mouth with a hand.

Livia smiled, showing a few broken teeth,

and shook her head.

'What is it?' Flavia said. They were using pestles and mortars, and the smell of crushed spices was heavy in the air. 'New instructions?'

'No, girl,' Agrippina said. She waved her own mortar, full of something – Flavia could not see what – towards the unlit oven. 'See if you can get that thing in there to stop whining. Take him out in the yard.'

Flavia could hear nothing and it was obvious that her four fellow slaves – the only family she had ever really known – wanted her gone. What were they keeping from her? She almost asked, but did not want to pry, especially as a shout of 'Gaius!' from the tablinium had the old slave growing pale.

'Best be quick,' his wife warned as Gaius limped from the kitchen, calling, 'Coming, sir!'

Pitying his fear, Flavia knelt by the cold oven and drummed her fingers on its roof. 'Here, boy.' Her heart sank as she heard the low growl in response.

'Been in there all night. Gaius forgot to block the oven bottom and he crept in. I have tried to tempt him with a honey cake, but he will not eat,' Agrippina said, resuming her grinding with a practiced hand. 'Honestly, he is a blessed nuisance with his pining – the master will want fresh bread for dinner and we will have to clean out the dog hairs first.'

Flavia nodded, understanding that this would be her job. She clicked her fingers and tried to sound like Lady Valeria. 'Nero! Come!'

The soot-grimed head of a white terrier appeared in the arched oven doorway, followed by a scrawny body as Nero trotted out across the beaten earth floor. Sniffing Flavia's outstretched hand, he whined and turned tail.

'No!' Moving almost as fast as a catapult ball in her eagerness to protect her kitchen, Agrippina planted herself in front of the oven, a raised long spoon ready to fend off the trembling animal.

'I've got him.' Enduring scratches and nips, Flavia gathered up the thin little beast and carried him off into the open air.

Crouching in the shadow of the columns where she had tried to hide from Marcus that morning, Flavia cuddled Nero in her lap. She stroked him slowly, feeling the ribs under the sparse fur. Poor Nero, who did not understand that his mistress had gone.

Rubbing her eyes, Flavia sat on a stone bench and began to tease out another length of wool from her spindle, working awkwardly in the winter air and with the dog on her knee. Only last month, Nero would have been grabbing at the spindle; now he had no interest in play. She took a crust of stale bread – her own breakfast – from the folds of her baggy dress and balanced it on her knee. 'Here, boy.' She hoped to coax Nero into eating.

Nero never stirred. As Flavia spun, she watched the comings and goings from the house. Everyone was seen and dispatched in a brisk way – with military precision, she thought, caught between a smile and a frown.

Soon there were only a few people left waiting to see the new owner of Lady Valeria's town house. In the middle of the courtyard, a huddled knot of favor-seekers stamped their feet and blew on their hands, their breath hanging in the still air. A balding Celt with his right arm in a sling walked out of the house, his interview with Marcus Brucetus at an end. The man's plain face was full of wonder as he stared at the bag of coins in his hand.

'Where is that girl?'

Agrippina emerged from the kitchen door, her dark eyes narrowed to slits as she scoured the figures in the courtyard-garden. About to rise to her feet, Flavia heard the cook cry, 'Ah!' and watched her march down a gravel path towards a slim young woman who had waved from the street.

Who was that? Flavia could not see the stranger's hooded face, but she was well dressed in a rich fur cape and blue gown. She and Agrippina talked a moment together by the villa gate, and then the cook passed the stranger a small parcel. The young woman slipped away and Agrippina returned to the kitchen.

Intrigued, Flavia waited to see where the stranger went, but lost her in the milling crowds out in the street. Staring through the villa gate, she spotted a small, dark slave girl running with a wooden crutch towards the healing shrine and great baths and remembered her own impending visit there. She frowned and Nero whimpered.

'It is all right,' she said, again offering the scrap of bread.

The little dog still made no move, but shuffling footsteps behind her had Flavia turning on the stone bench, her hand automatically shielding Nero.

Stopping beside a border of roses, old Gaius scowled at her. 'Where have you been?' he demanded, his voice hoarse with worry.

'Agrippina told me to bring the dog here,' Flavia reminded him, laying Nero gently on a sunlit part of the bench. 'Who was the young woman she was talking to?'

Gaius shook his head, his light blue eyes seeming to bulge slightly in his thin, tense face. 'A butcher's girl–'

'So finely dressed?'

'A spice seller, then. No one important.' He beckoned. 'You have been missed.'

Gaius always clenched his hands when he was trying to lie and he was doing it now.

Rising to her feet, Flavia noticed more. 'Your clothes...' She pointed her spindle at Gaius' long tunic and thick cloak.

Gaius touched his new bright wool tunic, fondling it with obvious pride. 'The master bought them for me this morning when a tailor called in, asking if *he* needed anything. Sulinus has a cloak and Livia and my Agrippina fresh shawls and gowns.'

Flavia smiled, thinking of how the plump, darkly handsome Agrippina loved to dress up, whenever she had the chance. 'That will please them.'

'Yes. Now, come.' Gaius beckoned again.

'But–' She glanced at Nero, disliking leaving the unhappy little dog alone and unsure whether to leave him outside. 'Does Livia need me? Agrippina?'

'Perhaps both, in time,' came a new voice. 'I am more interested in why you are so laggard with me.'

Marcus stepped round a column and stood looking down at her, tapping his fingers against his belt.

'Gaius, send my other people home. Tell them I shall see them tomorrow,' he went on, giving the older man a brief smile. Gaius set off towards the little group of lingering people, his scrawny arms raised in a shooing gesture.

There was no such smile when Marcus turned to Flavia again. 'Perhaps you are one of those females who are always late,' he mused aloud.

'It was not Gaius' fault,' Flavia said, although Gaius had not made clear who had summoned her. 'I – I didn't hear.'

'It is perfectly plain to me that my house steward is not to blame,' he observed, a remark that made Flavia blush. Dropping angry eyes from this Roman's annoyingly unreadable face she glanced across to the gate where Gaius was shepherding the last of the visitors out of the grounds.

'We shall be joining them, once I have decided how to ensure your good time-keeping. But, no: I will let it pass for now.'

Marcus' deep, faintly amused voice had Flavia angrily knotting her fingers on her spindle and, soldier that he was, he noticed her movement.

'What in the name of Mithras is that?' he exclaimed, naming the favorite pagan god of Roman soldiers. Before Flavia could react, he had lifted spindle and wool from her hands, staring at the thread. 'What do you use this for, bandaging? It is thick enough.' He gave the spindle a shake, a strange half-smile sliding across his handsome mouth. 'My Drusilla would not have this anywhere near her, except perhaps for kindling.'

'Perhaps you should summon her here, then, instead of me,' Flavia responded, thoroughly nettled. She knew her spinning was not of the best. 'My Lady Valeria required a scribe, not a seamstress.'

She gasped as Marcus caught hold of her wrists, imprisoning both in a one handed grip that she could not begin to break. He dragged her to him and lowered his head.

'I give you fair warning, little Celt,' he said softly, his strong jaw pressed against her ear. 'Drusilla was my wife. You will not speak her name.'

Flavia felt hot with shame. She heard anger in his voice and an unexpected pain. Perhaps they had been divorced. Perhaps the perfect free-born Drusilla had found someone else.

Suddenly Marcus was speaking Latin, his words softer still. 'Her grave is in Germania. Her headstone tells the world her virtues, hers and the child's.'

Silent, his mouth brushed against Flavia's hair, the touch of his lips gentle. His iron grip loosened around her wrists, releasing her when just for an instant, she would have stayed as they were, heads bowed together.

Her desire to comfort him startled her, although not as much as what Marcus did next. Breaking from her with a muffled exclamation he stepped away, then spotted the little dog on the stone bench. To Flavia's surprise, he crouched. 'Hello, there, lad! No greeting for your master?'

Hearing the Latin, Nero whined and

hauled himself onto his feet on the stone bench, his thin body showing up starkly in the bright winter sun.

'There, lad, there.' Marcus stroked the terrier. 'How long has he been like this?' he asked Flavia, in her language.

'Since my mistress–' Flavia could not go on.

'And he will not eat for you?' Marcus was gently checking the dog's teeth.

'No, sir.'

'Scarcely surprising, given those rations,' Marcus muttered, picking up Flavia's scrap of bread and throwing it into the garden for a pair of scurrying sparrows. He waved the spindle in front of the dog, clicking his tongue when the terrier did not react. 'What is his name?'

There was no help for it. Flavia caught hold of one of the ends of her plaits, something she did when nervous. 'My lady called him Nero, sir.'

'She would! A chance to command another male, and one named for an emperor –Valeria would not have been able to resist. Although, when I suggested to her in Rome the first time we met that she get a guard dog, I had a heftier breed in mind.' Chuckling, Marcus rose and plucked the dog off the bench, cradling Nero as the white-haired terrier gave a squirm and then settled, his tongue licking Marcus' forearm.

The man smiled, and this time his smile included Flavia. 'Some meat for this fierce brute and then we go,' he told her. 'This morning's tailor had nothing in his pack that I thought would do for a female scribe, but he promised I would find more suitable clothing at his shop. So we shall see.'

On their way through Aquae Sulis, Flavia kept watching for another glimpse of Agrippina's mysterious spice seller, but did not see the caped young woman again. Soon the wonders of the city itself were clamoring for her attention – she had rarely wandered in these fashionable parts, close to the great bath itself. Certainly not in the company of a man with whom she almost had to run to keep up: Marcus' smooth, flowing stride covered a great deal of ground. Flavia trailed in his wake as he wove effortlessly through the close-packed buildings and the bobbing mass of tourists, grizzled soldiers and trinket sellers. She was breathless and over-awed when they came to the tailor's shop, conscious of her shabby clothing and flyaway hair.

One of a block of three, the tailor's was a smart establishment, built within sight of a three storey hotel and the great new barrel vaulted roof of the main baths. Set between a Gaulish wine shop on one side and a potter's selling fine tableware on the other, it was roofed with tiles rather than the more common thatch, and was in two storeys with smooth plastered walls and large wooden shutters, now fully open.

Crossing in Marcus' shadow to its open door and supercilious-looking owner, Flavia felt even more out of place. Around her, she could smell a heady swirl of perfumes as people came and went from the baths and hear the sound of sawing and the masons shouting to each other within the precincts of the shrine itself. There was always building going on in Aquae Sulis, ancient place of healing and now a Roman spa.

Telling herself that she would one day walk these cobbled streets as a free Celt, Flavia tilted up her chin, determined to show no nerves.

'Flavia.' Marcus had kept glancing round to check that she was with him and now he turned back to her, blocking the view of the bowing tailor. 'Before we are overwhelmed by offers, we should have a plan of campaign.' He grinned, making the ragged scar close to his lower lip disappear, making light, too, of his own words and laughing at himself. *An attractive trait*, Flavia thought.

'Do you?' he asked softly.

She had done it again, missed a question. Perhaps it was his largeness, his maleness. She stared at the hand now clasping hers, her own palm dwarfed in his. 'I don't know,' she murmured, for something to say.

A gust of wind cut through her patched dress, dragging several strands of Marcus' glossy dark-brown hair across his forehead. Was it as tough and unyielding as it looked?

'You are shivering, we must go in. But if no favorites, then a color you particularly dislike – surely you have that?'

'Yes, imperial purple,' Flavia said promptly, returning his look with a steadiness she did not quite feel.

He laughed aloud. 'A pert reply! Very well, little Celt, your scruples will be respected. Come.' He drew her into the shop with him.

Inside, the tailor was all anxiety and courtesy, shaking Marcus' hand and thanking him for honoring his shop as he ordered his two elderly male assistants to plump up the cushions on the blue couch in the middle of the shop, opposite the open door and window, 'for special customers'.

'A glass of spiced wine?' the tailor continued, as Marcus sat on the couch. 'Or a local warming tisane?' He stared at the bigger man's plain dark red tunic and short cloak with barely concealed astonishment. He himself was dressed in a formal toga of rich heavy wool and, Flavia noticed, was also wearing socks.

'Later, perhaps, thank you,' came the reply. 'I find it warmer here than in Ebora-

46

cum, or on the northern wall.' A muscle in Marcus' cheek twitched, as if with suppressed amusement. 'Hadrian built the wall to preserve the imperial peace we all enjoy, in spite of the Caledonians beyond our northern border, but even the emperor could not change the weather!'

'Ah, but you will find the climate much more congenial in Aquae Sulis,' said the tailor rapidly, picking a pair of scissors from a nearby long table strewn with pieces of cloth in a bewildering array of colors.

Flavia, who had not missed the teasing jibe against her, thought it wisest to say nothing. She crossed the mosaic floor as Marcus beckoned and stood beside his couch while he and the tailor chatted about the northern frontier. The green walls of this place made her think of trees, something she sorely missed in the city.

She suddenly became aware that Marcus was giving her the same considering look he had given her at Lady Valeria's funeral. She trembled slightly, conscious again of what was at stake for her, Gaius, and the others.

'Something simple for the girl?' asked the tailor.

'Hardly that.' Marcus stretched, crossing his long legs. Catching the tailor's puzzled frown, he said, 'Ask Flavia. She will be wearing it.'

'Ah – more daring?' the tailor asked, still

not looking at Flavia. 'I have a wonderful tunic of the lightest Egyptian linen.'

'An appealing idea,' Marcus agreed. 'She should have that.'

Indignant and irritated, Flavia felt herself blush and stared at the floor mosaic. It showed a water goddess lying on a water lily, an image that made her feel more self-conscious. There was a wine jug on the window ledge and she thought about bringing it down on Marcus' dark head until another of his comments had her stiffening in shock.

'But for less personal occasions–' He smiled as Flavia whipped her eyes from the floor to glare at him. 'I think something more understated. A female scribe is enough of a distraction to an old campaigner like me.

'In fact–' He rose, gently tugging Flavia onto the couch in his place. 'There's a veteran in the street of the armorers whom I promised to see. You will do better with me out of the way. Shopping's not a man's business.' He placed a bag of coins on the long table and lowered his head to whisper.

'I look forward to studying the results, especially the fine Egyptian linen.'

Still smiling, he said his farewells, arranged to meet Flavia outside the shop at midday, and left.

Marcus had been right, Flavia thought an hour later, as the tailor's two assistants made up a parcel of clothes in a badly-dyed piece of linen. The tailor, another Gaius, had relaxed considerably once they were alone and had even thawed towards dealing with a slave. The money bag had helped, but, as the tailor explained as he handed her garments to try on behind a small cur-tained-off area of the shop, it was a pleasure to deal with an appreciative customer.

She chose a long-sleeved gown first, of yellow linen that made her think of sunlight. With the gown was a narrow belt, dyed in blue. Over both she cast a palla, a shawl of soft red-brown wool.

'Excellent!' the tailor said, when she drew back the curtain of the changing chamber. 'But you have spent hardly any of the money he left you. Let me show you more...'

She bought under-tunics in white linen, another gown in brown and a blue fillet and horn combs for her hair. Using a comb, she re-did her plaits and was glad to cast away the rags that had clothed her feet, stepping into the enclosed sandals with cork soles that the tailor sent for from a cobbler's: 'A friend of mine,' he explained. 'He will be glad of the commission.'

'Stroll about by my shop and I will be in your debt,' the tailor said, brushing aside her thanks. 'Wander out and smile. Go on!'

Flavia walked the length of the row of

shops, stopping by the potter's to admire the red Samian ware. It was rare for her to have so much free time, an uncomfortable voice reminded her, a voice which also whispered that she would be disappointed if Marcus did not remark on her new clothes.

He was coming. She could see him striding up the street towards her, head and shoulders above the crowds. Her stomach did a strange lurch and she felt suddenly light-headed. Of course, that was because she had eaten no breakfast. It was nothing to do with the fact that Marcus was smiling at her.

Another few steps and he was there beside her, looking down at her. 'Better,' he said simply and Flavia smiled back at him, finding more pleasure in his soldier's sincerity than in the tailor's fulsome compliments.

'Although that object spoils the effect.' He took the clothes bundle from her, swinging it out of her reach. 'You need your hands free for your writing,' he reminded her. 'You have stylus and tablets with you, I presume?'

'Of course,' Flavia answered, her professional pride piqued. She tapped the small bag hanging from her belt.

'So easy for a desk worker,' Marcus muttered. Then, as Flavia wondered how to respond, his mood seemed to lift as swiftly as it had come, his face clearing as he pointed down the street. 'There is a tavern just past the stone mason's,' he said, giving a beggar a silver coin. 'A little wine and bread before we enter the fray of the great baths will do us very well.'

The tavern's crusty bread and wine and honey were good, but Flavia ate little, apprehensive about their coming visit to the great bath. She had been there before, with Lady Valeria, and seen old soldiers, gnarled farmers injured by accidents, and hobbling Romano-British matrons all carefully splashing about in the warm curative waters. She had swum there herself and thought nothing of it. The baths of Aquae Sulis were healing baths: a swift dive into the central pool and she was modestly immersed; no one had ever gawped at her. But it would be different with Marcus Brucetus.

'We will visit the shrine first.' His voice interrupted her anxious reverie. 'People go there to plead for cures. That is where we will find Lady Valeria's apothecary, along with the other miracle-workers and fortunetellers, all on the make.' He stretched his arms above his head, and then drained off his wine.

Flavia put down her bread, unable to nibble another bite. They were eating at one of the tavern's indoor tables and she was glad to be sitting down.

'Drink up, girl: we need to be moving.' Marcus prodded her wine cup, grinning as she hurriedly finished the rest of her wine.

'Not too quick! I want you to have your wits about you when we question this healer.'

Flavia wanted the same, but for a different reason. Drawing her new shawl more closely around her shoulders, she was careful not to meet her companion's eyes as they set out again. She was wary of what the apothecary might say, but still more wary of the shrine itself, the place of the goddess Sulis, who might resent her Christian presence. She had never ventured into the shrine: her independent Lady Valeria had insisted on making any offerings herself, without an entourage.

Flavia's sense of disquiet increased as they entered the bathing complex, crossing the open precinct in front of the baths and the temple to the goddess. Although of clean design, in beautifully painted stone and marble, the temple seemed a dead-looking building. Before she had converted to Christianity, she had prayed to her Celtic gods in the open air. *There should be trees here,* she thought, struck afresh by the number of Romans who visited this place as she glanced about the cobbled precinct with its sacrificial altars and booths selling bath oils. Rivers and waters were sacred to her people, but the Romans had enclosed the spring here, perhaps not even knowing that all springs were a gateway to the world of the dead.

Flavia shivered. Three steps ahead of her, very grim as he dismissed an importunate healer who had approached offering to sell him the secrets of immortality, Marcus cut through the gaggle of would-be worshippers and bathers that filled the precinct. A man on crutches, limping away from a smoking altar, was jostled by the same crowd and slipped. Marcus caught him, supporting the smaller man until he had regained his footing.

'Thanks, friend,' the lame man said in mangled Latin, showing toothless gums in a leering grin as he stared at Flavia. 'How much for the little blonde?'

'You could not afford her, citizen,' Marcus shot back. 'Come, girl.'

Flavia suddenly found a hard hand fastened round her wrist as she was hurried away indoors, into the hot, dim heart of the shrine itself. Their progress was so swift that she was out of breath when Marcus stopped on the platform above the steaming waters.

'Now, my girl, you can start earning your keep and the cost of those fancy new clothes,' he said shortly. 'Is Lady Valeria's healer here?'

Flavia was so angry at his unfairness that she forgot her awe of a sacred place. 'I have already earned my keep in the faithful service of my mistress,' she hissed, peering about amongst the shadowy figures thronging close to the waters of the goddess. 'Now give me time to look.'

Standing directly in front of Marcus, her

back against his chest, she felt his quiver of amusement. 'Well spoken, little Celt,' he said, in a warmer voice than before. 'Take all the time you need. I will pay our dues to Sulis Minerva.' He gave the goddess' name in the Roman way and there was a flash of gold as he flipped a coin over her head into the waters, murmuring an invocation Flavia tried to ignore.

There were many gathered on the platform overlooking the shrine, men, women and children, some seemingly hale, others bowed down with dry coughs, peeling skin and twisted limbs. Attendants, conspicuous by their haughty bearing, bustled about strewing flowers around a statue to the goddess, supervising the lighting of candles, writing messages to the goddess on tiny lead tablets, and bringing water from the spring in small cups. Flavia was pierced by the sight of a boy with a withered hand throwing an ivory model of an arm into the shrine, his face bright with the hope that this offering would make his arm well. She prayed silently to Christ for the boy's healing.

Raising her head, she saw the apothecary whom Lady Valeria had favored in life padding towards them, his shaven head shining in the flickering candle light. She shivered, knowing that this was the man who had given her lady her means of death and disliking him for that, and for his harsh face and avid black eyes that never warmed, even when his lips were pulled back, as they were now, in the largest of smiles.

'Welcome!' Staring at her, the apothecary addressed Marcus, his Latin clipped and flat. 'Do you require a healing charm? Has someone stolen from you and you wish to curse the wretch? I have the means ready.'

He flourished a small lead tablet before Marcus, who stood quietly beside Flavia, watching with raised eyebrows. She pressed her shoulder warningly against his chest.

'This is the one,' she whispered in her own tongue. She felt his fingers lightly touch her elbow, acknowledging her message.

In the temple precinct outside, there were shouts as a sacrificial goat broke loose and careered amongst the stalls and trinket sellers. The apothecary eased his voice up another notch and continued his sales pitch.

'Or if it is relief from toothache, stomach-ache, head-ache, back-ache–'

'We are after information,' said Marcus in a dangerous voice.

The healer froze, his thin face darkening. 'What kind?' he snapped.

'I can pay, man, so you will have your fee.'

'The secrets of my art are not for every-one.'

The two were glaring at each other by now. Sensing that Marcus was losing them the chance of finding out the details of Lady

Valeria's last visit to the healing baths, Flavia almost let the matter go. Beside her, looming over the healer and with one hand touching the place on his belt where his sword would be, Marcus made to draw her behind him, but she side-stepped his reaching arm. It might not be wise or safe to question, but she wanted to know about her mistress.

'You knew my former mistress, the Lady Valeria, Master Healer,' she said, smiling up at him with a candid, open look. 'She praised many of your tinctures, especially the ones you brewed her for relief of pain.'

'Especially the ones using hemlock,' Marcus broke in, blunt where she would have been subtle. She wanted to yell at him in frustration, especially when the healer reacted as if stung, his hooded eyes taking on a yet more guarded look.

'I know nothing of this,' he said, shuffling back from them.

'But she bought cures from you,' Flavia cried. Her voice rang in the chamber, causing worshippers to turn and stare.

'That is enough, Flavia,' said Marcus. 'Perhaps your lady's healer will be more keen to talk to one of the city magistrates.'

'She told me she bought hemlock for rat poison,' put in Flavia, determined to have one final attempt at persuasion. The healer stared at her a moment and then he nodded.

'Ah, yes. She may have done that – Flavia?

56

A pretty name.' He smiled at her, his black eyes shining in the gloom of the shrine. 'But only if I sold hemlock – which I do not.' He gave her another smile, adding, 'Let us take a turn in the air.'

'Too crowded here for you?' asked Marcus.

'For some things, yes,' said the healer shortly. 'This is a holy place.'

They returned to the temple precinct, finding a corner out of the wind to talk. The healer would not admit to having sold hemlock, but he took the news of Lady Valeria's death in his stride, merely asking, 'You kept the cup that she used? I could tell you for certain what her last drink was, from the dregs.'

Flavia blushed. 'I threw the dregs away,' she said, aware of how suspicious that might sound to Marcus, who for much of their conversation had been glowering at the healer. 'The cup is buried with her.'

The healer stared at his fingernails, stained with many potions, and cleared his throat. 'A wise precaution, Flavia. I am always careful of my own cups and pestles and mortars.'

Uncomfortably, Flavia was reminded of Gaius and the others at home, none of whom seemed to be without a pestle and mortar these days. What were they doing? She thought of their silences. What were they hiding?

She risked a glance at Marcus, who stared

at the healer with open dislike. 'And you still claim you did not sell Lady Valeria the hemlock?' he demanded.

'As I told your pretty Flavia, I am a healer. I do not deal in poisons.' The healer gave Flavia another long, considering stare. 'Prudent and pretty. A distracting combination. You are fortunate, sir. I bid you both good day.'

He bowed to Flavia and set off across the precinct, entering the temple.

'A wasted interview.' Marcus dropped the bundle of clothes to catch Flavia's shawl, which was threatening to slide off her shoulders. 'You have done enough flaunting. Cover yourself.'

'I've done nothing of the sort!' Flavia retaliated, snatching the shawl from his hands and wrapping it tightly about herself. 'It's your fault if the healer would not admit anything – threatening him with the magistrate.'

'Shock tactics work,' said Marcus. 'Your way would have had him pawing you, as well as leering, if I had not been here.'

He was jealous. Even as she goggled at the idea, Flavia said angrily, 'No man touches me!'

'Indeed?' His blue eyes darkened almost to black and as she tried to avoid him, he caught her, his arms shackling about her like fetters of stone.

Marcus was in a storm of mixed feelings:

amusement and an odd kind of sympathy at her reckless challenge, rage at the gawping healer and that other fellow earlier, who'd had the impudence to ask her price; astonishment that Flavia did not realize the effect she had on men, and exasperation that he had helped in this transformation. Yet he could not allow loyal servants to dress so poorly, and fresh clothes for all of them had been essential, including new gowns for Flavia. But it was not simply her fine new clothes that made her so noticeable: she blazed with life. His own wife, Drusilla, with her hair the color of fire and her serene beauty, had never stirred men as this girl did. He could sense them watching now.

'By Mithras, you are a provoking wench,' he growled. She began to answer yet again, but he wrapped his arms tighter still and half-lifted her, drawing her up to the tips of her toes. He saw her widening eyes as his mouth claimed hers, taking the kiss that he had wanted all that morning – no, from the instant he had seen her, a small shabby mourner at a funeral.

He felt her shock. Her mouth trembled beneath his, her soft breath mingling with his own, and the thought returned to him: Flavia knew nothing of men. What could she know, living in an old woman's household with four elderly slaves?

Clasping her gently, Marcus kissed her

again, trying for a brotherly embrace, and then he lifted his head. He had expected to teach her a lesson, give fair warning, but instead he felt a curious sense of shame. 'We should go,' he said, kissing the top of that astonishing golden hair, drawing her shawl over her head and then retrieving the bundle of clothes. 'Come.'

She followed him silently into the great baths.

Chapter 3

Stumbling into the great bath complex, Flavia was cruelly aware of Marcus: of his height, of his watchful blue eyes, of the breadth of his shoulders and the strength of his body. He had plucked her from the ground as if she weighed no more than a cobweb.

Over and over in her mind she saw his head lowering, his keen eyes gleaming above that aquiline nose, and then his mouth, kissing hers. She had not known that kisses could be so tender, yet so powerfully sweet, almost intoxicating.

Don't be a fool, she warned herself. *Remember his wife.*

'I wonder what our Decurion looks like,'

Marcus remarked, checking his stride to match hers, so they would enter together. 'Are you ready for Lucius Maximus?'

How could she tell if she was ready? thought Flavia in a spurt of irritation, in that free way she seemed to feel only with Marcus, before she realized that he was teasing her. 'Yes, sir,' she said, making her voice servile.

'Don't go shy on me. Lucius Maximus needs that subtlety you wanted me to show against the healer and if your eyes are studying the floor tiles I might forget myself.'

'You will not,' Flavia murmured, blushing and reluctant to look at him. She did feel shy, and wary. She thought of the healer, who claimed he had never sold hemlock. Was he telling the truth?

'Flavia.' A warm hand drawn across her middle prevented her from moving forward. 'Please, I'm serious. You are a clever creature and I need that cleverness. Lucius Maximus is an aristocrat, someone who has risen through connections, who has never had to go on campaign.'

'A desk man, then?' Flavia asked pertly, unable to resist and raising her head to see how he took it. *In excellent part,* she thought. At least his colour never changed and his jawline did not tighten, signs of anger she was learning to watch out for. Instead, he looked at her solemnly for an instant and then he grinned.

'Yes, I deserved that, but I have my reasons. Still, we have no time now for explanations.' He took her hand in his, nudging her gently out of the way of a group of chattering Romano-British women, who left the baths in a swathe of fresh perfumes. Ignoring their clear interest in him, Marcus lowered his voice. 'Since it seems impossible for us to deal with each other formally as master and servant, I have a favor to ask. Will you be my guardian spirit, little Celt? I need that good sense.'

'Of course,' Flavia said, absently brushing her thumb over Marcus' hand. All at once she was proud that he needed her, and that he had recognized their unusual relationship, too, one that was almost free, at least to her. They moved along the narrow corridor leading to the great bath. Flavia jumped back as the door to one of the hot sweat chambers swung open, sending a blast of dry heat into her face. Marcus grabbed the door, calling 'Wait!' to whoever was in there, and shepherded her past.

'Are you all right?' she found herself asking.

'Naturally! And you react quickly, for a scribe.'

'Thank you, sir. I will take that as a compliment.' Flavia watched the stern face above hers break into a smile, thinking how young Marcus was; certainly no more than thirty. He was clasping her hand like a youth and she felt young herself, light-hearted for the first time in weeks.

I must be careful, she told herself again, but it made no difference.

They walked further, stepping round a towel-draped woman who was examining the contents of a small bottle by one of the wall lights. Ahead, Flavia could already hear the noise of the great bath: people splashing, people singing and greeting each other.

People bathing... She felt herself blushing again and thought of the man beside her, finding it disturbingly easy to imagine how that tanned, lean body would look, the muscles shining like bronze in the steam from the great bath.

They were closing on the dressing room. Would he make her strip? *I will wrap myself in a towel,* Flavia thought, smiling grimly to herself. Her people had been warriors and healers and poets: she was not going to be confounded by a little bit of water.

The curtain to the dressing room shifted and one of the young bath attendants, touting for custom, put his head out.

'Clothes, jewels, perfumes – all safe here,' the youngster cried, in a sing-song kind of chant. 'See, I put them in this dresser and guard them. No thieves get past me! I'm the one you should ask to keep safe your things, whenever you visit the baths...'

'Indeed,' remarked Marcus, grinning

down at the slave's shaggy dark hair with the same indulgent look he had given to Lady Valeria's old dog. 'What is your name?'

'Rags,' came the answer.

The dressing room curtain was tugged back and a small, skinny boy in a ragged loincloth bowed to them. He silently held out a hand and Marcus pressed a coin into it.

'May we come in, Rags?' Flavia asked, conscious that slave or not, this was his domain.

The boy looked at her. His face, like the rest of him, was very pale and thin and his big eyes – the little she could see of them between the narrowed lids – were as empty of expression as a dark flint. Feeling that a smile might insult him, she nodded a greeting.

'You are Lady Valeria's girl,' the boy said, head on one side as he scanned her new clothes. 'You used to come with her on old lady day – that is when most of the old women visit the baths,' he added, speaking to Marcus.

'I am that lady's heir,' said Marcus gravely.

Flavia was aware of being sized up once more, Marcus and her together, and then Rags seemed to relax.

'Enter and welcome.' He moved aside and pointed to a large wooden dresser at the back of the rectangular dressing room. 'I can help you to undress.' His narrow chin came up slightly, light from one of the upper windows striking across his forehead, showing a fading bruise. 'Or should I call one of the toga girls or older bath boys?'

'That will not be necessary, thank you,' said Marcus, glancing round the tall narrow chamber lined with screens and alcoves.

Rags nodded, giving Flavia another rapid look as if trying to work her out. 'I will put your things high, away from rats and thieves.'

Flavia kept a straight face at the mention of rats, part of her astonished that she had never noticed this tough, strutting little slave before today. But then always in the past her attention had been fixed on her mistress.

'How old are you, Rags?' Marcus asked, wadding his cloak into a ball.

'Eight, nine, ten.' The boy shrugged. 'Old enough.'

'Indeed,' said Marcus, continuing to smile as Rags watched him.

'I've always lived here,' the boy went on. 'I was a stoker before, now just promoted to a clothes-keeper.'

Flavia felt a sudden chill, despite the warmth of the dressing room. Beneath these floor tiles ran a heating system serviced by child slaves such as Rags. And what had his life been like, if he could count looking after clothes as promotion?

She looked at Marcus, who was looking serious again, although when he spoke to the boy, his voice was gentle. 'Very well, young man. I shall leave you my cloak and this bundle and Flavia will give you her shawl. We are heading for one of the private rooms at the east end: there's a party going on there, hosted by Lucius Maximus. Seemingly, the Decurion is having his dining room rebuilt, so today he is showing off his status at the baths, rather than his home.' Marcus seemed amused by this. 'Do we still walk through the main bath?'

An obvious question, Flavia thought, and one he must have asked to be kind, for when Rags said, 'Yes,' Marcus gave him another coin. She was glad of that kindness and relieved that she would not be shedding her gown.

Leaving her shawl with the unsmiling Rags, she followed Marcus into the great bath, hearing behind her the slap of sandaled and bare feet as new bathers began gathering for the tenth hour – the time any fashionable citizen of Aquae Sulis would aim to be at the baths.

'Wait there a moment, please.' Marcus stopped by one of the pillars close to the rectangular pool and expanse of the great bath and shouted something in a German tongue at a blond, rangy swimmer with only one eye, who raised a fist from the steaming waters and yelled back an answer, in obvious delight.

'I know Otho from Germania – this won't

take long,' he said hurriedly to Flavia, grinning as he stepped down the top step of four broad steps at the water's edge and stood waiting, immersed up to his knees, for his former comrade, both arms spread wide in greeting.

Amused at their back-slapping antics – Otho seized Marcus' hand and tried to drag him under the water – Flavia left them to their incomprehensible talk and took in the scene around her.

The great bath was a wonder, she thought, grudgingly acknowledging the powers of the Roman engineering. Set in a huge aisled hall with a soaring barrel vault overhead supported on massive columns, the great bath was surrounded by four deep steps on all sides and its aisle walkways were lined with massive white limestone flagstones. After the dimly-lit corridors leading here, the bath was dazzlingly bright, the light from huge arched upper windows reflected by white limestone columns and smooth plastered walls. The steaming water itself, a pale green, shimmered with light making the statues lining the bath seem alive.

In the water or waiting in the colonnade were the bathing attendants: slaves holding towels or bottles of scented oil, or strigils to scrape off the oil; masseurs calling out their prices; hair-pluckers flashing their tweezers.

Flavia studied the bathers with narrowed

eyes, resting her chin on one hand as she crouched by the base of a statue. She had never been in the baths so late before and she soon understood why, and why some of the women were leaving. The men flooding fast on her heels into the great bath were not elderly veterans. These were a different breed.

She picked out a few figures in the bobbing, chattering mass. There was a magistrate, whom she recognized from one of Lady Valeria's rare dinner parties, swathed in towels as he swept along the side aisle with his entourage and various cronies trailing behind. There was a rich young nobleman with a bored, sulky look, being lifted directly from the bath onto a waiting litter, which bore him away into one of the hot sweat rooms. There was a massively fat man with a scarlet nose eating a sausage and singing while floating on his back in the water. He was being propelled in the bath by an elderly slave whose back was still raw with lash marks.

'Don't stare, he is not a forgiving man,' said a familiar voice by her ear. Flavia turned on the damp limestone. Crouching beside her, his German friend nowhere to be seen, Marcus jerked his head towards the eastern exit.

'Let us get this visit over with and go home,' he said.

Lucius Maximus' party was in one of the smaller eastern chambers usually used by the masseurs. Warmed by underfloor heating and crowded with benches, couches, small low tables and a dozen people, it smelt overpoweringly of lavender. The door opened at Marcus' knock and Flavia coughed, the scent catching the back of her throat. Marcus gave her a quick concerned glance, then turned his attention to Lucius Maximus, who had strolled across the patterned floor tiles. The letter of introduction in Maximus' hand had been penned by Flavia that morning, just before they had set out for the city.

'Well met, noble tribune,' said Lucius Maximus in a light, pleasant voice, stopping a man's length from Marcus and snapping his fingers.

Around him the room fell silent, those in it turning to watch.

'We are prepared for your coming,' said Lucius Maximus, raising a languid hand as if inviting applause. 'The masseurs have just left, so we are ready for our next diversion.' He smirked, making no attempt to shake hands.

Astonished by such bad manners, Flavia shot an anxious look at the tall tense man beside her. Flicking dark eyes in her direction, Marcus tapped his belt with his fingers and then said evenly, 'Allow me to present my gift to you, Lucius Maximus.'

From a wallet at his belt he produced a heavy gold ring. The splendor of the gift had several guests craning forward on their couches for a closer look. Flavia felt proud of Marcus' self-control and also in his choice – Lucius Maximus had no option but to approach properly to receive his gift.

The two men finally shook hands, giving Flavia the chance to compare them. Marcus Brucetus and Lucius Maximus were about the same age and of similar height and muscular physique, although Marcus was the taller and, Flavia sensed, leaner and stronger. She had thought Marcus dark, but Lucius Maximus was still more so, with an olive complexion, even features that were already blurring with good living, a pair of knowing brown eyes, plucked black eyebrows, and wavy black hair. Following a more recent Roman fashion he sported a trimmed black beard and wore a light toga made of the very rare eastern silk, a garment in a cream color, artfully draped.

Lucius was handsome, Flavia conceded, but Marcus had the more decisive, striking looks. She could hear the women in the party whispering, stretching invitingly towards him on their couches. She bent her head to the writing tablet and stylus at her belt, then decided that unless asked she would make no notes of this meeting until they had left this hot little room. Instinct warned her that Lucius Maximus was not to be trusted and that he himself would be easily suspicious, quick to take offence.

'You are the youngest of four sons, I understand?' Lucius Maximus went on, wresting his fingers from Marcus' and walking up and down in a swish of silk. 'That must be a problem for your father in his division of his estate. Land is so essential for a Roman gentleman. But of course you have time to acquire land. You have served with one of your older brothers in Germania?'

'I have had that honor.' Marcus' features were now as unbending as if they had been cast in bronze.

'No doubt winning many captives, gold and treasure?'

'Certainly that last,' said Marcus. 'I have now finished my duty as tribune and was due to return home.'

He meant Rome, Flavia thought, her heart sinking, although that was what she had wished for only that morning.

But Lucius Maximus was talking and she felt she should pay attention. 'Who would not wish to return to Italy, to civilization! Have you seen the theatre here?' He raised an eyebrow. 'A farce. But good enough for our little Brits.'

There was a polite tittering from the guests, although Marcus did not laugh. Chilled at the man's arrogance, Flavia heard Lucius

Maximus say something even more surprising.

'But perhaps being a North Italian you feel an affinity for these Celts? Or perhaps the Celtic connection in your case is deeper? You are unusually tall for a Roman, perhaps from your mother's family.'

Marcus moved, but Flavia moved too, clutching at her side with a sharp cry. 'Forgive me,' she panted, as Marcus stopped, bristling, less than a sword's length from Lucius Maximus and stared at her. 'I have a stitch.' She hoped her grimace of pain looked convincing.

Marcus' blue eyes lightened and he almost smiled, plainly seeing through her feint, but going along with it as he took her hand. 'May we sit down, Decurion?' he asked formally.

Lucius Maximus' even features had twisted in definite alarm, but now he gave a shudder. 'Do not remind me of that appointment; even here in the baths I cannot escape people moaning about their taxes. But yes, by all means, sit down on that striped couch, you and your lady.'

One of the hovering slaves leaned down to his mistress on her couch, whispering into her ear. The woman giggled and pointed at Flavia.

'That is no lady, Lucius,' she called out, her perfectly made-up face shining with malice. 'It's the Lady Valeria's slave girl, whom our naughty tribune was not going to introduce.' *Was not going to admit she was a slave,* the woman's eyes said, while her voice said, 'Perhaps he is ashamed of her.'

'Indeed not, madam,' said Marcus. 'I would never be ashamed of Flavia.'

He turned and plucked Flavia off her feet, carrying her to the couch Lucius Maximus had so grudgingly indicated. He laid her down gently and, kicking off his sandals, came beside her.

The door to the chamber opened again and more slaves filed in, carrying platters of food and glass flagons filled with wine.

'Excellent! Our dinner has arrived, good guests, and all from my own kitchens!' cried Lucius Maximus, his sallow features taking on color as he savored this moment. 'This is where we can really begin the entertainment!'

Gratified by these arrivals, he hurried amongst the new slaves, ordering them where to place each dish on the various low tables. Amongst the guests there was a buzz of anticipation and calls for napkins and finger bowls.

Flavia, lying on a Roman couch for the first time in her life, felt as though she was in a dream, in a dangerous golden daze. Against her breast the couch cushions were soft and her new clothes softer than water against her skin. She could hear exclamations of, 'Roast

73

goose, expensive!' and 'Stuffed dates! My favourite!' and she could smell all the rich scents of the banquet, but all these things faded to nothing against what Marcus made her feel.

His touch made her tremble. Lying next to him she could feel the hairs on his legs, his manhood pressed against her bottom, his breath on the back of her neck. He kissed the side of her throat, close to the collar of her new gown, and her entire body blazed with sensation, all new.

'Steady,' Marcus murmured. He smiled and put an arm around her middle, giving one of her plaits a tug, both a tease and a reminder that there were others in the room.

His warning came just in time. Lying on the couch next to theirs, beside the woman who had called Flavia a slave, Lucius Maximus raised a silver goblet.

'Sweet young wine.' His gaze lingered a moment on Flavia. 'You will not have tasted such delicacies in your north Italian provinces or Germania, Marcus Brucetus. You must have some now.' He snapped his fingers and a slave approached with a second goblet.

'My thanks, Decurion.' Marcus placed the goblet on the low table beside his and Flavia's couch, but would not drink. So far he had taken no food, either. Too distracted herself to eat, although hungry again, Flavia was grateful that Marcus did not ask her to try any of the plates of goose, dates, or chestnuts that the slaves kept carrying round the couches.

Lucius Maximus fingered the new ring on his hand. 'I would exchange this for her.' He stared at Flavia in a self-satisfied way that made her skin crawl.

'Flavia is not for sale.'

'You keep her in remembrance of the British princess? Because, of course, you are Valeria's heir, are you not, tribune? So some land has come your way. How pleasant for you, so long as you do not interfere in local politics.' Lucius Maximus smiled, his silk toga whispering around his body as he lounged on the couch, taking up most of the space. 'Old Valeria could not refrain from meddling, and these local matters are ... tangled.'

Flavia had felt Marcus stiffen at these insults to the Lady Valeria and at the veiled threat, but he said simply, 'The estate seems in good order.'

'Excellent!'

Was that relief in the Decurion's voice? Flavia was careful not to watch Lucius Maximus as he took a drink of wine, in case he sensed her scrutiny.

'You met Valeria in Rome?' he continued. 'That is the rumor running round Aquae Sulis. Bit of a man-hater, was not she?

75

Rather like that Iceni witch who burned Londinium a hundred years ago.'

Hearing her own lady and Queen Boudicca mocked was too much. Furious, Flavia sprang at the glib face – or she would have done, had Marcus' arm not tightened in a lung-crushing grip about her middle.

'Calm, little Celt,' he growled in her tongue. 'Think of snow.' Aloud, he said in Latin, 'Our Emperor Septimius Severus found her gracious.'

'Yes, but he is African, not Roman,' brayed the woman beside Lucius Maximus. She shrugged as Lucius Maximus stared and returned her attention to her napkin full of stuffed dates, gesturing for a slave to feed her.

Marcus cleared his throat. 'As a matter of coincidence, I met Lady Valeria in Rome outside Nero's baths. A thief had run off with a scarf she particularly liked.' His mouth quivered in private amusement. 'A purple scarf made of silk, like your toga.'

'And you caught the thief and returned the scarf to her,' said Lucius Maximus, voicing Flavia's own thought. 'How kind.'

'Lady Valeria thought so,' said Marcus. 'She was a relative of yours, by marriage, I believe?'

'Unfortunately,' Lucius Maximus sighed.

'Being a family member you would perhaps know where her more important papers have gone?' Marcus went on, relentlessly polite. 'I believe she has passed them to a close relation for safety.'

Just in time, Flavia schooled her face into an empty shell of docility. Lucius Maximus knew no such restraint, sitting up so rapidly that his toga threatened to tumble off one shoulder altogether.

'What papers?' he demanded.

'Her daily journal. Valeria was scrupulous in keeping it.'

Flavia knew of no such thing, but if she was wondering what Marcus was doing, Lucius Maximus was angry. His olive complexion darkened.

'I have no idea,' he snapped. He swung himself down off the couch, kicking out spitefully at a passing slave, and started for the door. 'Where is the red wine? Where are the toga girls? Must I do everything?'

Flavia touched Marcus' arm, but he had already recognized the moment, as she had, and was smoothly making their farewells and thanks.

As they walked through the great bath, Marcus said, 'An impatient man, and cruel. Detestable.' He cracked his fists together.

'He's hiding something,' Flavia said. 'Why else was he so concerned about Lady Valeria's papers and that fictitious journal?'

'Ah, so you knew I had made that up!' Marcus put an arm about her shoulders and steered her towards the shimmering waters. 'You are right, though, and so was Valeria. That is not a man to be trusted.'

'I wonder why he warned you off politics.'

'I'm wondering that myself.'

As they closed on the top step of the great bath, Flavia sensed a new kind of danger and tried to forestall possible trouble. She lifted the small wax tablet attached to her belt. 'Should I make a note of anything, sir?'

'I think not.' Gently, but inexorably, Marcus turned her to face him. 'Thank you for shackling my temper, little Celt.' He bent and kissed her forehead. 'When he spoke of my mother–' His fingers tightened around her shoulders, instantly relaxing as if he realized what he was doing. 'Forgive me.'

To her own amazement, impelled by a sense of sympathy she hardly dare acknowledge, Flavia touched a hand against his chest. 'There is nothing for you to be sorry about,' she whispered.

His hand brushed against her head. 'Amazing stuff,' he said, running a loose tendril of her hair through his fingers. 'Like foam.' He lightly kissed her nose and then, as she laughingly protested, her mouth.

A passing bather made a ribald comment, which Flavia did not hear. She was in Marcus' arms again, her own arms floating shyly around his middle, tightening as he groaned and gathered her closer.

She closed her eyes and lost herself in the kiss, her lips becoming ever more sensitive as their embrace deepened. His arms were locked about her, his sensual mouth both taking and offering, his tongue tracing her teeth, the inside of her lips.

'Flavia,' he breathed, as his hands spread across her back and waist, one dipping lower and stroking exquisitely slowly over her bottom. She gasped aloud, wanting yet not wanting to break free.

'Hey, soldier!' yelled another bather. 'Have pity on the rest of us!'

Horrified, suddenly aware again of exactly where they were, Flavia tried to draw back, but Marcus followed her, his mouth smiling against hers. 'Not yet,' he murmured, 'Just one more.' He kissed her again and lifted her in his arms, half-threatening to drop her into the great bath.

'No, please!' Flavia squirmed, the rising steam dampening her clothes as she was lowered helplessly close to those pale green waters. 'I will bite your arm!'

'Do that, my girl, and your backside will regret it,' growled Marcus, sitting on a marble bench close to the top step with Flavia on his lap. 'Now be still a moment and stop scandalising the bathers – the few that are left.'

'The baths close soon after sunset here,' Flavia reminded him, leaning her head against his shoulder. She felt a disturbing mixture of shame and exhilaration, but overall she was grateful for the respite, a breathing space for her overwhelmed senses. Watching the emptying waters of the great bath with Marcus, she told herself that she could not afford to be close to him. Yet she had heard of masters who had freed and married their slave girls – a beguiling thought.

Marcus watched her, taking in her warm, bright eyes, her flushed face and prettily reddened lips. She dovetailed so snugly in his lap it was a pity to move. *Delicate,* he thought, watching the shadow of her long lashes falling across her high cheekbones, but surprisingly passionate. A water spirit, very much in keeping with their surroundings.

He scowled, disquieted by his own thought. He had never been sentimental before. He remembered Drusilla his wife, an honored spouse, whom he had treated from the very beginning with respect, good-will, and loyalty. This girl was not even his own race.

She licked her lips, one hand absently pressed against her stomach.

'Thirsty?' he asked. 'And hungry no doubt.'

'Not for any delicacy provided by Lucius Maximus,' the girl said quietly. Marcus applauded her principles: she had great spirit.

He patted the marble bench. 'Wait here. I will find us a drink, at least.'

'Thank you, sir.'

She left his knee and although that was what he had asked for, Marcus was frowning again. She had called him the slave's term of respect, as was his due, but he was disquieted as he set out through the rapidly emptying baths in search of a wine-seller. He had discovered that he did not really want Flavia to call him 'Sir'.

Flavia removed her sandals and dangled her feet in the water, thinking how easy it would be to fall in love with someone like Marcus. She had thought him so alien and yet, it seemed he was not Roman enough to a man like Lucius Maximus. Even the mystery of his parentage was intriguing.

'You should be more modest,' she told her reflection. Surely as a Christian she should not be this way? Wanting him to embrace her? Wanting to kiss him? She kicked a foot in the silken warmth of the great bath, hearing bats fluttering above through the open ends of the barrel vault. Nearby, a small slave was lighting lamps to stand along the edge of the aisle walkway.

It was Rags, the slave-boy keeper of the dressing room. She recognized him by that strutting walk and his ragged loin-cloth. Glad of a familiar face in these very Roman, increasingly silent, and rather eerie surroundings, Flavia drew in a breath to speak

81

to him.

The child looked up as if he had heard her, and smiled a genuine smile of welcome. She smiled back, and he marched from the wall side of the walkway towards her bench seat at the edge of the bath.

As Rags crossed the walkway, his oil lamp and lighting candle held aloft in both hands, a tall, well-fleshed figure clad in a towel stalked from the growing shadows and careered straight into the boy, knocking him off his feet. His candle shattered on the flagstones and his oil lamp flew from his grasp and landed in the bath, sinking in a spluttering puff of smoke and steam.

Flavia was already up and darting in to help, but the new figure was interested only in blame. 'Fool! Did you not see me?' he raged in a mangled mixture of Latin and Flavia's own tongue, 'You stupid Celts are all the same. You should have stepped out of my way, slave! You should have been on your knees when I passed!'

'He didn't see you, sir,' Flavia pointed out, moving to stand in front of the huddled boy, who had rolled onto his side and tucked in his head and legs. 'It is becoming dark and neither of us noticed–'

Behind her she could hear Rags whimpering and her heart went out to the boy but she dare not turn her back on this angry Roman, who had sustained no injury whatsoever except possibly to his dignity.

'Please, forgive us, sir.' She bowed her head, hoping a show of submission would placate the man.

'Should that not be master?' he answered in perfect Latin and Flavia stiffened. Stripped of his silk toga and using that fearful mixture of languages, she had not recognized him until now.

Lucius Maximus stepped out of the shadow of a column and whispered an order to one of his own slaves, who had just arrived with oil flask and strigil. The slave ran off, disappearing back into the small series of chambers at the eastern end of the baths.

'Please, master,' Flavia whispered, dreading what was coming. Marcus was nowhere to be seen and Lucius Maximus had clearly summoned more of his own people.

'Run,' Rags whispered, coiled at her feet, his teeth chattering.

'Step away, girl,' Lucius Maximus ordered, his hands bunching into fists. 'This wretch will have such a beating that he will be sorry to live.'

'No!' Flavia spread out her arms, shielding Rags.

To her deepening horror, Lucius Maximus smiled. 'Another slave who does not know her place.' He snapped his fingers at his returning scurrying attendants. 'Take her back to my chamber.'

Three male slaves grabbed at her. Flavia kicked and yelled, but it was three against one and the few remaining bathers showed no interest in interfering. As she was dragged away, she heard the sickening sounds of fists on flesh and Rag's piercing shrieks.

'Stop it!' she cried in her own tongue, but one of the male slaves slapped a hand over her mouth, gripping so tightly she could hardly breathe. The other two hauled her off her feet, carrying her out of the great bath into the narrow corridor leading to Lucius Maximus' room.

Half-smothered, Flavia continued to struggle, but could feel herself weakening. *Help me,* she prayed, wanting just a chance to break free. A chance for her and Rags.

There was the sound of more running feet, this time from the direction of the main entrance: a heavy, but agile man, sprinting along the walkway.

'That is more than enough, Lucius,' said Marcus.

Flavia jerked her head, but could not loosen the slave's hand over her mouth. He and the others stopped, though, and turned to watch. Carried like a parcel between the three of them, Flavia could also see.

Marcus was standing where she herself had been, shielding Rags from his attacker. 'Leave the lad alone, Decurion,' he said, his jaw clenched in anger.

'No one orders me,' roared Lucius Maximus, lunging at the taller man.

Marcus reacted so swiftly that from her half-upside-down, suspended position, Flavia see only that he seized Lucius Maximus and forced his right arm behind his back. Kicking futilely, Lucius Maximus failed to free himself, his face dark with pain and frustrated rage.

'You are sweating, Decurion,' said Marcus, his every word falling like a catapult stone in the now-absolute silence of the huge, vaulted chamber. 'You should take a bath.'

With an easy push, he thrust the man away with such force that Lucius Maximus tottered and had to snatch at a statue to keep his feet. His large towel had unraveled from around his middle and he was forced to use his other hand to keep the towel from falling away entirely.

Marcus meanwhile had gathered the shivering little body of Rags into his arms. 'Steady, lad. I have you now.'

Taking advantage of the slaves' shocked stillness, Flavia lashed out again and this time wrestled herself free, dropping painfully on hands and knees onto the tiles, but able to scramble out of the men's windmilling reach. Marcus' head whipped round at the new commotion.

'By Mithras—' His eyes widened as he saw her. 'Don't touch her!'

His order rang out like a call to arms and the three slaves froze.

'I am all right,' Flavia told him, as she limped towards him. 'Please, can we go?'

Marcus looked again at her and Rags. 'Only because you have both had more than enough,' he said sternly. 'Walk in front of me.' He did not move until she had gone several steps ahead of him, rushing as quickly as she could for the dressing room and the exit.

Back in the dressing room, Marcus retrieved their things and wrapped Rags in his own cloak. 'You are coming with us,' Flavia heard him say. 'It is all arranged.'

Raising his head and meeting Flavia's eyes, Marcus added, 'I had already decided to get him out of here, even before this.'

'You, you—' Hope Flavia could scarcely believe flared in her.

'I have bought him.' Marcus shook his head. 'Don't look so shocked, girl. I cannot be worse than Lucius Maximus.' He tossed Flavia her shawl. 'Come.'

Flavia fumbled with her shawl. Now that she had escaped from Lucius Maximus' men, reaction had set in. 'Is he – is he all right?' she stammered. Rags was standing now, bundled in Marcus' cloak, but he had not spoken.

'He will be,' Marcus said. 'You both will.' His expression softened. 'Come, my

86

Flavia. Be a warrior a little longer. I am sorry I have no wine for you – that is lost somewhere in the bottom of the bath, where I threw it – but I've ordered a litter to take us home. We need only step out to it.'

No doubt in a similar situation his wife Drusilla would have behaved like Queen Boudicca herself, thought Flavia, appalled at her own spite. But the spurt of anger was enough to make her come alive again, to shake the chilly bonds of shock from her limbs.

She moved, her bare feet cold on the cooling tiles. Her bare feet, Flavia realized. 'My new sandals!'

'No.' Marcus moved to intercept her. 'You stay here and I will fetch them. Where are they? Where you were sitting? Stay here.' He clasped Flavia's hand in his and placed her hand on Rags' bony shoulder. 'Tell him about the garden,' he said, slipping back for the third time into the great bath.

Flavia coaxed Rags into sitting with her on the floor, in a shadowy corner. She sat with her back against one of the cupboards, took off her belt and offered it to the boy to tie round his middle. 'Your cloak will be warmer, then,' she explained.

Silently, Rags lifted the belt from her hand.

'That's it,' Flavia encouraged, wondering how long it might be before the boy would speak again. Peering at him in the dim light

87

she saw fresh bruises on his face and more on his arms and legs. He had been beaten horribly.

And Marcus had saved him. He had stopped Lucius Maximus from brutalizing a small, insignificant Celtic slave for no other reason than to stop cruelty – there had been no personal advantage for him, but rather the reverse, for a man like Lucius Maximus would certainly see his action as an insult. 'He is such a man,' she murmured, her voice stopping as she caught, far off, but approaching, the tapping of a pair of soft shoes on the tiles.

Flavia breathed out. It was not Marcus, but neither was it Lucius Maximus. She rose and moved to the threshold. Rags was in no condition to deal with any requests for clothing; whoever it was would have to make do with her.

With a whiff of rose perfume preceding her, a woman glided into the dressing room. Tall, she moved gracefully in her delicate slippers. She wore a short linen toga and had the glossiest red-gold mane of hair that Flavia had ever seen, set off by silver combs. She had lively hazel eyes, their uptilting corners enhanced by green make-up, an impudent, upturning nose and a mouth that looked made for laughter.

'Do you work here?' she asked Flavia, smiling at the huddled Rags and shrugging when the child made no response.

'For now,' Flavia said, guessing that this was one of the toga girls who worked in these baths. Lady Valeria would have disapproved of her talking to such a girl – by Roman custom only men and courtesans wore the toga – but Flavia felt a kinship with her. This comely woman would certainly be a slave.

She smiled at the tall stranger. 'Can I help you?'

'I am only passing on a message,' the woman said, examining her painted fingernails. 'A woman in the laconicum wants you to bring her sandals with the red string ties in cupboard fifteen.'

An easy request, Flavia thought: the laconicum, a hot dry sweat room, was only next door. She would be there and back long before Marcus returned. Rapidly retrieving the sandals, she nodded to the toga girl. 'Thanks.'

The woman shrugged. 'It's only a message. I am Messalina, by the way.'

'Flavia.'

'Then good luck, Flavia.' Messalina walked through the door with her and turned along the narrow corridor to the great bath.

Flavia hurried to the laconicum. Opening the door on the stinging dry heat, she saw a cloaked man closing on a cringing woman, his hand raised as if he would strike her.

'Stop!' Flavia shouted, astonished when the woman raised her head.

It was the haughty, thin-lipped woman who had shared Lucius Maximus' couch and she was laughing. 'See, Lucius?' she cried, plucking her own cloak from the nearest wooden bench, 'I told you an actress never loses her touch! What a show I made for this little fool. She is all yours now.'

Sensing movement behind her, Flavia ducked, ran back several steps and hurled the sandals at the looming Lucius Maximus. She pelted for the entrance, hearing the man raging. 'Insolent Celt! You will be whipped!'

Flavia ran along the corridor, Lucius Maximus gaining on her with every step. He and the former actress must have made their way to the laconicum while she and Marcus were comforting Rags in the dressing room. Hooded and cloaked, they had passed unrecognized from the eastern end of the bathing complex and set up this charade, deliberately to trap her.

Lucius Maximus grabbed one of her plaits. 'Got you!'

Flavia screamed, feeling a fearful pulling on her hair.

'You will not escape me again, slave!'

He caught her and slammed her against the wall, thrusting himself against her. Under the cloak he was naked.

'Your half-breed master should take better

care of his property,' he said, yanking savagely on her hair again. 'But then he will not be your owner for much longer because I shall buy you. Then you will learn what a true master is like.'

He pawed at her, enjoying Flavia's disgust, her shudder of revulsion. 'You are only a slave, my insolent Celt. Only flesh bought for money.'

Flavia choked as he breathed over her, his mouth stinking of wine. He was well on the way to being drunk and clearly a man accustomed to his own way, to cheating and to buying everything he wanted.

He tried to kiss her, laughing as Flavia turned her face desperately to one side. 'Perhaps I should sample the goods here?' he gloated.

'Let her go,' said Marcus harshly. 'Now.'

Opening tear-streaked eyes, Flavia saw Marcus standing in the corridor, with Rags carried piggy-back on his shoulders.

Lucius Maximus gave an evil smile. 'Of course, tribune. She is yours – for the moment.'

Running a hand insolently across her breast, he stepped back from Flavia and made to pass by Marcus, but then a knife glittered in his hand.

'No!' Flavia yelled.

Marcus lunged at the same instant as his attacker, driving a fist into the man's groin.

With a strangulated mew of pain, Lucius Maximus dropped the knife and toppled onto his knees, retching and clutching himself.

Marcus picked up the knife and gave it to Rags, whom he still carried on his back. He held out a hand to Flavia.

Quickly, stepping round the prone and moaning Lucius Maximus, Flavia went to him. 'I was tricked,' she began.

'I guessed as much,' Marcus said. 'But we should leave, before his people come.'

Flavia nodded and together they hurried from the baths, aware that they had made an enemy.

Chapter 4

That day marked a beginning. As the winter deepened, Flavia and Marcus learned whatever they could about each other.

Marcus told Flavia about his three older half-brothers, who were now all smaller than him. He told her about his childhood in the north of Italy. He remembered walking in the forum with his father, holding onto his father's little finger, and gathering wild flowers in the hills for his mother. He said she was his father's second wife, who came from a land across the Alps, close to Gaul, and never felt the cold. A Roman citizen, his mother spoke Latin with an accent, but he would not say, and Flavia did not ask, if she had been born a Celt.

For Flavia Marcus drew sketches of little Aurelia playing with her favourite doll. He spoke of his daughter with real affection. Drusilla, his wife, he described as smiling and even-tempered, skilled in cooking, the brewing of cordials, weaving and spinning. They had married when Drusilla was fourteen and he was a raw eighteen. Little Aurelia had been born a year later.

Flavia pitied him for his loss and acknowledged fearfully that she was far older than the serene Drusilla had been when she and Marcus first met.

For her part, Flavia told Marcus about reading poetry for the first time. One day she told him of a summer when no rain had fallen in Aquae Sulis and the river had slowed to a trickle. On another, she told him of a wandering teacher, a Celt, who had lived just outside Lady Valeria's gate for two seasons, begging and taking odd jobs and always teaching. 'A gentle man. A good man,' she said. Flavia did not say that this teacher had been Christian and that she had learned her Christian faith from him. In the Roman world she and Marcus lived in, Christianity was seen as the faith of slaves and subversives; Christian beliefs of equality seen as dangerous.

She has made the best of everything, Marcus thought. He wondered if she would ever share her secret, whatever it was she was hiding.

Meanwhile there were the child and the dog. Flavia had suggested that Rags might look after Nero as a way of helping both and slowly the pair were beginning to bloom. To show the boy that he would never be sent back to the baths, Marcus had renamed him. Rags was now Hadrian, trim and fresh-faced in a deep red tunic the same color as Marcus' own, and only the cook complained of his constant eating. Marcus bought Hadrian stuffed dates and sweet honey cakes from morning visitors who came selling and laughed to see the lad romping in the garden with an increasingly fast and noisy Nero.

Three weeks later, Marcus decided that it was time to begin teaching Hadrian a little of what he knew. Returning one mild after-noon from the fullers' with an armful of newly-cleaned laundry, Flavia found them in the garden, with Nero snapping playfully at their heels. Marcus had set up a target close to a lavender bush and he and then Hadrian were hurling javelins at it.

'Look, Flavia!' Hadrian yelled, and in a scramble of arms and legs the boy threw the javelin. It landed wildly off-target in an old wicker beehive and Hadrian shot off to retrieve it.

'Don't run with your spear!' Marcus warned, jogging down the main path to speak to Flavia. She however decided to speak first.

'Battle training, sir?' she asked, thinking that Hadrian would be better learning his letters. Something of the thought must have shown in her face because Marcus frowned.

'Why not? The army's an honorable life.' Towering over her by more than a foot, Marcus stood before her, arms folded. 'I am teaching Hadrian to defend himself. Would you have him set upon by every sneak thief in Aquae Sulis? If the Caledonians and other tribes from across the border came spilling down here from the great northern wall, would you have him helpless against them? I have seen what carnage their raids can do!'

'Of course not,' Flavia said quickly, recognising everything Marcus said and yet still uneasy. Her Christian creed forbade the taking of life. She bit her lip, wishing that she had not antagonised Marcus and aware that her fears were more than that of faith. 'He is so young, so small,' she whispered.

The stark face above hers softened. 'Like another we know.' Marcus brushed a speck from her brown gown.

'I did well enough against Lucius Maximus,' said Flavia stiffly.

'Indeed.' Marcus continued to stand in front of her, although Hadrian was waiting, juggling his javelin from hand to hand.

Flavia was unsure what to do. Although she and Marcus talked, a certain coolness had developed between them. Even her fellow slaves had noticed. Only that morning, Agrippina the cook, hurrying out to the gate to meet the mysterious spice seller in the rich fur cape and hood had snapped at Flavia, in passing, 'Do us all a favour and go to the master's bed tonight. Honestly, why not?' Another time in the kitchen while kneading dough, Agrippina had turned aside Flavia's questions about the mysterious spice seller by saying, 'The gods alone know why master's waiting for you to give him a sign but he is. Who are you, slave, to be so proud? Tell him you like him.'

'She is jealous,' fellow slave Livia had muttered, which may have been true but gave Flavia no comfort. She was shy of Marcus and of herself. She knew their relationship was unusual in its lack of formality but perhaps Marcus was no longer interested in her. Perhaps it was better if he was no longer interested. What future could there be between them?

'I don't like you wandering alone in the city,' Marcus said now.

Flavia tore her eyes away from him and took a closer grip on her armload of freshly-laundered washing. 'What are you teaching Hadrian?' she asked, unhappy at the tension between them, but uncertain how to resolve it.

'Riding, sword-play, spears, the use of shields. How to tend wounds. Wrestling–'

Marcus broke off, staring at the small bowed head. A memory of the girl's face shocked with fear, swimming with tears, flashed through him. For the thousandth time he cursed Lucius Maximus, vowed that he would never provoke such a look of dread. But she was so tempting in her little drab brown gown, no cosmetics, no fancy combs in her hair, no perfume, nothing except a body Venus herself would have begged for, with pert round breasts, a waist he could span easily with his hands, hips that made his mouth go dry with longing and beautiful soft, silky skin.

'Perhaps I should teach you to wrestle,' he said.

Her head came up at that, to check if he was teasing. Marcus kept his face straight.

'Would you, sir?' A certain wicked look he had not seen for the last three weeks came into her eyes. 'Sword play, too, and riding?'

'Wait!' Marcus held up both hands in mock surrender. In truth, he found it impossible to think of Flavia as a slave, much less treat her as one, and now he was relieved that their earlier banter was back. 'Very well, a little about how to handle weapons. But no riding.'

'Why–' Flavia stifled the rest of the question. She would be learning to wrestle with Marcus, feeling that lean, tanned body against hers. The thought made her blush, but she also felt like laughing. She looked at him again, thinking how handsome he was, and how far out of her reach.

He tapped his fingers against his belt. 'There is one condition.'

'Yes, sir?' said Flavia, a suspicion forming swiftly and confirmed by Marcus' ready answer.

'If you are to join Hadrian, you will need a short tunic.' He ran a thumb along his dark stubble, the small scar near his mouth disappearing as he smiled. 'That new tunic of fine Egyptian linen will do very well.'

'It is winter!' Flavia protested.

Marcus laughed. 'I will be working you hard, little Celt. You will be warm enough.'

'I cannot,' Flavia said, suddenly nervous. 'Not today. I – you wanted me to read you more of Lady Valeria's final letters,' she added, rapidly recalling one of his earlier instructions. 'The ones you said you have not yet read fully.'

Marcus showed his strong teeth in a knowing grin. 'They will keep.' He shouted and beckoned to Hadrian and Nero, adding, 'I want you back here, in your tunic,

98

within ten javelin casts. Go.'

'Yes, sir.' Blushing furiously, Flavia turned and sped off into the villa.

Changing in the damp little room which she now shared with Hadrian, Flavia was reminded of two things. The first was the clear and increasing confidence of the former bath boy. For three nights after coming into his new home, Hadrian had woken with nightmares. Flavia had taken him into her own bed with her, singing to him softly, rocking him, until he slept again. As the bruises from Lucius Maximus' savage beating had faded, as he had played with Nero, and since Marcus had never raised voice or hand to him, the boy began to settle. His eyes were losing that hard, flinty cast and his face softening, so that he looked closer to his true age. Marcus treated him like a small younger brother and, of all the household, Hadrian was the only one who called Marcus by name without turning a hair.

The second change, Flavia thought, smoothing the linen shift over her hips, was going to happen to this very room. Marcus had inspected all the slaves' quarters and had decided they must be rebuilt. The stone masons would begin work after the midwinter festival of Saturnalia.

Flavia straightened, feeling very exposed in this scandalous, sleeveless v-necked tunic.

She glanced down at herself, tugging nervously at the pale white cloth, so fine as to be almost sheer. It stopped far short of her knees and was so light she felt to be wearing nothing.

'He does not like women who are late,' Flavia told herself, but her limbs still moved as if she were underwater as she forced herself to return outdoors.

Back in the garden she saw that the javelin target was gone. Old Gaius had brought Marcus' horse from the small stable block and yard set at the back of the villa, and he was leading the tall black round the gravel paths. Hadrian, with a squirming Nero held tight to his chest, was asking if he could lead the massive stallion and Gaius was shaking his head, his wispy red moustache seeming to droop even more than usual over his wrinkled chin.

She heard a twig crack behind her and automatically twisted sideways, stepping back several paces. Marcus shadowed her, running his thumbs lightly down the sides of her arms, a brief caress that made her tremble.

'Do I tell you well done?' he teased, bringing his head close to hers. 'The cracked twig was an obvious warning. I would have been disappointed if I had caught you after that.'

'But you did not,' Flavia said, and that odd burst of defiance that she only ever seemed to have with Marcus made her add, 'Even I know not to let an enemy creep up behind me.'

'Enemy, eh? And what about a friend?'

Flavia looked him straight in the eye. 'A friend would not do that.'

'Maybe not, but I am trying to teach you. Perhaps next time a harder test would be more ... appropriate.' Marcus scratched at his chin, then suddenly his same hand snatched at Flavia's wrists. She danced back just in time – straight into his other arm, which coiled lazily about her middle.

'Remember, Flavia, that a man's reach is longer than yours,' he said, lifting her off her feet and giving her a tiny shake. 'A man's fighting space will be bigger than yours, so you need to back up that much further.'

'Or attack that much closer,' Flavia answered, stung into a response by sheer exasperation. From the corner of her eye she saw Gaius tether the black stallion by the gate and come hobbling towards them.

'I know,' said Marcus, as she opened her mouth to inform him. 'I can recognise Gaius' bandy-legged walk anywhere. And Hadrian has scurried off to the kitchen with Nero, no doubt to grab more food before we set out.' He raised thick black eyebrows. 'What lesson am I teaching now?'

'Always know where people are,' said Flavia, conscious of the powerful flank and thigh pressed close against her own. 'You and Hadrian are leaving, sir?' To her disgust she sounded young and rather pathetic.

'We are riding to the farm. Freedman Valens has just sent word requesting my immediate presence there and Hadrian has clamoured to come along, too.' Setting her down on her feet again, Marcus flicked one of her plaits, making her feel even more absurd. He called out, 'That is fine, Gaius,' and waved the man back into the warmth of the villa. 'I will be back before sunset,' he said then.

'Of course,' said Flavia, ashamed that she should now envy Hadrian.

'I will consider the letters tonight.'

Flavia nodded.

'I am sorry about our fighting lesson.' He looked her up and down. 'I like the way your tunic clings and I like that length. You have excellent legs.'

She had almost forgotten the tunic. Becoming fully aware again of her immodest new outfit, Flavia crossed her naked arms protectively in front of herself, trying to hide behind her hair as she covered her exposed thighs with her hands. Reluctant to face those knowing blue eyes, she mumbled an excuse about having to help Livia and prepared to leave.

'I expect to see you wearing it when I return.'

Flavia said nothing. Absently at first, she stared at the black stallion cropping a few blades of dry grass at the gate and then she frowned. Was there something strange about the animal? A prickle of unease ran through her – suddenly she wanted a much closer look.

'Let me walk you to your horse, sir,' she said, ignoring her companion's raised eyebrows and quiet, 'Be my guest.' Hurrying ahead, she slowed only when the horse pricked back its ears.

'Easy,' she murmured in Latin, taking care not to move behind the stallion as she checked it over. Lady Valeria had never owned a mount like this, so Flavia dredged through her reading memory: bits of Virgil and the writings of that tyrant Julius Caesar. War horses. How was the saddle secured, the harness?

She glanced over the saddle and saddle cloth, coming closer to the stallion, but not touching it. Moving to its head, she put her hand out flat for the beast to smell her, to recognise her as a friend.

After a moment, the horse lifted its head from the sparse ground, nuzzled a soft, hairy mouth across her palm and then returned to its browsing.

'You like horses, then.' Coming beside her, Marcus patted the black's long reaching neck.

'I do,' Flavia breathed. Before today, she had only watched Gaius harness the stiff old mule for Lady Valeria's small cart. This shining, spirited creature was entirely new. She scratched its stiff mane and shoulder, astonished by its beautiful large dark eyes and delightfully furry winter coat.

'Alexander seems to like you, as well.' Running a gentle hand over each of the horse's legs, Marcus was lifting and checking each hoof.

'Yes.' Watching his strong, searching fingers, Flavia recalled his touch with a tiny shiver of pleasure, almost forgetting what she was supposed to be doing. Tearing her eyes away from his dark, intent head, she looked at the harness. There was a dangling, loose piece of leather close to the horse's cheek that did not look right. She touched the leather strip and the horse snorted, tossing its head, jangling its harness.

'Should the harness move that way?' she asked, stroking the horse's flank, crooning as the beast quietened again.

'That is it, keep him occupied,' Marcus said, patiently checking the bit before running his hands this way and that over the harness. 'By Mithras, you are right.' Quickly, he re-secured the piece of dangling leather. 'Gaius must have forgotten this one. We could have had quite an accident with this, if Alexander had decided to bolt.' He patted the black's neck again.

Flavia imagined Marcus and Hadrian riding off in all innocence, the stallion shying and bolting, out of control. She shuddered, her mouth full of the iron taste of dread. She could not bear the idea of Marcus or Hadrian being hurt in any way.

'Flavia?'

She turned, so that he would not see her ready tears.

'You are trembling.' Marcus unhooked his short cloak and wrapped it around her narrow shoulders. 'It is all right, it was only a mistake,' he was saying, 'And because you saw it there is no harm done – no harm at all.'

He cupped her elbows, then gently wound his arms about her.

'Thank you,' he said, looking down into her eyes. 'I am in your debt.'

'You would have checked yourself,' Flavia stammered. 'You are a horseman.'

'Hush! Don't be so modest.' He ran a teasing finger over her lower lip. 'Do you still wish to learn to ride?'

Still thinking of what might have happened had she not spotted the loose harness, Flavia stared at him. He gave her a slow, broad smile, clearly far less concerned with the incident than she was.

'It will not be so difficult to teach you as well. You are scarcely bigger than Hadrian.'

He grinned at her indignant snort and stooping, stole a swift, tingling kiss from her mouth. 'Until this evening.'

Chapter 5

The glossy black horse and large and small russet-clad riders trotted off towards the river ford, with Nero streaking on ahead. Flavia clapped her hands together.

'That's it, then,' she said under her breath, aware that she should be about her cleaning but reluctant to step out of this bright, mild afternoon into the villa. She lifted the edge of the short cloak Marcus had draped over her, inhaling his crisp, masculine scent from the cloth. She felt foolishly pleased to be wearing something of his, even if this 'short' garment brushed her calves.

She turned and saw Livia approaching, snug in her own fresh gown and shawl. Lady Valeria had been a fair mistress, but there had never been sufficient money when she was alive for new clothes or even extra food. According to the arrogant Lucius Maximus, Marcus was land poor, but even so he had means and he was generous.

Would he be equally generous with her, Flavia wondered, if he knew what she had done? If he learned of her desperate forgery? Marcus trusted her. By saying nothing was she not betraying that trust? More and more she wished the secret was not between them. She wished she was free, and his equal.

Putting these unhappy thoughts aside, Flavia ran back to Livia.

'Where would you like me to begin sweeping?' she asked. As the youngest and most agile of the household, Flavia deferred to Gaius, Agrippina, Livia and Sulinus and was content to do so. Until Marcus had come into the villa as a new, decisive master, she and the others had looked out for each other. Agrippina had always been brisk and domineering in a well-meaning way, but never jealous, as she was now, especially of Flavia.

Conscious of these changes, Flavia was glad when Livia answered easily, 'You can start in the master's study, but not yet.' She smiled, her once handsome face meshing with wrinkles, and rubbed a weather-beaten hand along her jaw, close to the site of a missing tooth.

'Come,' she said, catching Flavia's concerned expression, 'Agrippina has made us all a hot elderberry tisane. It is waiting for us in the kitchen.'

Relieved to be included, Flavia fell into step with the taller woman. They had reached the peristyle when Livia frowned and said, 'No, we go this way,' and veered away from the narrow outer door that led directly to the kitchen, moving instead towards the main villa entrance.

Something in her manner reminded Flavia of Gaius' fist-clenching, whenever he tried to lie. She took a rapid backward glance and was disappointed, but not confounded, to see a slim, rather stately figure, robed in a hooded fur cape, gliding through the open villa gate. Livia and the others clearly did not want her to meet this stranger, but Flavia was determined to learn more. Aware that Livia would tell her nothing in case she upset the sharp-tongued cook, she thought of a way.

'Ah, my new sandal!' She crouched and made great play of fiddling with the sandal ties on her left foot. 'You go on, Livia. I will catch up. It is just a pebble in my shoe and the tie is knotted.'

She kept her head down and fingers busy as Livia walked on. She knew she was being sly, but this way she had not forced Livia to tell any lies or to break any confidences. Quickly, she stole back to the peristyle and waited, hidden by the villa's shadow.

As before, the mysterious spice seller wore her hood up, but this time Flavia could see her face. Walking steadily towards the kitchen entrance was a young woman of between twenty and twenty-five, with a brown fringe, long, rather elegant features, dark eyes and a face slightly reddened by the winter's day.

Not a native, Flavia thought, for the sunny afternoon seemed mild to her.

About to work her way closer, Flavia froze when the young woman stopped on the gravel path, a look of puzzlement crossing her calm, intelligent face. She lifted a hand to her hood, smoothing the fur away from her forehead, then nodded and turned to leave.

Flavia was not interested in whoever had signalled from the house; she set off after the young woman, walking lightly on the grass and soil and praying that the stranger would not look back. She trailed her to the gate outside the villa, where the young woman threaded her way along the street in the same direction Marcus had taken earlier, towards the river ford with its small settlement for workshops and houses.

Aware that she would soon be missed in the villa, Flavia darted straight up to the stranger.

'Excuse me, my lady,' she said breathlessly, as if she had just run hard, 'But do you have more to sell? We need more.'

The young woman's wind-reddened features sharpened into a glare of suspicion. 'I buy, not sell,' she said coldly. 'Agrippina and the others know this. Why do you not, slave?'

With a proud tilt of her chin and flip of her fur cape, the woman was gone, leaving Flavia dumbfounded in the middle of the street. The bellow of a passing carter forced her to move and she pelted back to the villa, still smarting over that derisive 'slave' and even more worried. She had seen the woman's hands and realized that, like the apothecary who lurked around the baths, the haughty female *buyer* had heavily stained fingernails.

Was she also a potion maker? If so, what were Agrippina and the others selling her? What was going on?

In the kitchen, her fingers wrapped tightly around a wooden beaker of hot elderberry tisane, Flavia asked the cook the same question.

'Who are you to ask, Lady Curious?' Agrippina was peeling parsnips, preparing Marcus' favourite dish of honey-glazed parsnips, and now she pointed her knife at Flavia. 'Honestly, you sit there, drinking my tisane, sampling my biscuits–'

'And I am grateful,' Flavia said, as alongside her Gaius tugged at the ends of his thin red moustache. Further along the table, the gardener Sulinus was using his knife to clean under his fingernails.

'Stop that!' Agrippina skidded a wooden spatula across the scrubbed board at the stocky man, who had the grace to look embarrassed.

'Honestly, I have meals to make and you...'

Flavia, Gaius, Sulinus and Livia glanced at each other, trying not to smile. Agrippina's complaint was as familiar as her excellent cooking. There was no genuine ill-will.

Sulinus scratched his hair under his hat and mumbled, 'We all work hard, Pina.'

'I know that,' Agrippina responded. Laying the peeled parsnips in a cooking pot, she pointed to the basin of freshly-milled flour that Flavia had ground earlier that morning and added, 'Thanks for that, girl. I know you always do it to save my back.'

Wishing she did not blush so easily, Flavia met the cook's brilliant black eyes. 'It is nothing,' she said. Reminded of Agrippina's kindness when she was sick last summer with heat stroke, she was ashamed of her formless suspicions.

'Please tell me what is happening,' she said. 'I do not like to be excluded.'

At her honest appeal, the four older servants shuffled uncomfortably on their seats, the two men hiding their expressions behind their wooden beakers as they drank.

Livia leaned across the table and patted Flavia's arm. 'It is not that we don't trust you–'

'So Marcus doesn't know what you are doing,' said Flavia.

She might have said more, but was interrupted by the cook's irritated, 'Marcus, is it? Well, it is certainly clear you are the master's

111

favourite,' she went on, bustling from table to shelf to retrieve a small jug of freshly-made garum sauce. 'Look at you, wearing his clothes as if you were born in them. Honestly, you will be giving us orders next!'

Agrippina broke off, her dark complexion colouring slightly. 'Sorry,' she said, sloshing the garum sauce round and round in its jug. 'I am sorry, that was unfair.' She shrugged, absently touching her thumb between her full, heavy breasts. 'I would be a liar if I said I was not envious.'

'Now, now, wife,' said Gaius, giving Flavia a wink. 'I think you have said enough on that subject.'

Everyone gave a nervous smile and drank from their beakers. After a moment, Livia touched Flavia's arm again.

'These are early days,' she said. 'It is for the best.'

Old Gaius tapped the side of his long nose. 'What you don't know cannot hurt you.'

'I am not a child. Please do not treat me like one.'

Gaius shook his head. 'Trust us, Flavia. We are not doing anything wrong.' He puffed out his skinny cheeks. 'Just give us until the end of the month, and then we will explain everything. I promise.'

His faded blue eyes were fixed upon Flavia, his thin mouth trembling with tension. Flavia looked at him and the others and knew she had no choice. 'Then I will wait,' she said.

Trying to forget the female potion trader, Flavia busied herself in Marcus' study, mopping down every tile and the table. As she shook the wolf skin rug out in the courtyard-garden, she thought of his swift, teasing kiss as he had left.

'He would not have treated the perfect Drusilla like that,' she muttered, giving the rug a final, savage flap. 'I am sick of being treated like a child!'

Hot-eyed, she retired indoors and lingered over the polishing of his study couch and chair, wishing that Marcus would kiss her as he had before – properly and with feeling.

Later, passing the room that had been Lady Valeria's bedchamber and which still contained her things, Flavia stopped and opened the door. For a moment, she felt as if she was invading her former mistress' room, but then she walked in – whether for comfort or in that mood of defiance which seemed to be affecting her more and more of late, she was not sure.

She touched the bed where Lady Valeria had slept, then turned and hurried to the dressing table under the shuttered window. The light was fading, but she could see the circular hand mirror that she had held up for her mistress, and the pins that she had used to dress her lady's iron-gray hair.

She ran her fingers over the curved lid of the jewel box. Her lady had been wearing her favourite pieces when she died, but the jewel box still contained some earrings and bracelets.

Prompted by a memory of Lady Valeria ordering, 'Tuck that awful gold bangle out of sight – it is hideous,' Flavia opened the jewel case lid. She remembered the wide, heavy bracelet, a gift from one of Lady Valeria's grateful dependants, but rarely worn. Recalling its chunky, ornate gold work, and its rare but gaudy gemstones, Flavia smilingly shook her head. Valuable the piece might be, but Lady Valeria had been right – it was ugly. She would look at it again and applaud her mistress' good taste.

It was not there. Frowning, Flavia lifted out each bracelet, but the ugly-expensive bangle was not in the jewel box. The other glittering pieces slid away from her suddenly nerveless fingers. Where was the bangle? Had someone taken it, someone in the house?

No! Flavia's mind rebelled, revolted at the idea of there being a thief in the villa. 'A thief would take the whole jewel case, or at least all the pieces,' she said aloud, which was as true for a burglar operating from outside the household. But then who would have taken it, and why?

'What are you doing?'

114

Marcus' icy demand filled the bedchamber. Whirling about to face him, Flavia dropped the jewel box. Thin gold bracelets scattered like blown leaves over the floor tiles.

'I am not stealing!' she burst out. Had he heard what she had said? Dare she tell him about the missing gold bangle?

Marcus raised his eyebrows. 'So what are you doing in here?' he said, in a less glacial voice, folding his arms across his chest.

His tall, strong body blocked the doorway, but Flavia had no wish to escape, only to convince him that he could trust her. She hated the idea of his not believing her.

'I came to look, that is all,' she said, knowing how lame the truth sounded. She thought of Gaius and the others, accepting that they, like her, would never have stolen any jewel of Lady Valeria's, and confessed. 'A golden bangle with amber and ruby stones is missing from my lady's jewel box, sir. I do not understand it, seeing–'

'Seeing that no one in the villa would have taken it,' Marcus finished for her. 'No, that is a mystery.'

'Perhaps Lady Valeria gave the jewel away,' Flavia suggested.

'Knowing Valeria, that is entirely possible.' He tapped his fingers on his belt and nodded, his black brows unbending as he continued to look at her. 'Thank you for sharing that with me, girl. Now, gather up those spilled trinkets and meet me in the study. Wait.'

He strode into the room and unfastened the brooch pinning his own short cloak to her slender shoulders. Deftly, he removed the cloak from her, brushing her arm with his thumb and saying, 'You look warm enough to me now. And I am glad you remembered my wishes.'

'Thank you, sir,' said Flavia faintly, conscious yet again of her short, diaphanous tunic as his eyes raked over her figure.

He gave a grunt of amusement. 'You only call me that when you are unsure of me.'

'You only call me girl when you are angry with me,' said Flavia. Her breath stopped as he ran his fingers under her chin, raising her face to his.

'Not angry, Flavia. Exasperated, bemused, amused. Not angry.'

He brushed a flyaway wisp of hair away from her forehead and stepped back. 'Remember those baubles.' He tossed the cloak over his shoulder as he left.

Marcus had lit two lamps in the study, so that she could read in a good light. Lady Valeria's old wicker chair had been draped with the wolf skin rug and the blue and gold couch lifted away from the wall to within a foot of the desk – an easy arm-stretch for Flavia.

'As I am sure you remember, I do like my

116

people to be comfortable.'

Facing her across the desk, Marcus was shadowed in the narrow shuttered room, but not for long. He rose and approached her, flicking the door curtain across the entrance behind her. In his hand he held several wax tablets and a bundle of rolled papyrus.

'A prodigious correspondent, your lady,' he remarked, nodding at the couch. 'Hop up there and we will begin once I have poured some wine. Reading aloud is no pleasure with a parched throat.'

Flavia's mouth was dry but for a very different reason. She prayed she would not be asked to read Lady Valeria's 'last' letter again – her own forgery.

She boosted herself onto the blue and gold couch, her feet dangling as she perched on the edge. Couches were Roman and she was neither Roman nor free, but as Marcus sat beside her, handing her a cup of wine, she was vividly reminded of the last time she had shared a couch with him.

'Drink,' he said. 'It is not poisoned.' He scratched the blue-black stubble along his jawline. 'Why so stiff? My words were only a foolish joke.'

'Of course.' Dismissing thoughts of the female potion buyer and the sinister apothecary, Flavia drank deeply from her cup, keen to prove that she trusted him. The wine was as smooth as honey, rich without being

cloying, slightly fizzy and very strong. Surprised, she coughed as a track of fiery
sweetness burned its way to her stomach.

'Steady, little Celt,' said an amused Marcus beside her. 'That is unmixed Veliternian
you are tossing down your throat. Take
some water with it next time.' He poured
her another third of a cup, filling the rest
with fresh water from a small jug.

Flavia sipped the wine.

'Like it?'

'Very much.' She drank more, not caring if
she was beginning to feel light-headed.
These days, Marcus made her feel that way
on his own and now he was smiling at her
too, shaking his head, but smiling.

'I think we had better start on these letters,' he said. From the couch beside him,
he drew an open wax tablet and dropped it
into her lap.

'I received this from Valeria while I was
stationed in the northern city of Eboracum.
Now that we have both seen Lucius Maximus, I would be interested to know your
thoughts on what she says about him.'

Marcus pointed to several spindly lines
below her own regular scribe's hand. 'Her
text begins right after your own. It will be a
message you have not read before.'

Flavia nodded, uncomfortably reminded
that until Marcus had burst into her life
she'd had no idea that Lady Valeria had

regularly added more than just her seal and signature to the ends of letters. She had believed that her mistress told her everything; that although she was only a slave scribe, she had been privy to Lady Valeria's thoughts. It was a bitter, uneasy thing to learn otherwise, sharpening her old longing for freedom.

Forcing herself to concentrate, she read aloud:

Young Flavia gives you all the farewells in the correct order, so I will not bother to repeat those. There's a new Roman amongst the high-living classes at Aquae Sulis, one Lucius Maximus. He is about your age, Marcus, and I wondered if you might have heard of him. He is married, but he and his rich wife are separated. The rumour in Aquae Sulis is that he has come to Britannia to fleece a fortune from us Celts.

An acquaintance of mine called on Lucius Maximus. Found the man in a silk toga, lounging on a couch while receiving guests in a huge, statue-filled atrium – a hall large enough to take my entire villa, according to my sober informant.

From their conversation it appears that Lucius Maximus claimed a blood-tie with me, which is regrettable, as I do not like the sound of the man. He kept my elderly acquaintance waiting for hours, offered no refreshment or chair, and bragged endlessly about his collections of gemstones and antiques. It seems our Lucius is a keen hoarder of ancient gold. He showed my friend a necklace he was wearing, made of gold, which he

119

claimed to have taken from a local alder tree growing over a spring.

'It was simply entangled in the branches, swinging about in the tree above the water and no use to anyone where it was,' Lucius Maximus told my friend.

Reading, Flavia stopped. 'That necklace was surely a sacred offering,' she whispered. 'It was meant for the deity of the spring.'

'As Valeria said, an unholy man,' remarked Marcus. 'Read on: it gets worse.'

Lucius Maximus' entrance hall is crammed full of antique statues and small monuments, including one particularly fine gravestone from Londinium and a Greek female nude in marble which Lucius Maximus regularly caresses.

Flavia's frown was answered by Marcus' scowl. Together they raised their cups and drank, the study silent except for the steady fizzing of the oil lamps and their own breathing. Silently scanning the rest of the letter, Flavia picked out 'natural conspirator', 'looks for his cut in everything' and, darkest of all, 'He has stolen another man's slave, violated the girl and passed her to another of his cronies.'

'What?' Seeing her expression change, Marcus took the letter from her and cursed. 'I forgot that part. I would not have had you read it.'

'Why not? It shows the man. He clearly has a taste for other people's property.'

120

Flavia tried to jump down from the couch, but her abrupt movement made her head swim and in the next instant Marcus had his arms about her.

'You try running now and you will fall flat on your face,' he rumbled softly against her ear. 'I warned you – Veliternian is not supposed to be drunk like water.'

'You gave it to me,' Flavia protested, one hand clasping the wax tablet while the other treacherously hovered upwards to stroke Marcus' tough dark hair. Astonished at her own impulse – though she had experienced such feelings before – she snatched her hand back, turning her head to stop staring at his ruggedly handsome face and dark blue eyes.

Lowering her face, she noticed Lady Valeria's closing phrase: 'I give you my love, Marcus, and my good wishes.'

I would do the same, Flavia thought. She shivered and ducked her head lower, afraid and yet at the same time amazed, feeling never more alive.

She had done the worst thing possible. She had fallen in love with Marcus Brucetus.

Chapter 6

She loved Marcus. She loved him for his kindness, energy, courage, generosity and strength.

She loved him for tender, foolish reasons. For the way he strolled about on his long legs, leaving everyone in his wake. For his drawing of fishes and monsters in the gravel for Hadrian. For his endearing habit at meal-time of leaving his parsnips until last, a final delicacy.

The revelation of her love welled like a spring in Flavia, so powerful that she was convinced that something would show in her face. But she must not let that happen. Marcus was a free Roman citizen, proud and honorable. She was a slave born of slaves with no knowledge of her ancestors; nothing to give him.

Nothing to give him but myself, she thought, trembling a little at her own arrogance. Yes, she knew he found her pretty, but what was that? There were many pretty girls in the Roman world: she was not special. But it would be wonderful to lie with Marcus, to please him.

'Perhaps the wine was a mistake,' Marcus

said, as Flavia struggled to compose herself, a scalding blush sweeping over her throat and cheeks. She was afraid of meeting those watchful blue eyes in case he read this new love in hers and was pitying – or worse, embarrassed. Compared to Drusilla, his beloved wife and the mother of his child, she was no more than a useful tool. Like a stylus, she thought, glancing across the nearby desk at one of the many pens.

She must have acted on her thought, leaned and reached over, for Marcus enfolded her stretching fingers in his own large hand.

'I doubt if you could write a true or fair line now, little Celt,' he said.

Marcus brushed the girl's shoulder with his other hand – only a touch, but Flavia reacted as if she had been burned, flinching away and then hunching into a tight coil of shielding arms.

Cursing his clumsiness, Marcus swung his legs off the couch and came to stand in front of his tough, but definitely nervous Flavia. He wanted to say to her that he didn't believe in life-slavery, that to him loyalty in a servant should be rewarded sooner rather than later by freedom. Given his own past, how could he not think that? But then Flavia didn't know that part of his personal history, and she might think less of him when she did.

But what did that matter now? Most of all, Marcus thought, he wanted her not to be afraid of him. He planted his arms one on either side of her tight, seated figure and gently kissed her forehead.

'Flavia.' She would not look at him yet but he knew she was listening. 'I think you like me, as a man–'

She said nothing, but with a soldier's quickness, Marcus noticed her right hand tilt very slightly towards him, a tiny movement, rapidly smothered. It gave him hope.

'I have called you provoking. I could also say distracting. To be blunt–' Marcus heard his own voice roughening with desire– 'I want you. You please me very much and I would pleasure you.'

She looked at him then, her golden hair a halo to her flushed, sensitive face, her gray eyes wide and bright, her soft lush mouth hovering on the edge of a smile. He wanted to snatch her up there and then, rip that taunting, slinky tunic right off her body and have her on the couch, and make her yield to him totally.

'But there is no rush,' he said, ignoring the hardness in his loins, the hunger in his mouth to kiss her lips, her pink-nippled breasts, lower...

Behind her back, Marcus gripped the edge of the couch until his fingers cracked, repeating the words *slow down* in his mind.

He made himself smile, although he wondered if the result would be 'Daddy's grave grin', as little Aurelia had called it: his smile when he was angry, or fighting other strong emotions.

'Not all Romans are like Lucius Maximus,' he said.

'I know that.'

She sounded almost impudent, tossing her head.

'Careful, young Flavia,' he warned, but then he opened his arms.

She came to him at once, stretching up on the couch and wrapping her slender white arms around his neck. Astonished and delighted at her unabashed response, Marcus scooped her off the couch, cradling her and kissing her.

'You taste of honey and Veliternian,' he said, kissing her again.

He laid her back on the couch and came beside her. It was the warm trust in her eyes that gave him the control he needed.

'Say my name,' he said, feathering a fingertip down her forehead, nose, lips, chin, and throat. He wanted to hear her say it.

'Master Marcus,' she said shyly, and then quite clearly, 'Marcus.'

He wanted her to know that they were equal, that he would never force her to do anything. He needed to keep her trust.

Lying beside him, glowing with more than the wine, her head nestled in the crook of his arm, her small yet surprisingly well-figured body tucked against his, Flavia smiled.

'Marcus,' she said a third time, running a strand of his hair through her fingers, a curious look of mingled triumph and concentration lighting her pretty face. She knew they were not betrothed, not even equal in the eyes of the law and yet, she did not want this moment to end.

Slowly, in answer to her touch, he trailed his finger from her throat to the shadowed cleavage between her breasts. In the flickering lamp light her skin had the silken, creamy shimmer of a pearl. Through her gossamer tunic he could see the perked, tender rosettes of her nipples and below her taut waist, the dusky blur where the material pooled seductively at the meeting place of the tops of her thighs.

At this sight, his mouth, already cinder dry with desire, gaped. He shut his eyes, thinking of the most boring drill manoeuvres he could imagine, and willed himself not to flip her tantalising little body over on the couch and plunge into her, like a stallion to a mare.

'Flavia.' He touched the delicate bones at the base of her throat. She deserved so much more than a rapid, clumsy tumble. He was not a raw cadet, nor an over-eager youth: he should explain.

'Flavia, it will be all right. I want you, yes, but not without your consent. Let me cherish you, show you part of a delicious journey.' Deftly, his fingers untied her tunic belt and he lowered the shoulder straps, slowly exposing her to the waist.

She sucked in a breath as his hand cupped each breast and then she pressed her palm against his chest, stroking her hand slowly across his middle. Even through his rough tunic, her tentative caress hit him like a lightning bolt: heat and pleasure scorched through him.

'May I touch you?' she whispered, suddenly stopping, a new blush darkening her almond-blossom complexion. 'Is it permitted?'

'By Mithras, yes!' Marcus groaned, hugging her tighter. His mouth found hers and her lips parted under his. Their kiss was long, hot and sweet. Striving for self-control, he broke away, only to be drawn back by the perfection of her breasts. Drawing her up on the couch, he lowered his head and flicked his tongue across her nipple. She moaned and arched towards him, her legs entwining with his, her hands stroking over the length of his back.

'Flavia,' he crooned, gently exploring and caressing. Her skin tasted of salt and a kind of milky, baby sweetness that was rapidly driving him wild. Full yet firm, her breasts invited his hands and mouth again – he could not stop now.

Flavia's breath snagged in her throat as his mouth nuzzled her breast again, his tongue softly sucking her nipple, tasting her. Her body felt at once drained and energised, as if she would simply sink into the couch, then rush from the room in a dazzling blaze of movement. For the first time in her life she knew she was truly desirable.

Wishing her master – her Marcus now – would feel the same, she caressed him in return, sensing his taut sinews and flesh beneath his tunic. He was her stark opposite, hard where she was soft, rugged and strong. She tapped his breastbone, feeling his heart pound in answer, as if it might burst from his chest to meet her fingers. Suddenly it was no longer enough to feel him through the cloth; she must touch him, him alone, print her hand upon the mighty shield of his ribs. She began to untie the belt of his tunic.

'Gods!' Marcus exclaimed, his hands cupping her, his fingers shimmering over her breasts, gently squeezing and tickling. Flavia, one hand still fumbling with the belt, could only gasp, falling onto him, wrapping her free arm about his back. She caught a glimpse of his bushy black eyebrows – she loved his bushy black eyebrows – and then his mouth was on hers once more and he was lifting her, drawing her closer still. 'You are a quick learner, little scribe.'

I have a good teacher, she thought in her own tongue, kissing him as he kissed her, aware of the spitting oil lamp, and the dry ache in her throat, a moist, fiery ache between her thighs

She kissed the side of his nose, laughing as he wrinkled it, smiling as he playfully pinched her nose in turn, gasping as he patted and pinched her bottom.

'Now that you know some of the characters of loving, perhaps you can write something for me,' he said, his voice indulgent.

'For you?' she breathed, wondering if she dare add, 'Or on you.'

She swallowed and ran tongue over her dry lips, gearing herself to speak, when outside the study door there came a hectic slapping of rushing feet. Jerking back from Marcus, she watched in appalled frustration as Hadrian tried to burst into the room.

'Marcus, there's a messenger come!' the boy yelled, promptly enmeshing himself in the hanging door curtain.

Marcus raised his eyes heavenwards and rumbled something in his own language. He looked aggrieved and dishevelled as he muttered, 'No peace anywhere in this house.'

Sensing her shrink, he turned to her and smiled: rather a grim smile, but far better than a frown. 'Are you all right?'

Fastening her tunic with trembling fingers, Flavia nodded, grateful to be asked and relieved when Marcus chose to be amused. 'Good, then!' he said, briefly touching her cheek with his fingers. 'Now let us get this thunderbolt out of his netting.'

Speaking, Marcus had already moved to the door and swiftly untangled Hadrian from the heavy curtain. 'Your report, soldier?' he demanded, as the boy's grinning face emerged from the blood-red hanging.

'Marcus, there's a rider from your old barracks at Eboracum! He is carrying a message for you from your commander! He has ridden non-stop from the north, changing horses–'

'He has been given food and his mount stabled?' Marcus interrupted, but Hadrian was not to be quenched.

'Yes, yes. And he says he will go to the baths before moonrise. He is going to sleep in your room tonight, with you. Can I join you, Marcus, please?'

With her tunic snug again on her shoulders, the cloth seeming to scrape against her sensitive breasts and painfully erect nipples, Flavia turned to the couch to retrieve her belt. She and Marcus exchanged a glance. Marcus' tunic hung on him like a piece of bad tailoring and a tuft of hair was sticking straight out, close to his ear. She motioned

130

with a hand, and he flattened the hair, drumming the fingers of his other hand on his partially untied belt.

'The rider will be tired tonight, my lad, and likely to snore,' he said. 'You stay with Flavia tonight.'

Hadrian's smooth face crinkled with distress. 'But he is a dispatch rider with a bronze cavalry helmet that he has already let me wear. He has tattoos on both wrists!'

'Believe me, Hadrian, you have the better bargain,' said Marcus, shooting Flavia another regretful look.

Flavia felt herself blushing and said nothing.

Leaving the study behind the striding Marcus and bobbing Hadrian, Flavia did not see Marcus for the rest of that night. The cook was waiting for her in the kitchen and she was kept busy preparing warming drinks and snacks for the household and the new guest. Later, Marcus took the rider out to the baths and then to one of the city's taverns. The two men did not return until long after moonrise. By then, Hadrian had finally settled and was asleep, but Flavia remained wakeful. She heard Marcus bidding the rider good night and shivered under her rough woollen blanket, although she was not cold.

In the morning, after helping Sulinus hoe the vegetable and herb patch in the garden close to the stable, Flavia was summoned to the tablinium.

The dispatch rider from Eboracum was already gone. Standing at the entrance to the dining room, Marcus was now saying good-bye to the plain, balding man who earlier that month had called at the villa with one arm in a sling. Today, the man shook Marcus' hand with both of his and nodded to Flavia as he skirted past the dining couches and out into the courtyard garden.

Marcus looked her up and down as she stood hesitantly by one of the room's low tables. 'Back in the brown, I see,' he remarked, nodding at her modest gown. 'It will serve, since we are going out.'

'Yes, sir,' Flavia said, turning to fetch her shawl. He seemed distant today, preoccupied, and she did not want to presume.

Do not be clinging or tiresome, she thought, wishing that he would smile at her. Marcus had changed her world forever, but he might not feel the same way about her. Perhaps he regretted what had happened last evening. Her stomach churned at the idea and she longed for the floor tiles to open and swallow her.

'Flavia.' He walked across to her, stepping in front of her so that she was forced to raise her head to him. She stared at him proudly, determined to show nothing of her pain and disappointment.

'We will have no time together today, you and I,' he said. He touched her shoulder, his face solemn. 'Will you do something for me?'

Anything, thought Flavia, nodding.

'Your new hair comb. Wear it for me today, while we're in town.' He gave her shoulder a squeeze and then released her, sending her on her way with a brief pat in the middle of her back. As she looked round at him, still trying to guess his mood, a quizzical light blazed in his eyes. 'Go on, then, or must I direct my hand-pat lower?'

'You...' Flavia snatched up the hem of her gown and stormed from the tablinium, Marcus' bark of laughter ringing in her ears.

The weather had turned frosty again when Flavia followed Marcus into Aquae Sulis. Hadrian had wanted to come with them, but on hearing that they would be visiting a sculptor the boy lost interest. Marcus was leaving him his sword to polish, which pleased Hadrian mightily, although when Flavia questioned this, Marcus replied in typical fashion: 'If he cuts himself, he will learn to be more careful.'

Flavia could scarcely believe what he was saying. 'Hadrian's only eight years old! How can you be so irresponsible?'

They were walking through the garden under a looming gray sky that looked heavy with approaching snow. Flavia had on her new shawl and hair comb, and even Marcus had chosen to wear a longer cloak. Now at her indignant statement, he turned back from examining one of the withered lavender bushes.

Without waiting to see his expression, Flavia backed up several steps, wishing wildly for a second that the snow had already fallen so that she might fend him off with snowballs – a foolish, futile idea.

'Good, you remember a man's fighting range,' said Marcus, his deep voice sounding amused. Flicking open his cloak, he produced a small dagger in a leather sheath, holding both up so she could see them, his black brows drawn together over his fierce, intent eyes. 'I want you to keep this in mind, also. It is a man's duty to protect, and for that he must have weapons. I was younger than Hadrian when I received my first sword.'

Flavia said nothing.

Whistling, Marcus tucked away the dagger, let down his cloak and strolled on through the gate. Out in the street he waited for her.

When he held out his hand, Flavia discovered that she could no longer be angry. He was Roman and this was the Roman way. She placed her hand in his, thrilling anew at the warm strength in his fingers.

'Hadrian's clever – like his room-mate,' Marcus observed. 'How are you at reading monuments?'

Flavia blinked at the rapid subject change but refused to be wrong-footed. 'Very good,' she answered, promptly, skirting a pile of steaming blood and guts in the road as they walked quickly past a butcher's shop. Stray dogs and red kites were already gathering for a feast.

'I need a headstone and inscription for Lady Valeria.' Marcus gave a coin to a one-handed beggar. 'Something appropriate.'

And he wanted her help, Flavia thought, hugging that idea to herself as they turned away from the great bath complex and moved into the side streets of Aquae Sulis. Passing a smaller hot spring, enclosed by a wall and dedicated to the healing god Aesculapius, she was reminded of a secret place of sanctuary close by, a place she sensed she would never need while she was with Marcus.

Comforted afresh and guided by an increasing din of chiselling and hammering, she and Marcus made their way to a series of builders' and sculptors' yards, a place in the narrow city streets where colored smoke from large fires lingered in the cold air.

'This one,' Marcus said, pointing to a yard enclosed by a tall wooden fence. Opening a small door in the fence, he sneezed violently. 'Sorry.'

Opening her mouth to say, 'That is all right,' Flavia coughed as the gritty limestone dust choked her. There was gray dust everywhere, coating everything.

A chalk-white figure in a grubby loin cloth stumbled out of the maze of half-finished statues and headstones that filled the yard almost to bursting and gave a screech. Dropping a rag into the frosted gray mud, the figure scurried to a small lean-to hut in the corner of the yard. Disappearing inside, he reappeared a moment later with a stocky, bearded man, dressed in dusty brown leggings and tunic – the master sculptor.

'Customer!' bellowed the master sculptor and the other five loin-clothed, wretched figures instantly stopped their chiselling. A relative silence fell, punctuated only by the sound of a hammer from a neighbouring builder's yard.

'Greetings, sir,' said the master sculptor in heavily-accent Latin. 'Dexter, stonemason of Aquae Sulis at your service.' He came forward and shook Marcus' hand. 'I have wine or ale – it is a brisk day, is it not?' He clapped his hands together. 'What is your pleasure?'

'Perhaps some wine at the conclusion of our business?' said Marcus, glancing round the yard at the urns, statues and headstones, some undercover of rough awnings.

'A man after my own heart! Very well, Master...?'

'Marcus Brucetus. This is my scribe, Flavia.'

Surprised to be introduced and as a scribe, Flavia was more startled when the sturdy master sculptor marched up to her with a rolling seaman's gait and shook her hand.

'An honor, little mistress! You will write a good report of me, I trust?'

'I will try,' Flavia answered, disarmed by the man's sparkling brown eyes and generous smile. Dexter's enthusiasm was infectious and, now that she had grown used to the floating dust and the chips of limestone that appeared to line every nook and cranny in the place, she realized that the workers, although filthy, were well fed. None bore any lash marks and, leaning on their hammers or against half-finished statues, they watched quite openly. One jabbed a chisel at her, saying something in Greek that made Marcus stiffen.

'That is enough.' Dexter had spotted the taller man's disapproval and now he waved to his workers. 'Quiet polishing, my people and then we will have a bread and beer break.

'Now, Marcus Brucetus,' he continued, leaving his workers to resume their tasks in their own time, 'You require a gravestone? An inscription? A statue? An orn–'

'An inscribed gravestone for my adopted mother Lady Valeria, who is recently deceased,' said Marcus quickly, before Dexter recited his entire range of goods. 'You know the lady?' he added.

137

Flavia, who had also seen Dexter's round cheerful face become thoughtful, rather than simply composed into an expression of conventional grief, listened carefully.

'I know of the lady, of course. She will be sadly missed in this city.'

Dexter knew more than that, Flavia guessed, as the master sculptor glanced at the still-open door leading out from the enclosed yard into the street. 'You perhaps had dealings with her, sir,' she said. 'When her husband Petronius died and she came here for a headstone?'

'Of course, that is it,' said Dexter, rather too quickly. 'We have so many funerals here in Aquae Sulis. I have so many clients—'

'Yes, one of my dependants recommended you,' said Marcus dryly, a reminder of mutual obligations. 'May we see the kind of work you do? Something appropriate for an aristocrat?'

As Dexter nodded vigorously and ambled through the yard with his seaman's walk, Marcus lowered his head to Flavia. 'Well done, little Celt,' he said quietly. 'The man didn't want to admit he'd had dealings with Valeria.'

'I will keep an eye on him,' Flavia said, her heart beating quickly as a rush of joy flooded through her at Marcus' praise. Do not be foolish, she told herself. A few kind words mean nothing. Do not lose your heart

138

any further. But she knew it was already too late for that.

A few minutes later, she had to steel herself for a more testing exchange with Marcus, over what was 'appropriate' for Lady Valeria's headstone. Dexter had taken them to a windy corner where, in the shadow of a marble fountain head, a workman was polishing a half-finished headstone.

'This is for a retired centurion's wife,' the master sculptor said, taking the workman's place and polishing rag and giving the tall headstone a proud flick with the cloth. 'Very suitable for a lady – shows off her status. Look at the depth of the relief carving! None of the other city sculptors can match us.'

Flavia ignored the rest of Dexter's sales patter and focused on the headstone. The inscription was full of conventional platitudes about so-and-so being a perfect mother, but with no true sense of the real woman beyond the centurion's wife. Above the lettering was a carved figure of a woman seated on a couch, dressed in a fine gown and jewels and holding a fan.

'Yes, I like the size and the clarity,' Marcus was saying. 'The fan's impressive, too: the way all the folds are shown.'

'Naturally, we would produce the same standard for Lady Valeria's memorial,' Dexter said, rubbing his hands together as if he was already scenting a sale.

'Then we are agreed,' Marcus said, nodding approval. 'And the price?'

Let it go, Flavia thought, as Marcus squared up to the bearded sculptor to begin haggling, but she could not. 'My lady never used a fan,' she said.

At her low distinct voice, the two men stopped in mid-bargaining and stared at her.

'What was that?' Marcus demanded, his eyes narrowing.

Flavia did not know if he was irritated at being interrupted or angry at being reminded of Lady Valeria's true character, but she persisted. She loved Marcus, but she had loved her mistress, too, and to have a memorial that captured so little of that lady–

'You cannot have a headstone showing her with a fan.'

'They are very fashionable,' said Dexter, smoothing a smear of chalk-dust from his beard.

'Only women of substance are shown with fans.' Marcus took a step towards her, his jaw clenching ominously. 'Would you have your lady shown as less?'

'I would have her shown as she was,' said Flavia. 'She considered such things–' and here she waved a hand at the carved figure – 'as total frippery. If you must show her with anything, show her with a book!'

'We can do that,' said Dexter rapidly, glancing from Flavia to Marcus.

140

Marcus was shaking his head. 'By Mithras, you're a stubborn wench,' he growled.

Flavia swallowed but did not budge, or flinch as Marcus stooped beside her, shading his eyes as he glared at the headstone from her eye-level. 'What fuss,' he muttered.

'Would you be shown with a fan?' Flavia retorted.

The instant she spoke, she bit her lip, not daring to smile, but Marcus' shoulders shook at her suggestion. 'All right!' he exclaimed, laughing, throwing up his arms. 'Let the Lady Valeria be carved holding a book!'

'And the inscription?' asked Dexter.

'Ask Flavia,' said Marcus laconically, but he was smiling. He scratched his stubble along the length of his jaw and chin. 'You mentioned wine?'

'An excellent notion.' Dexter appeared to unfreeze from his shock or bewilderment after witnessing how Marcus and Flavia dealt with each other. Confirming quietly to Flavia, 'You will write an inscription for us?' the master sculptor snapped into motion, hurrying through the yard towards his hut and chattering all the while.

'I do recall the Lady Valeria now quite clearly. A most assertive woman with very decided opinions. She brought her house-steward with her on her first visit, but on her second, she came alone to my yard...'

Flavia knew this. Her mistress had ex-

141

cluded her here, too. Trying to compose a fitting epitaph to her lady, her mind kept returning to how Lady Valeria had described her to Marcus as, 'A mettlesome little thing. May need watching,' and felt bruised and drained. Her lady had been so independent – or had it been a reluctance to trust anyone else?

Perhaps she simply did not trust me, thought Flavia, slogging around the statues, roof cornices and marble benches in the sculptor's yard. She wanted to talk to the old lady, to cry unfair, unjust: but there again, was Lady Valeria so wrong?

Flavia felt a guilty blush creep over her face. She had not told Marcus everything. She had trusted in his fairness over the missing jewel, but even though she loved him, dare she trust him over her forged letter?

Why did you do it? she asked the dead Lady Valeria for what felt to be the thousandth time. If only she had known what her mistress had intended, perhaps she could have persuaded her not to go ahead. If only she had disobeyed Lady Valeria, followed her on her solitary trips to the baths and here...

Inside Dexter's windowless, dusty hut, sitting on a stool amongst faded ledgers and broken cups, Flavia wrote something for the inscription. She was far from satisfied with it, but Marcus gave his terse, 'Better,' and the master sculptor summoned a workman to begin transferring her letters into a permanent memorial. Marcus also had her jot down a few notes regarding Lady Valeria's appearance for the workman to follow.

'Sitting, or moving, my adoptive mother was always very straight,' he said. 'She was a thin, handsome woman. She dressed her hair very plainly. She loved rich fabrics, though, and jewels – yes, and little filmy scarves.'

He smiled at Flavia as he said this, and as she wrote it on a scrap of papyrus ferreted out from a corner by Dexter – the master sculptor had no desk in his hut – she was glad of that shared remembrance. When Dexter produced three chipped cups and a flagon of wine she willingly joined in Marcus' toast to her lady.

The wine was surprisingly good. Flavia sipped it slowly as Marcus and Dexter concluded a price. She wondered if Marcus would try to find out more about the master sculptor's dealings with Lady Valeria – why especially he had been so reluctant to admit that he knew her.

Idly, her gaze fell on one of the ledgers of accounts close to her feet. Some were rolls of papyrus, stuffed into a crude open-fronted dresser, but some were tiny, thin sheets of lime-wood, made into a book or stacked in no particular order into rough mounds. The small pile of records by her right foot was topped by a thin wooden sheet on which was scribbled a man's name.

Determined not to pry or turn her head to read the name by the light filtering in through the open door, Flavia was not surprised when Marcus, accepting another cup of wine from Dexter, asked, 'Did my adoptive mother ever mention a family member of hers who has recently settled in Aquae Sulis? Lucius Maximus?'

Flavia blinked, wondering if some kind of transference of thoughts was occurring between Marcus and herself. Because now, as she stared at the small wooden sheet on the beaten earth floor, the name Lucius Maximus swam into focus.

'I have never heard of him,' said the master sculptor, shifting heavily from one foot to the other. 'More wine for you, little mistress?'

Addressed directly, Flavia was forced to raise her head to answer Dexter, but not before she had deciphered more of the thin wood tablet. 'No, thank you.' An image of Lucius Maximus' smiling, drunk face and then of the terrible beating Hadrian had received at the man's fists flashed before her. Lucius Maximus was a brute and bully – if she said nothing, was she not failing her brave mistress' memory? Was this ugly piece of accounting that lay at her feet what Lady Valeria had also discovered about her distant kinsman?

Flavia wet her lips with her tongue. 'Does the word "insurance" mean anything to you, Master Dexter?'

The sculptor moved to retrieve the wooden tablet, but Marcus was there first, snatching the thin sheet off the floor, raising his eyebrows as he read the name. 'Perhaps there is another in this city named Lucius Maximus,' he remarked.

'You do not understand.' Dexter's jovial face had lost its humour; his paling mouth seemed to have almost disappeared into his thick brown beard.

'I have seen dues like this before,' said Marcus, his tanned features hardening and darkening as he read aloud. 'Fire insurance to Lucius Maximus for three months – fifteen sesterces. One month water insurance to Lucius Maximus of five sesterces. Twenty sesterces to L.M. for the six month safety of his workers' hands.'

Flavia glanced at her narrow fingers and shivered.

'So this is where his money comes from,' said Marcus, and, as Dexter seemed to sag, 'I will help you fight this man. I have been a tribune. I know people. I know which official to contact. We can put a stop to this.'

'No, you cannot,' said Dexter, snatching the wooden tablet from Marcus. 'That is what she thought, your Lady Valeria, but she could not get anywhere. Do you not see?'

Dexter raised his hands in a pleading gesture. Flavia could see a muscle jumping in his face, under his beard.

'There is no proof,' he gabbled. 'He never sets his seal to anything: it is all done by go-betweens; men who come at night, in hoods. He knows everything that is going on, too: both here in the city and elsewhere.'

'How extensive is this "business" of his?' Marcus demanded, moving so that Dexter could not escape through the door.

'I do not know. I swear I do not know. Other people are too scared to speak out. Do you not see, tribune? It would be my word against his!'

It would be your death, thought Flavia, sickened and understanding only too well. *As it must have been for my lady.* In a flash of insight she realized everything. Lady Valeria had not taken her own life. Had she done so, she would have left a suicide note: her mistress had always been careful and exacting. No, it was worse even than suicide. She had been poisoned, most likely on the orders of her own distant kinsman, Lucius Maximus. She had tried to move against Maximus and his corruption: that was what Dexter meant when he spoke of Lady Valeria not getting anywhere. Instead, she had failed in her brave attempt at seeking justice and had been stopped in the most brutal way possible – by murder.

'Please, sir—' she began with Marcus, hoping that he too would understand the risk of crossing someone like Lucius Maximus, but then a new voice interrupted her.

'There is much more to Lucius Maximus than extortion. I know by personal experience.'

The speaker was a woman, whose shawled and veiled figure was outlined briefly in the doorway as she entered the hut. She nodded to Marcus, acknowledging that he had seen her coming across the yard, and walked up to Flavia. 'We meet again,' she said.

She lifted her hands to her covered head and a waft of rose perfume mingled with the scent of stone dust. Flavia recognised her by it, even before she lowered her veil.

'Messalina! How are you?'

'I am well, as you see.'

Messalina turned on the spot – more for the men than for her, Flavia knew, although she was interested to see the toga girl again. Today Messalina was wearing a more modest costume of a white gown and shawl, but her lively, mischievous face was made up to add depth and lustre to her eyes and lips and the inviting cleavage in her bosom was highlighted in rouge.

'Good health to you, Flavia,' she said, 'And to you, Master Dexter,' she continued, extending a braceletted hand for the sculptor to kiss. 'I came to ask after the progress

147

of my statue, but this is a more interesting discussion.'

Her eyes flicked to Marcus and travelled languidly up and down his tall, strong frame. 'You are a military man?' she asked, her painted lips crinkling into a dimpled smile.

Watching, Flavia was unsure whether to applaud her performance, but Marcus smiled back broadly and said, 'I am, or rather I was. I am between duties at present.'

He gave Messalina a bow, adding, 'Tribune Marcus Brucetus at your service. Your statue must be very beautiful, Messalina.'

He spoke her name as if he were tasting it. Flavia clenched her teeth, praying she would not blush and loathing her own jealousy. This was only male-female banter, she told herself as her stomach and eyes burned, but then Marcus surprised her. Stepping away from Messalina, he said, 'It seems you already know Flavia.'

This time, his smile included her. Flavia felt her breath stop in her throat as he took her hand. 'How did you meet?' he asked.

'At the baths, of course,' said Messalina at once, removing the rest of the veil and shaking her head. 'I owe your Flavia an apology.'

'Why?' Flavia asked, as Marcus stared at the toga girl's luxuriant plume of red-golden hair. Had the perfect Drusilla been blessed with that brilliant color? she thought, wishing that the dim interior of the hut was

148

darker still. 'Why?' she repeated, removing her hand from Marcus' and forcing herself to attend to Messalina's words. 'You have done me no injury.'

'I sent you to Lucius Maximus and that is injury enough.' Messalina glanced at the master sculptor. 'I owe her an explanation, Dexter,' she said, in a calm, flat way, quite unlike her earlier flirtatious manner. 'You should tell your story, too–'

'Tell yours and be done,' said Dexter. He gathered up the wine cups, an obvious sign that he wanted this meeting concluded as rapidly as possible.

Messalina needed no further prompting and spoke directly to Flavia, woman to woman. 'I owe you an apology, because when I passed on that message in the baths I knew what kind of man I was sending you to.'

She gave Flavia a searching look. 'You must understand that I had no choice but to deliver Lucius Maximus' message. I saw what he once did to another toga girl who disobeyed him.'

'Messalina!' snapped Dexter, hurrying to the open door and looking out to ensure that no one else could hear.

'It does not matter,' Messalina said, holding up a hand against Flavia's protest. 'I know that you and your tribune have guessed what I am, so there is no need to pretend any more about my being here for any artistic reasons.' Her lips quivered in amusement and then she sighed. 'You have probably guessed who owns me.'

She took a deep breath. 'I am a courtesan in the employ of Lucius Maximus. I am popular and so he tends to leave me alone.'

'I would buy her freedom,' Dexter broke in, 'But he will not sell.'

'Lucius Maximus made me dye my hair to this.' Messalina tugged at her red-golden mane. 'He is a cruel man, taking pleasure in pain.'

She raised her head and faced Marcus. 'If you can defeat Lucius Maximus, there are many in this city who will be grateful.'

Marcus nodded, his strong features stern and impassive. 'I swear I will do everything in my power to stop him,' he said.

Hearing his promise, Flavia felt both proud and afraid. *Help him,* she prayed, as she and Marcus left Dexter's work hut. *Help us all.*

Chapter 7

'Lucius Maximus cannot be allowed to continue as an imperial official,' Marcus continued, as they walked away from the sculptor's quarter. 'My old commander

150

Pompeius Gellius is a good man who understands the importance of fairness and honor. I will speak to him, stress that Lucius Maximus must be removed as Decurion.'

It was on the tip of Flavia's tongue to confess her insight, that Maximus had probably murdered Lady Valeria, but then she stopped herself. There was no clear proof and no witness, and even if there were, for a man as powerful as Lucius Maximus there would only be removal from office and possibly exile. If that was already going to happen, was it wise to say anything? Maximus would certainly counter-accuse her and the other house-slaves. They could be tortured, indeed, if they were questioned by the authorities, they would be.

For the first time since hearing Messalina speak, Marcus smiled. 'Pompeius is a friend of the Governor of Britannia and, what is more, he is travelling south today from Eboracum.'

'The rider from last night,' Flavia said, leaving her suspicions unspoken, 'Advance word of his coming?'

'Exactly. The northern tribes beyond the great wall are quiet at the moment and he and his wife are travelling to Londinium for a family birthday party, but diverting and stopping off here first. It seems they want to see the famous baths of Aquae Sulis.'

Holding her hand in his, Marcus swung

151

his arms as he walked. Out in the sunlight again he looked younger, less forbidding. He looked like a man with a purpose, Flavia thought, glad that she was with him. Every moment that they spent together was precious to her.

I am harming no one, she told herself, then heard Marcus say, 'By tomorrow night, Pompeius Gellius will be my guest at the villa.'

The rest of the day was taken up with finding a professional chef who would work in the villa's kitchens while the northern commander was staying with them. As Marcus pointed out, Agrippina and the other elderly slaves would enjoy directing the professionals and there would be too much work for the household without employing help.

'Pompeius Gellius travels with his wife and a retinue – they will be billeted in hotels and taverns, but he will expect to stay with me and he will expect a banquet,' Marcus explained. 'He and his wife dislike drinking dinner parties and wild revels – I will need to ensure that he's appointed Master of the Feast, so that he can dictate what goes on – but they both adore exotic food.'

Marcus was ready to hire a pastry chef whose shop was in the cluster of houses and workshops close to the river. Flavia disagreed. Their conversation was conducted in whispers across a nearby tavern table, with Flavia clutching a beaker of warm mead and Marcus a cup of the rough local wine.

Speaking with some exasperation, Marcus said, 'His pastries are superb. Pompeius' wife loves such food. He is not just a pastry cook, either: he provides the first and second courses, the wines and the sweets.'

'He is arrogant and impatient,' Flavia countered. 'He will not understand that Hadrian likes to lurk about the kitchen, tasting everything.'

'You don't like him because you saw one of his under-chefs beating a clumsy wine-server.'

'The boy slipped on the shop floor tiles! He spilt nothing! Would you have this professional chef or one of his sneering minions beat old Gaius?'

Straight to the root of things, as ever, thought Marcus, hiding a smile behind his cup. Part of him was always amazed and half-admiring at how she stood up to him, nearly always on behalf of others. He had faced tough centurions down and made countless soldiers quail, but this slip of a girl – woman was like no other. Flavia: provoking and beguiling – brilliant as a battle-standard now, her face flushed as she waited for his answer.

'You are right,' he conceded. 'We will find another chef.'

With a professional chef finally hired, Flavia and Marcus returned to the villa. Another messenger-rider from Pompeius Gellius was waiting there for Marcus. This time Hadrian had his wish to spend time with a rider as he went off with the two men to spend the evening at an old soldiers' club.

Flavia scrubbed and polished, aired bedding, and made the villa ready for receiving guests, continuing to work as Gaius, Livia and Sulinus all said their goodnights and retired. Agrippina was panicking at the prospect of entertaining such high-ranking Romans, even with professional help, and Flavia spent much time offering reassurance. In the end, Pina succumbed to a headache and Flavia insisted that the cook bed down in her room.

Working in oil lamp light, massaging Pina's stiff shoulders and back with a mixture of olive oil and ground-up lavender, Flavia was tempted to ask again about the mysterious potion buyer, but Pina was pale and tearful, so she let the matter go. Tired from her cleaning and the day's revelations, she lay on Hadrian's bed and much later, was only dimly aware when Marcus entered the sloping roofed chamber and laid the small, limp, sleeping form of Hadrian beside her.

The morning dawned with pewter-colored skies and brief showers of sleet that drummed on the roof-tiles and the garden statue of Pan. After seeing the latest rider off, Marcus had few people calling in such dismal weather and his guests were not due until the late afternoon.

Strolling through the villa, he found Flavia and Hadrian in the kitchen, nervously awaiting the arrival of the professional chef and his staff. 'You look much better today, Pina,' he told the cook, straight-arming the giggling Hadrian right off his feet and tossing him in the air. 'Let us go, my warriors – we will have a fighting lesson in the stable. Flavia: you will need to change.'

Back in her short, sheer tunic, Flavia joined Marcus and Hadrian in the stable. The gardener was taking a break from hoeing and, bundled into his new cloak and old hat, was walking Marcus' black stallion down to the river. Marcus, meanwhile, had lit lanterns to give them the best light in this gloomy morning and had cleared a space in the hay for them to begin their latest weapons training.

'We use these for practice in the army,' he said, handing her a wooden sword. Running round the cobbles outside the stable, happily oblivious to the falling sleet and a biting wind, Hadrian was already fending off imaginary Caledonians with his.

'Hold it properly!' Marcus called after him, shaking his dark head. He beckoned to Flavia. 'Here, little Celt, you are not yet quite close enough. That is it!' He surveyed her. 'It is good that you have tied back your plaits, but you need to change that belt. It will get snagged as you practice. I have brought you a sash instead.'

He wrapped a long red sash deftly around her middle, crossing it over her breasts, and knotting it in the back. He flicked one of her tied plaits. 'All done.'

Flavia turned and found herself in his arms, staring helplessly as a tanned, lean face bent inexorably to hers and a full, firm mouth claimed her lips. Shocked at her own dazed compliance, she thought for one instant of fighting him – to at least make it less easy – but the blazing tenderness of his kiss undid her. She dropped the wooden sword and took his head between her hands, kissing him deeply in return.

'So here is the way to disarm you,' he chuckled, his lips ranging with a devastating, brutal softness across her face and throat.

'And you,' Flavia responded, standing on tip-toe to recapture his mouth. Her reaching hands gathered round his waist and, growing daring, teased lower. She felt his stifled exclamation as her fingers explored the hard, sinewy curves of his buttocks. His own practice wooden sword went clattering onto the stable floor.

'Hadrian,' he groaned, gathering her still closer.

Fighting herself, Flavia surfaced from the sensual world of their embrace, her whole body trembling. Her skin prickling, her mouth feeling almost like a ripe fruit, she forced her legs to take a step back.

Slowly, moving with obvious arousal and some discomfort, Marcus retrieved their swords, returning hers hilt-first with an almost formal bow.

They stared at each other as Hadrian pounded back into the stable, yelling, 'Come on, Marcus, she is just a girl! I want you to watch me fight!'

Flavia enjoyed the lesson. Marcus showed her and Hadrian how to grip their wooden swords, and how to stab and slash with the blade. He had them leaping up and then ducking down behind pretend shields, running forward and back exactly in step so that their battle 'line' of two would be orderly. He made them attack one of the stable posts, striking it with the sides and points of their swords. He finished by staging mock attacks on them, moving with ponderous slowness so that they could see and understand his approach.

'Good! Better!' he told them when they stopped.

Hadrian collapsed panting into the straw, his shaggy black hair tousled into impossible knots and his dark red tunic covered with bits of straw and dirt. He wiggled a small front tooth with his thumb and bounced to his feet.

'It is loosened!' he crowed. 'This will be coming out soon! Wait till I show Gaius – he has promised me a bronze coin for it!'

'Where is Gaius?' Flavia asked, sitting on the straw with her head on her knees, and her arms shielding her legs. In spite of the growing cold, she was hot, sweaty and aching in places she didn't know she had, but overall she felt marvellous. Marcus had been endlessly patient and she knew that he had never used his full strength on her or Hadrian. He answered her now, his tone indulgent and even, as it had been through-out their impromptu 'battle' drill.

'Gaius is out, walking with Nero to the spice market.' He was standing above her with folded arms, leaning against the stable post they had used for target practice, and scarcely out of breath.

'That is right.' Hadrian flopped back onto his front amongst the rough bales of straw, using his wooden sword to jab into the spiky yellow mounds. 'I told Nero to go with him as a guard dog.' He wiggled the loosening baby tooth with his tongue, his large dark brown eyes widening in contemplation. 'I didn't feel that he would be happy seeing us trying to stab each other.'

'The term is "lunge" or "strike" with a

sword,' rumbled Marcus, his teeth showing in a half-smile as he clearly tried not to laugh at Hadrian's strange military language or the idea of Nero as a guard dog. 'But, yes, that was a good strategy. Nero would have interfered.'

'I thought so, too.' Hadrian grinned, glowing under Marcus' praise.

'Wrestling tomorrow, both of you,' Marcus went on, holding out a hand to help her up. He was watching Flavia closely, almost as if he sensed her ambivalence. 'No absences allowed,' he added, his face alive with amusement.

The day wore on. Returning to the villa and changing back into her long woollen gown, Flavia found that although she had been warm 'fighting' out in the stable, she quickly became cold indoors. The villa seemed full of icy corners and chilly spaces.

She was not alone in feeling the chill. Coming in from the market and the riverside, Gaius and Sulinus tottered about with gnarled hands thrust deeply into the spare folds of their tunics. Dusting the dining room and the candle-lit study where Flavia was trying to teach a yawning and inattentive Hadrian to read a few more words and to copy out a few more alphabet letters, Livia wore her shawl wrapped about her head and mouth. Even the white terrier

159

Nero curled up on top of the wolfskin on Lady Valeria's wicker chair and showed no sign of being dislodged from such a snug, draught-free spot.

Marcus had braziers carried into every room, lighting them himself and checking the shutters and the door curtains. He found extra rugs and cushions and placed them throughout the house. He instructed Pina to prepare fresh bread and Livia to refill all the oil lamps. He had Gaius and Sulinus scrub down the outer villa steps and joined them making garlands of holly and ivy and crowns of rosemary. He burned fresh incense at the household shrine.

He was out in the stable, checking the animal fodder and the water and stabling for Pompeius Gellius' horses, when the professional chef arrived with his entourage.

The professional chef was a tall, lanky man from northern Gaul. Like the apothecary who had claimed he had *not* sold Lady Valeria hemlock, the chef had a shaven head, but he was smiling and pink-cheeked where the apothecary had been gaunt and colorless. Earlier that morning, when Marcus and Flavia had hired him, the chef had been dressed in a simple undyed tunic, but now he swept into the villa like an exotic bird, bright in a saffron-colored long tunic, glittering gem-studded brooches, and blue leggings.

Re-introducing himself as Clodius, he

charmed Agrippina by praising the layout of her kitchen and quality of her stores. He impressed Hadrian by carrying several of his spits and cooking pots himself, slung around his wiry frame on slings. He took command of the kitchen and dining room with several disarming smiles and a few choice instructions to his own retinue of under chefs and servers.

To Flavia's private amusement, he suggested that Marcus and the other men go spend the rest of the afternoon at the baths, having themselves oiled, shaved and massaged for the evening.

'You will be the better for the attention, my lord tribune,' Clodius told Marcus. 'Go! Your banquet is in hand and you must be prepared to enjoy it.'

Clearly, Marcus decided that a tactical withdrawal was in order, Flavia thought, for he, Gaius, and Sulinus departed soon after. She watched Marcus lead the way into the city, head bowed against the sleet, his big, agile body swathed in the long hooded cloak. Shamelessly, she longed to be going with him, to oil and tend him. To bathe him...

Clodius had a different task for her. Before he told her what it was, the chef roasted chestnuts and set Agrippina, Livia, and Hadrian to peeling them at a small trestle table that his staff had brought with them into the kitchen. He also gave them wine and a hard salty cheese to 'sample'. Soon, it was not only Hadrian who was devouring most of the chestnuts and enjoying the cheese and the Gaulish wine. Even Nero was given a saucer-full.

'And now they are occupied, I can turn my attention to you,' Clodius said, examining Flavia as he had earlier scrutinised the kitchen and the stores. 'Will you walk with me to the dining room?'

'Of course,' said Flavia.

On the way there, Clodius paused in the corridor. 'The tribune has instructed me to say that you are invited as a guest to this feast. His guest,' he said in a low voice. 'Or you may retire with the others. He was insistent that the choice be yours.'

Astonished, Flavia began, 'Why did he–'

'Why did he not tell you this himself? I think because he wished to give you the clear choice, and the time to consider your answer.' Clodius resumed his progress to the dining room, adding, 'The tribune is a gentleman in this matter, but speaking as a man of the world, I believe he will be very disappointed if you do not join him as his lady for the evening.'

Touched and even a little surprised by this latest showing of Marcus' sensitivity and concern, Flavia did not know what to say. Recalling Pina's jealousy and the other servants' aloofness, she was disconcerted at being singled out. She was at the same time pleased – much more than that, she was thrilled and delighted – that Marcus wished her to join him. Surely that must signify that she meant something to him? Then Clodius shattered her hope by saying, 'The tribune knows the value of a pretty woman at a grand dinner.'

Was that all she was to him – a kind of trophy? The idea brought Flavia back to reality with a jolt. Still no closer to making a decision, she followed Clodius into the dining room, hastily composing her face to hide her disappointment.

In the small, sloping-roofed chamber she shared with Hadrian, Flavia dressed herself for the banquet. She had decided to attend, mainly to please Marcus, but that did not stop her from being apprehensive. Lady Valeria had entertained few grand dinner guests. What if she made a mistake in custom? What if she unwittingly offended Pompeius Gellius and made Marcus' task in obtaining justice against the corrupt Lucius Maximus more difficult? Please do not let him be disappointed in me, she thought, wondering if it would be better if she pleaded off with a headache. Heart-ache more like, she reflected wryly, admitting that her own pride and a certain stubborn belief in upholding Celtic courage and freedom compelled her to go through with this.

As the villa gradually filled with delicious cooking smells, Flavia changed into what she considered her 'best' clothes: her yellow gown and blue belt. Lady Valeria had no cosmetics she wanted to use or would suit her colouring but, aiming for a more sophisticated look, she swept her plaited hair up into a low bun with soft tendrils defining her ears, and pinned her fringe into waves. She had no jewels and longed for some of the roses of summer to tuck into her belt. A small posy of the bright, bead-like hips of a wild rose, pinned to her left shoulder where a Roman matron might show off a rich brooch, worked almost as well.

She had no means to check her appearance. Emerging from the tiny room in search of a mirror, she hurried to the nearest window. Peering through the shutters she saw no one – Marcus had not yet returned and today the female potions buyer was seemingly keeping her distance.

Why? Flavia thought, stepping back and moving towards Lady Valeria's old room, now prepared for Pompieus Gellius. Why, if the potions buyer and her fellow servants were doing nothing wrong were they so secretive? She had promised them a month, but Flavia was uneasy.

Then there were these strange connections between Lucius Maximus and Lady Valeria. They had been family, but estranged and with no contact between them until Lady Valeria had stumbled upon her kinsman's protection business. Had the formidable old woman confronted the Decurion with her suspicions? It would be like her, Flavia thought.

And the Decurion had responded by having her murdered.

Can I find proof? Flavia wondered. *Can I stalk Lucius Maximus, find some way into his house or question his people?*

She discarded these foolish ideas at once. Marcus would not allow her to go off alone. She could easily be spotted by Maximus, who had noticed her too much already, at the baths. His people would not talk to her, a slave.

And what if she was utterly wrong? Yet, if that were so, why had her lady chosen to end her life at that moment, when she was involved in discovering the extent of Lucius Maximus' corruption? When Marcus had been coming to join her and to offer his own support?

She was back with that hopeless question of why again, Flavia considered bitterly, standing at the entrance to Lady Valeria's room and surveying her former mistress' things. Her lady had always hated these long, cold winter months, when the pains in her joints would keep her restless and wakeful night after night.

The room looked different, arranged for guests. The bed had been moved and two of the three braziers removed. It smelt of dried mint and other strewing herbs. Although she herself had done this, Flavia suddenly did not want to cross the floor tiles to pick up the mirror from the dressing table. The room seemed alien to her; she felt like an intruder.

Lady Valeria dead. It did not seem possible, but the changed room was proof that it was. Flavia's eyes were pricking with unshed tears, her throat burning, her head feeling as if it might burst, her tongue feeling as if it might choke her. She swallowed the angry wail that was rising in her and turned away, blundering into a statue.

The statue moved and a pair of strong arms encircled her. 'What is it? What is the matter?'

It was Marcus, still in his cloak, with sleet melting and dripping from his thick dark hair. He was back and holding her, winding the cloak about her, too, and murmuring, 'It will be all right,' when she knew that it was not. She would never see her lady again, never hear her laugh. If she had not been murdered, then Valeria had done the worst thing in the Christian creed: she had taken her own life. Where would her spirit be now?

'How can she rest?' Flavia cried, and with that resentful, sorrowful question all the damned-up grief flooded out of her and she

166

began to weep.

'Flavia...'

Dimly, through her furious tears, Flavia was aware of being cradled, of Marcus crooning against her ear. She kicked against him in her own frustrated misery, despising herself for breaking down.

'It is all right to cry, Flavia,' Marcus whispered, not letting her go even when she struck out at him with her hands. Hitting him was like striking a piece of living marble; she hurt her fingers and made no impression whatsoever on him.

'Let me go!' She thrust her palms against his chest, trying to push him away, but could not budge him a finger-breadth.

'Not for all the gods in heaven.' He pressed her head against his heart and stroked her hair as she wept – Flavia did not know where all this water was coming from.

'I hate this!' she muttered, raising streaming eyes, her nose beginning to feel like an over-cooked turnip.

'Our tears honor the dead,' Marcus said.

To her amazement his dark blue eyes were misted, but he was also smiling and now he touched her cried-up face with his hand, saying, 'I wondered when this would happen.'

Speaking, he drew the ends of his cloak from her shoulders, swung her off her feet and bore her along with him, carrying her into a very different chamber.

Chapter 8

Marcus settled on a stool in his bedroom with Flavia on his knee. Recalling his own furious, bewildered hurt at Drusilla's and little Aurelia's deaths, he let her cry herself out before he said or did anything. As her storm of weeping subsided into occasional sniffles, he reached across his three-legged bedside table and pulled the water jug and basin closer. The water in the jug was cold, but still fresh from that morning: it would soothe her swollen eyes.

'Here,' he said, stripping off his long cloak and tossing it aside. 'I will find you a towel.'

She rose at once and washed herself, drying her hands and face on the towel Marcus found in one of the small clothes-chests. He guessed that she was coming back to herself when she glanced about the room, staring curiously at the bed.

'This used to be the guest room,' she said, her voice still husky with the crying. The tears had brightened her eyes and darkened her blonde eyelashes: she looked at him, all eyes. Marcus pitied her loss, but he would need to be dead not to find those big eyes and low, dusky tones attractive.

'It was,' he agreed, wondering how he might coax her onto the bed. She gave him an opening by pointing at the striped coverlet.

'Is the bed longer?' She was puzzled – bewilderment made her look eminently kissable, he thought, especially now, her cheeks and lips reddened with emotion. Reminding himself yet again of her inexperience with men, trying to ignore the surging blood in his ears and elsewhere, Marcus said that it was.

'I have put a table under the foot end,' he explained, striding over to the couch and patting the blanket-covered table. 'I like to stretch out in bed. It works very well – care to try it for yourself?'

She threw him a look that said she found his clumsy subterfuge quite transparent, but she did not stir. Encouraged by that, Marcus risked more.

'Were you looking for anything particular in the other bedroom?' he asked, walking back to her. He still had the sense that she was hiding something from him, something possibly important. He wanted to win not only her, but also her trust. 'You can tell me,' he said.

For an instant, Marcus was convinced that different words hovered on her lips, but then she sighed and lowered her head. 'A mirror,' she admitted hesitantly to his chest, as if this very feminine desire was a character flaw.

'Is that all?' Going to the three-legged table again, Marcus plucked a wine cup off a metal tray and held up the tray. 'Here. It is not a perfect looking-glass, but you should be easy. You are very pretty. Indeed, your costume puts my tunic to shame, so if I am to join you this evening, I had best change.'

'Yes,' she said, looking once at her reflection in the metal tray and then fixing her gaze back on him.

Seeing her calm again, Marcus could not resist a tease. 'Perhaps you can help me change into my dining mantle?'

She was backing away now, but her warm gray eyes shimmered with mischief. 'I cannot help you there, sir,' she said, reaching the threshold and lingering, 'The mantle is a Roman garment.'

With that final quip she left, her sandals lighter than blown leaves on the floor tiles.

Flavia returned to the kitchen, where Clodius spotted her and shouted, 'Away! Your companions are playing dice in the stables and await the arrival of the commander's horses. They have beer and bread and a promise of scraps. Join them if you will, but leave now. I have no room or time for amateurs!'

Wondering how Agrippina felt about being ejected from her own kitchen, Flavia was ready to hurry across to the stables when she heard footsteps in the darkening corridor behind her.

Marcus, carrying a lighted oil lamp, the shadows and light coiling round him. She had expected to see him a stranger in his Roman mantle and he did look taller and more studious, like a picture of an idealised Greek philosopher. His mantle was like those she had seen worn by upper class men in Aquae Sulis: a large, rectangular piece of bleached fine wool, almost as big as a bedsheet, draped around his left shoulder and around his back, enclosing both shoulders and covering his body almost to his ankles.

Under it, at his right shoulder and around his throat, Flavia could see that Marcus had also changed into a different tunic, dark blue and with thin darker stripes woven lengthways into the cloth as decoration. The blue matched his eyes and the snowy white mantle showed off his tan, she thought, wondering with a stab of envy if his wife had selected the outfit.

He saw her looking and flicked at the mantle with a strange, almost embarrassed smile. 'I can never drape the folds of these things properly.' He raised the oil lamp to see her face more clearly. 'Thank you for agreeing to join me this evening.'

'You could have ordered me,' Flavia murmured, wanting to acknowledge this. She tilted up her chin. 'Thank you for *asking* me.'

Inspired by his very human moment of shyness, she confessed, 'I have not served at a grand dinner and never attended one as a guest. Is there anything I should or should not do?'

'Be yourself. That is more than enough.' Marcus looked as if he was about to rumple her hair after that rather cryptic comment, but stopped himself, muttering, 'Why do you women torture your heads with these pins? You are more like a siege engine than a girl.'

'Then loosen it!' Flavia snapped, nettled at the dismissal of her more elegant style and disappointed after his earlier praise. So much for his calling her pretty! 'Loosen it,' she repeated, not caring that she goaded. 'After all, you own it.'

His eyes darkened, almost as if he had been struck, but Marcus reached out and touched a single hair pin with the tip of his finger, nothing more. 'Surely an owner would go further?' he asked softly.

'You have made your point.' Suddenly Flavia felt weary, tired of being a slave, weary of fighting this man and her own feelings.

Marcus looked at her a moment longer, then sighed and stepped back.

'You are right,' he said. 'That was a crass thing to do.'

'Yes,' said Flavia steadily. 'It was.'

At that moment, old Gaius hobbled in from

172

the stable block, his wrinkled face flushed with beer and anticipation. 'Pompeius Gellius' party has just arrived!' he exclaimed.

'I am sorry, Flavia,' Marcus said. He blew out the oil lamp and placed it on the corridor floor tiles, close to the wall. Slowly, he offered his arm to her.

Slowly, she took it.

Together, they walked after the excited house steward to welcome the newcomers.

Marcus' old commander Pompeius Gellius and his wife had already called at the great baths to wash away the dust of travel. They and their attendants retired briefly to Lady Valeria's old room to change – Pompeius and his lady into their dining clothes, the slaves into simple fresh tunics. The slaves were then led away by Gaius to the stables, to join the other servants and grooms who were eating and gaming there.

'I see that the Saturnalia has come early to this house,' remarked Pompeius Gellius, when he and his wife entered the dining room.

Marcus smiled at this reference to the great midwinter festival. 'I think rather that our chef for this evening prefers to serve the feast with his own people, sir,' he said, nodding to Clodius, who was hovering in the doorway. 'That is also acceptable to me.'

'Naturally, my boy,' said Pompeius Gellius,

smiling in return.

He and Marcus shook hands again and Marcus embraced Pompeius Gellius' wife, asking solicitously after her journey.

Standing beside him, uneasy and also curious as to how Marcus would introduce her, Flavia pondered the Saturnalia: a time of feasting and play, lasting seven days, when the normal 'rules' of life were suspended. During the Saturnalia, people took to the streets in carnival and all kinds of familiarities were permitted. Even the roles of master and slave were reversed for this one day.

Flavia doubted the reality of this last but, although she had never been out on the streets of Aquae Sulis during the festival, she knew that the Saturnalia was full of revels and luxury. She also knew that any Roman holiday allowed much cruelty and depravity, especially to slaves.

She shivered, almost dropping the crown of rosemary handed to her by one of the professional servers, smart in his uniform tunic of jet black wool. The other diners were also receiving similar crowns and she waited to see what they did with them.

Pompeius Gellius dangled his from a bony wrist. He was not quite what Flavia had expected, being a short, thin, fair-skinned, gray-haired man of about forty-five, more like a northern Celt than a Roman. He was dressed in a white tunic with a red and green mantle and, Flavia noticed, the muscles on his right side were slightly more developed than those on his left, perhaps because of years of soldiering, she thought.

Beside him, his wife handed her crown back to another passing server and nodded at a particular dining couch. She watched this second black-garbed server place the rosemary crown at the head of the couch and smiled her thanks. She was a little taller than her husband and younger, at about forty years old. She too was thin, with a hooked nose and square jaw, a commanding profile and very thick, glossy brown hair, fastened in a low bun in the nape of her long neck and dressed with pearls. In her manner, she reminded Flavia of Lady Valeria.

The woman turned to Marcus now and said, in Lady Valeria's typically forthright fashion, 'Don't keep us in suspense any more, Marcus – introduce her!' Without waiting for the men, she faced Flavia and put out her hand.

'Good health to you, my dear girl. I am Julia Sura. Please call me Julia.'

Her intelligent brown eyes pierced Flavia with their clarity, but her smile was genuine and her handshake firm enough to feel the callus on Flavia's own hand. Flavia blushed, knowing that Julia Sura had recognised much of what she was in that instant.

To her amazement, the older woman gave

no sign of it. Startling Flavia again, she gave her husband a decidedly playful jab with her elbow and said, 'This gentleman is Pompeius Gellius. I hope you will do as I do and call him Pompey. It is too bad that Marcus and all his former staff will insist on trotting out his full name or title; I frequently feel as if I'm living on a parade ground.'

Disarmed, Flavia laughed and bowed her head to each. 'I wish you both excellent health. I am Flavia.'

She glanced at Marcus, pausing in case he wished to reveal more, and conscious of the earlier quarrel between them. That tension still remained as Marcus silently returned her look. Was that disappointment in his eyes, or irony? Whatever it was, the moment was gone and his face became a handsome mask.

He is still angry with me. I am losing him, she thought wretchedly, even while acknowledging that he had never been hers to lose. The idea of eating a grand dinner with him before these admittedly kindly strangers, of acting some part of a gracious host, filled her with despair.

She forced a smile as Pompeius Gellius shook her hand. 'You must share our supper couch, Flavia,' he was saying. 'I am sure my tribune can spare you.'

'Not for this evening, I fear.' Marcus moved to intercept Flavia and his former commander even before they had stirred. 'I insist that Flavia remain with me, sir.'

Smilingly said, but there was steel in his voice. For a moment, Flavia hated him for sounding so proprietorial, then in the next she was confused by his touching her hand, a delicate, almost sweet, caress. Or was she deluding herself? Did his contact mean nothing?

The small silence was broken by Julia. 'If I am not mistaken, Marcus, your cook is ready for this banquet to begin,' she remarked, casting keen eyes between Flavia and Marcus to the hovering presence of Clodius in the corridor. 'Come, Pompey.' She extended a ring-adorned hand. 'You will have to make do with me as your couch companion for the first two courses.'

Pompey beamed, his eyes narrowing to amiable slits in his narrow, leathery face. 'As ever, my dear, your company is a delight. But should we not wait for Lucius?' His sharp hazel eyes widened again as he addressed Marcus. 'We saw Lucius Maximus at the baths today and he told me he was joining us for dinner. Of course, I knew his father back in Rome: an excellent fellow.'

Lucius Maximus' father, a friend of the commander. This was bad news, Flavia thought, her heart jumping as she realized how much more difficult Marcus' task of persuading Pompeius Gellius to act against

177

the corrupt Decurion had become. Marcus needed definite proof, or witnesses willing to speak against Lucius Maximus, and so far he had neither.

'As a guest he will be welcome,' Marcus said, giving nothing away as to his true thoughts but faithful to the Roman laws of hospitality. Lucius Maximus must have overheard the news of Pompeius Gellius' arrival at the baths and subsequent invitation and decided to invite himself. Or was it more sinister than that? Flavia wondered. Again her thoughts turned to her former mistress and to murder.

Unaware that he had caused consternation, the older man went on, 'I am delighted that you have already cultivated Lucius while you are here in Aquae Sulis. But tell me, Marcus, are you planning to stay in Britannia for long? You are a young man. The empire needs your talents in other places.'

Hearing the question which was beginning to haunt her spoken so plainly, Flavia dare not look at Marcus in case her own expression gave away her feelings, but she heard his cool, steady answer: 'I have not yet decided.'

'And of course, there is your own natural family at Faesulae,' Pompey continued, his every word acting on Flavia like the turn of a blade.

Beside her, Marcus said merely, 'I am also

the Lady Valeria's heir and owe her my loyalty – my family understands this.'

'Yes, yes, my boy, but you have duties to Rome, to the empire...'

'Pompey, you are holding up the feast,' his wife broke in firmly. 'If Lucius is late, then so be it – he strikes me as a man who is always late. Now please escort me to my couch.'

After washing their hands, evoking the gods, removing their sandals and relaxing onto their couches, Flavia and the other diners were ready and Clodius instructed his staff to bring in the banquet. While his servers, smart in their black tunics, ensured that the big dining couches were drawn up close enough to the central dining table and that each guest was supplied with spoons and cups, he presented Pompey, who had been elected as 'Master of the Feast', with a beautiful silver goblet, wine and water jugs, and a large mixing bowl in fine Samian ware.

'Your orders?' called Marcus, stretching out on the couch beside Flavia. As 'Master', Pompey would decide on the ratio of water to wine – wine was always diluted with water, and the proportions of each usually determined what kind of party the feast would be.

'We do not want a drunken orgy,' Pompey remarked mildly. 'One part wine to three of water, I think. And no foolish drinking games. Then we can enjoy our food and conversation.'

Smiling, he raised the silver goblet to Flavia. She was lying rigidly on the couch opposite, her rosemary crown forgotten and terribly aware of Marcus even though he was as stiff as herself, his long body tensed as if determined not to brush even a toe or fingertip against her. Around them, Clodius' servers were piling steaming dishes of food onto the sideboard and central table and bringing in more holly and ivy garlands and lighted oil lamps. There was light and bustle, the sound of rushing feet, the faint clash of metal or pottery on the sideboard, the smells of garum sauce, spices and hot meat and still the evening stretched before her.

She wondered how she would stand it – being so near to the man she loved, near enough to feel his breath on her shoulder and smell the warm wool of his mantle, and yet, so far apart from Marcus in mind and spirit.

Opposite, curled up beside her husband so they lay together like a pair of hand-clappers, giving off an ease that Flavia could only envy, Julia fingered her pearl necklace and earrings.

'They are still on,' Marcus said. 'Still there.'

He was smiling; Flavia could tell from his voice. Unable to resist his good humour, she rolled onto her stomach and twisted her head to face him.

'Julia's the busiest checker of her jewels of any woman I know,' he explained, passing her a cup of the newly-mixed wine.

The sight of him smiling at her almost robbed Flavia of her breath. She forced a weak, 'Really?' took the cup with clammy fingers and tore her gaze away from Marcus to the guests.

'What your brute does not say is that my pearls are heirlooms,' Julia replied imperturbably. She shrugged her violet-colored mantle off her right arm, showing the gap sleeve of her amethyst-colored wool gown, and drew back the sleeve. On her arm was a bracelet of pearls, of the same size and color as those round her throat. 'These were all my grandmother's.'

'They are beautiful,' Flavia said. 'They must be precious to you.'

'They are superb, Julia Sura,' said Lucius Maximus from the threshold of the dining room. 'Almost the equal of my mother's pearls. I would covet them greatly if I were a woman. Or if I were trying to please a woman.' His eyes rested on Flavia.

Elbowing a server out of his way, clearly conscious that his long, unbelted silk tunic and white mantle showed off his dark good looks, Lucius Maximus walked into the tablinium, straight up to the dining couch where she was settled.

These wide low couches could easily accommodate three people. Flavia had already fanned out her gown and sprawled as much as she could, praying that the man would move on. There was an empty couch, so he had no reason to stay...

Lucius Maximus smiled at her, his eyes cold.

'Good evening, Brucetus,' he said, without looking at Marcus, 'I believe my place is here.' Not waiting for a reply, he sat on the couch, almost sitting on Flavia's legs, and kicked off his sandals, lounging next to her.

Repelled by his proximity, Flavia said nothing – he was within the bounds allowed by custom and if she protested he would deny any kind of imposition. Worse, it would make Pompey think that she and Marcus disliked the Decurion for personal, possibly even petty reasons. It would undermine their serious accusations against him.

Clenching her teeth together behind the shield of her wine cup, Flavia fought for composure, mentally chanting lines of her own poetry in her head until she felt steady again. Lucius Maximus meanwhile was settling in. Reaching forward on his elbow, he took a honey-roasted dormouse from the central low dining table, popped it whole into his mouth and chewed it vigorously. 'Delicious!' he mumbled.

Trapped between Marcus on her left and Lucius Maximus on her right, feeling increasingly beleaguered, Flavia prepared herself for an evening of misery.

Chapter 9

Whether from jealousy or sensitivity or both, Marcus instantly tried to swap places with Flavia, a move vetoed by Pompey.

'As Master of the feast, it is much more pleasing to have Flavia in my direct eye-line,' he stated, spearing a sausage with garum sauce and dried damsons with his knife. 'A rose between two bears – what could be finer?'

Flavia dutifully laughed, although she disliked Lucius Maximus more and more as the evening unfolded. He expressed surprise that the dinner plates were of pewter, not silver. He wondered at the lack of music or jugglers. He railed at the servers.

Conversation was spasmodic. When Flavia noticed that Pompey was wearing fluffy white socks as part of his dining costume, Julia, who missed nothing said, 'Pompey's toes crucify him in this northern climate.'

Marcus and Pompey exchanged rueful smiles, while Flavia felt a sudden chill, reminded of the ultimate punishment for slaves. About to offer a sympathetic remark, she was cut off by Lucius Maximus.

'What a pity this villa has no underfloor heating,' he said. 'I am having some installed in both my winter and summer dining rooms at present.'

'Your summer dining room?' Marcus enquired. So far, he and the Decurion had exchanged less than a dozen words.

'Have you not noticed, tribune? Summers are frequently worse than the winters here in glorious Britannia,' said Lucius Maximus, rolling his eyes.

'Really, Lucius,' chuckled Pompey with evident affection, 'If you think Aquae Sulis is cold, how would you fare in Eboracum?'

Lucius Maximus made no effort to disguise a yawn. 'I would not set foot within a hundred miles of Eboracum.'

Out of sight of Marcus and the other guests, his bare foot pressed hard against Flavia's calf. Repulsed by his touch, but sensing that if she showed any open disgust it would only encourage him to attempt more, Flavia shifted backwards.

'Yes, Lucius, I think you are right in that,' said Julia Sura in a considering way, before Lucius Maximus could add any further, no doubt disparaging remarks.

'Germania was colder.' Marcus' face was grim.

184

His remark was greeted by silence. Flavia longed to comfort his grief, but all she could do was to distract Lucius Maximus by saying quickly, 'What do you think of the wild mushrooms in pastry, Julia? The chef is anxious to know: it's his own recipe.'

Julia was equally swift in making an answer and that moved the talk onto the safer topic of the feast itself, especially as the servers were now bringing in the second course. Pompey was enthusiastic about the venison with spicy garum sauce and pine nuts, dipping his spoon frequently into the communal pot on the central low serving table. He seemed an honest man, as Marcus had described, but too simple, Flavia thought, to take on a Lucius Maximus.

'Will you have some vegetables?' Marcus asked in a low growl. 'You have eaten less than a wren.'

He had spent most of the feast glowering over her head at Lucius Maximus, so how did he know? Disconcerted, Flavia murmured, 'In a moment.' She sipped her cup of mulsum, finding the honey and wine drink warming if not comforting. Everyone else was onto a Gaulish red wine by now.

Slowly, too slowly to her, the second course was eaten and cleared. Marcus rose from the couch to direct the traditional banquet-sacrifice to the lares, the household gods. While he, Clodius, and the servers were busy placing portions of the feast on the sideboard shelf designated for the household gods, Lucius Maximus turned on the couch, leaning now on his right elbow.

This was not according to custom, but what did he care? Flavia thought, avoiding his eye as she sensed trouble. She was glad that the former bath-boy Hadrian was out of this man's reach and safe with the others in the stable.

She did not flinch as Lucius Maximus lowered his head closer to her.

'Lentils and garlic would be more appropriate to a girl of your kind,' he drawled. Reaching out, he flicked the end of her blue belt. 'Read anything interesting lately, scribe? Any diary entries that Brucetus has told you about?'

He still believed Marcus' story about Lady Valeria's diary. Flavia felt her heart and mind racing as she thought of an answer. Of course a man like him would expect her to deny it, to lie to his face.

She raised her head, staring at the bearded, olive-skinned, handsome face, those cruel brown eyes. 'I do not know what you mean,' she said.

She did not move and certainly did not look towards Marcus, in case he sensed her movement. His gods were not hers, but the sacrifice was sacred: he should not be distracted.

186

Flavia remained still, but when Lucius Maximus grabbed at her belt, his manicured fingers digging into her stomach as he tried to drag her across the couch to him, she called out, 'More wine for the Decurion! The Master of the Feast wishes to propose a toast.'

'I do?' asked Pompey, trying and falling to catch his rosemary crown as it slipped from his gray head onto the floor tiles.

'You do, Pompey,' said his wife. She nodded to Flavia, an acknowledgement that she had spotted what Lucius Maximus had been trying to do and approval at Flavia's actions.

'Excuse me.' Lucius Maximus rolled to his feet and started for the door, his mouth wide in another yawn.

Waiting until he had gone out, Julia Sura said in a low but very distinct voice, 'A most disagreeable fellow.'

'I agree.' Back beside Flavia, Marcus was unsmiling again, but he looked her over with a rapid glance. She blushed at his scrutiny.

'Let us hope he drowns in the latrine,' Julia Sura continued.

'My dear!' Beside her, Pompey lowered his silver goblet. 'Now I have forgotten my toast,' he complained. 'Lucius comes from a very old, fine family, you know.'

Julia Sura touched the pearls at her throat again. 'Breeding is not everything,' she said, her square jaw taut with disapproval. She leaned closer to her husband, whispering something.

'Of course!' Pompey beamed and raised his goblet again. 'To Flavia.'

He and Julia Sura raised their cups and drank to her. Marcus also drank, his dark eyes never leaving her face.

Please let him like me, Flavia thought, suppressing the secret wish of her heart.

She left the dining room soon after, asking one of the servers if he had seen Lucius Maximus.

'Yes, going that way.' The server pointed – but not in the direction of the latrines.

It was as she had feared and suspected. With a sinking feeling, Flavia thanked the server and stood a moment in the corridor. Was Lucius Maximus prowling in this house because he was looking for Lady Valeria's supposed diary, or some other incriminating records? Or had he simply lost his way and gone in the wrong direction?

She did not think so. She had seen his rapid backwards glance as he left the room, the calculating expression on his well-groomed face.

Tell Marcus, the sensible part of her mind clamoured, but Marcus might consider that she was being nonsensical. He might resent being called from his own feast. Above all,

Flavia admitted to herself, she did not want to look an anxious fool. She could walk very quietly when she wanted to and she knew this house well. She could move in the growing darkness with confidence and be shielded by the twilight. It would only take a few moments – she would not be missed.

First find Lucius Maximus, she decided, and only fetch Marcus if the man is anywhere he should not be.

She set off down the corridor in pursuit.

She found Lucius Maximus in the study. The study door was closed, but she could see the flicker of a candle inside and hear the distinctive rattle of the man's nasal breathing.

Searching, she thought, catching the rustle of shifted papyrus, but not burning – there was no smell of charring. Her fingers traced the grain on the door. Should she knock, perhaps scare him into leaving? Better if he did not know yet that she had been here, to retain the advantage of surprise.

She glided back from the door – and found herself facing another man – Lucius Maximus' personal slave, whom she had forgotten. Worse, she had been thinking like a free person and had not taken account of this wiry, dark stranger, who must have followed his master into the dining room and out again like a faithful shadow. She had not even noticed him, Flavia realized, also realising her own danger.

She tried a smile. 'Your master has lost his way to the latrine,' she said.

'He knows the way,' said the stranger. He was calm, but his eyes were never still, scanning her face, the study door, the empty corridor.

'There are people who will hear you,' said Flavia. In the semi-darkness, she dug her fingers into her palms. Lessons in fighting taught by Marcus seemed forgotten, but as she thought of Marcus, her resolve stiffened, even as the stranger called softly, 'Master Lucius! The girl followed you.'

'I did not,' said Flavia, backing away from the opening study door.

'Here, girl.' Lucius Maximus stepped out, his arm already reaching for her. He shook his head at her flinching away from him. 'Insolent as always.'

There were two of them now, blocking her return to the dining room. She must go round another way, but without turning her back. The little of the rich food she had eaten threatened to rise in her throat.

'We will be missed,' she said.

'You are already missed,' said Marcus, rounding the corner of the corridor and lifting a lamp high. 'Take this and guide your master better this time,' he told the dark, wiry slave, holding the lamp out.

'My thanks, Brucetus,' said Lucius Maximus as his servant took the lamp, 'Without your timely arrival no doubt I would have been wandering these cramped little rooms for another hour – although of course I had company.' He smiled at Flavia. 'My offer for her remains, you know.'

'The sweets are about to be served, Decurion,' was all Marcus said.

He waited until the two men were forced to move, tramping along the corridor, and called after them, 'Clodius' people will direct you, if you still wish to relieve yourself.'

'He was in your study, going through things–' Flavia stopped as Marcus continued to look at her, his tanned, lean face half in shadow, his eyes piercing. There was no kindness in his glance. Unable to stop herself, her eyes filled.

'Lucius Maximus is very rich,' said Marcus finally. 'As you know, I have two treasure-chests. He will have a dozen.' His dark head swivelled round, tracking where the man had gone. 'I know women find him attractive.'

'Not this one!' Flavia snapped, indignation replacing hurt. 'Or have your forgotten that day in the great bath?'

'Did you follow him to give some kind of message?' Marcus went on as if she had not spoken.

'How could you think that of me?' Flavia whispered. She wanted to fly at him, to yell at him for his stupid male jealousy, in-security, pride and blindness. But she was blind herself. The threatening tears had come and were spilling out...

He would not see her cry, not again, never again.

Her head bowed, shoulders hunched, Flavia ran past him.

He sprinted after her, exploding into motion with that uncanny swiftness of his, his feet almost as light as hers, closing on her, running her down before she could escape into the garden.

'I am no mercenary!' she cried in fury, as he caught her, struggling, in his arms. 'I loathe the man – he disgusts me!' *He is a murderer!* She almost spoke her thought, drew in breath to do so.

'Hush!' Marcus muttered by her ear and, as she protested again, he began to kiss her deeply.

How could he do this and think her at-tracted to anyone else? The thought blazed in Flavia even as her body and lips responded. 'Marcus!' She said his name over and over as his hands caressed her shoulders, arms, waist, breasts. 'Marcus. Marcus.'

'Flavia,' he answered softly, his shoulders cracking as his arms tightened about her. 'My little Celt.'

Quarrels and doubts forgotten, they clung to each other.

Flavia remembered very little of the rest of the evening. Lucius Maximus called for his outdoor footwear and left as soon as he had consumed two blackberry and apple pastries, giving the barest thanks. Julia Sura and Pompey also quickly retired, claiming the weariness of travel.

Soon afterwards, in full darkness and in a blazing torch-lit procession, the cook Clodius and his retinue departed for their shop in Aquae Sulis. Marcus went with them, to be satisfied of their safety, he said.

Checking the study, Flavia discovered that although some papers and tablets had been moved and a wax tablet broken, there was no other sign of Lucius Maximus ever being there. She was glad of that. Back in her bare little chamber, she found a grubby, grinning, newly-gap-toothed Hadrian sitting cross-legged on top of his bed, eager to tell her everything. Slipping into her own bed, she fell asleep to his chatter.

Pompey and Julia Sura stayed on at the villa for another five days. Marcus was much involved in escorting his former commander around Aquae Sulis, and in taking him hunting. Hadrian pleaded and was permitted to go on these expeditions, while Flavia was involved in her usual duties. Julia Sura liked to spend most of the afternoon at the great baths and took her own attendants with her.

Pompey had brought a parcel of mail for Marcus from Eboracum, and Flavia had a great many letters to respond to on his behalf. It was the kind of role she had fulfilled with Lady Valeria but, working every afternoon in the silent study soon after midday, Flavia admitted that she had never felt lonely doing these tasks before. Now she did, and all because of Marcus.

She saw very little of Marcus, and certainly he had no time for any further fighting 'lessons', not even for Hadrian. Once, passing her in the kitchen, he kissed her forehead and whispered, 'No wrestling today, either, I fear.' To her own vexation, Flavia laughed, the tension lessening between them for an instant.

That was how it was now: an uneasy truce between Marcus and herself while Julia Sura and Pompey were in the house. What would happen when they left, Flavia did not know.

On the evening before she and her husband were due to leave the following morning for Londinium, Julia Sura invited Flavia for a pre-dinner stroll. Flavia sensed that the Roman woman wanted to share a confidence, a feeling which increased when Pompey joined them in wandering the gravel paths of the enclosed courtyard-garden. There had been a thin scattering of snow but the day was bright, with no wind.

'Let us hope it is like this at the Saturnalia,' Julia remarked, threading her arm companionably through Flavia's, her booted feet crunching on the snow. 'There is less than a month now to the festival.'

'Yes,' Flavia agreed, digging her free hand more deeply into the folds of her shawl, although she was not cold. She did not want to seem nervous.

Julia Sura, handsome in a green, gap-sleeved wool gown and heavy outdoor mantle, smiled at her. 'You are wondering why we're out here. Two reasons. I wish to compliment you on Marcus – he looks younger and happier than he has for months.

'My husband served for a time in Germania,' Julia went on, smoothly bridging the gap of Flavia's astonished silence. 'Pompey met Marcus soon after the deaths of his wife and child – you know about them? Yes, I see that you do.'

'Wonderful fighter, marvellous leader but a lost man,' Pompey broke in from Flavia's left side, making her start. 'I was sure he would grieve forever for them.'

'Hush, my dear.' Julia leaned across Flavia and gave her husband's arm a warning shake. 'We do not need to know your opinions of Marcus' state of mind.' She caught Flavia's pensive expression and gave an exasperated sigh. 'Really, Pompey!'

'It is all right,' said Flavia, hiding her face for a moment as she crouched and scooped a handful of small pebbles from the path. 'I knew that already.' She flicked a pebble at a snow-dusted lavender, and when she was certain she could fashion a smile, she turned to Julia. 'May I ask your second reason for speaking to me out here?'

Julia laughed. 'You don't let your sandals lie idle in the sun, as we say in Rome. But you are right: it is the moment to be frank with each other. And I say to you now, Flavia, that I like you very much.'

'My wife is an excellent judge of character–'

'Hush, Pompey. What I mean to say, Flavia, is that you and Marcus have many admirable qualities–' She held up a hand as Flavia demurred, '–But neither of you are good liars. Pompey tells me that Marcus has been on the brink of confessing something about Lucius Maximus on their every hunting trip. I know that you have no love for the man. So what is it?'

Flavia glanced at Pompey, who gave an embarrassed cough. He took a pebble from her hand and flicked it at another bush. 'Don't know what the fuss is, myself,' he mumbled. 'Excellent family. Impeccable credentials.'

'And if you said that to Marcus, it is no surprise he is close-mouthed,' said Julia briskly. She stared down her hooked nose at Flavia, tapping her hand against her leg, and then pointed at the stepped main entrance to the villa. 'And here is Marcus. Why do you not go meet him, husband?'

Without giving Pompey a chance to respond, Julia Sura clasped Flavia's shoulder and steered her firmly in the opposite direction. 'We have no time now for any kind of explanation,' she said rapidly. 'So I will say this. After Pompey and I have helped my sister to celebrate her birthday in Londinium, we're returning north to Eboracum. Write to me there if you need my help.'

'Thank you,' said Flavia, surprised and touched by the offer.

Julia Sura nodded. 'Take care of Marcus for us. We are very fond of him.'

'I will do whatever I can,' vowed Flavia.

Julia Sura smiled. 'You really mean that, don't you?' Stooping, she surprised Flavia again by kissing her. When she drew back, she looked surprised herself. 'Remember my words,' she said.

'I will,' Flavia promised.

Chapter 10

When Julia Sura and Pompey were gone, the villa seemed eerily quiet. The dawn was damp and foggy and all sounds and sights were deadened. Hunched over the heavy mill-stone, grinding the wheat for the day's bread, Flavia felt lonely again. Marcus and Hadrian had gone with Pompey's party for part of the way, guiding them onto the road to Londinium. It was likely they would be gone all day.

As she shopped for Agrippina, gardened with Sulinus, and polished the floor tiles with Livia, Flavia felt the hours drag by. She missed Marcus even though she knew he would be back by nightfall. In Aquae Sulis, she found herself wandering towards the tailor's shop that she and Marcus had visited on his first day with her in the city. In the garden, she picked a few small holly branches and strands of ivy to stand in a simple wooden beaker in Marcus' room. Back in the kitchen with Agrippina, she helped the cook prepare honey cakes for Hadrian. By this time, Pina was proud of the boy's voracious appetite, helped by his appreciation of her cooking. As she worked, Flavia imagined herself at another feast with Marcus: a Christian feast, where she was free, his equal, and he was her guest.

Slowly, the morning merged into the afternoon. A dim, spectral twilight came and still there was no sign of Marcus, no sound of his galloping horse, no glad shouts from Hadrian, no enthusiastic bark from Nero. Already uneasy from hours before, even though she knew that Marcus was not due to return until sunset, Flavia took herself out into the courtyard-garden and from there into the street.

Gaius came out of the villa and called her back. 'You know the master does not like you wandering about alone, especially at this hour,' he scolded.

'I was only just outside the gate!' Flavia protested. She felt she would go wild, waiting and being able to do nothing. 'I am going to walk out to meet them,' she said. 'I will take a lantern–'

'No!' The old slave gave her a quelling glare. 'He will be furious, and not just with you. You must *wait*.'

'That is what I have been doing all day!'

'So you will have had lots of practice.' Gaius took her arm in a grip that she knew would hurt him if she tried to break. 'Come on, Flavia,' he said tiredly, his wispy moustache drooping more than ever in the cold, damp fog. 'It will not be for much longer.'

Flavia looked at him. 'What about this potions buyer?' she asked, determined to resolve one thing at least today. 'What is going on? I know I promised you a month, but do you not trust me?'

At that moment it was the right question to ask. Gaius sighed heavily and patted her arm. 'I suppose to tell you a little will do no harm.' He glanced back at the quiet villa. 'Pina did not want you worrying.'

How typical of Pina to decide for me, Flavia

thought, but said nothing. At last Gaius was explaining.

'The potions buyer you kept asking about,' he went on, 'we have been keeping her supplied with unguents and potions to sell in the great bath. We have been doing it for months. As a way to earn our freedom,' he added, when Flavia still was silent.

'All of you busy with those mortars and pestles,' Flavia said at last. 'I never realized.' She had feared that their preparations might be more sinister. She had even thought, although never admitting to the thought, that perhaps one of them had supplied Lady Valeria with her fatal poison. 'But Marcus—'

'Knows nothing yet. We would prefer he remain that way for now.'

'I will not tell him,' Flavia promised, although even as she spoke she was wondering at the risk the old slaves were taking. What if their master discovered what they were up to and resented it? What if he punished them in some way?

And they were not going to tell me about this. They kept it from me for months. Do they really consider me to be such a sneak, running to Marcus with gossip?

I do run to Marcus, she admitted. And Gaius and the others know I like him. But for them to wonder if I would be such a blabber-mouth...

Seething with frustration and anxiety, Flavia stalked back into the villa.

Another hour snailed by and a messenger came to say that Marcus' horse had gone lame and that he and Hadrian would not be back until close to midnight.

'That is it, then,' said Gaius. 'We may as well all turn in and get some sleep before they come.'

Sometime later, Flavia woke in her room. Hadrian was snoring softly in the bed next to hers, with the wooden practice swords Marcus had given to him and Flavia clutched tightly in his fists. Nero sprawled across his middle, his white paws twitching in a dream. There was a strange, sour taste in her mouth, which made her wonder if the blackberry tisane Pina had given her just before she had retired might have been drugged with some kind of sleeping potion. How ironic, she thought wryly, considering what she and Gaius had been speaking of that afternoon. A potion would explain why she had slept so easily, and why she now felt peculiarly calm.

Marcus was safe.

Marcus had returned.

Flavia said aloud, 'Marcus is home,' and felt an overwhelming fountain of delight building within her – even a sleeping potion could not suppress that. She leapt from her bed, her drugged limbs tottering slightly, her head swimming, and saw a small posy of winter flowers lying on her pillow.

Suddenly, her legs would not hold her up anymore. Flavia flopped back onto the bed and reached with trembling fingers for the posy. The flowers blurred before her eyes and she almost cursed Pina for that sly sleeping draught, but the instant she felt it, her anger melted away into renewed joy. Marcus was safe, home again, bringing others safely home and bringing her flowers.

No one, no man, woman or child had ever brought her flowers before.

She lifted the posy. Beneath it were three slender bracelets, which Marcus must have bought on the way out of the city that morning, bought and given to her: her first jewellery.

Hardly daring to believe that any of these gifts were real, Flavia softly gathered them up and walked quietly to the chamber door. Stealing out into the corridor, she came to a window and opened the shutter a crack.

The fog had lifted and the moon was riding high. By its brilliant light, she could admire the tiny white flowers of chickweed, the delicate flowers and foliage of shepherd's purse. There were dried fennel stalks and a single daisy and two blue speedwells that must have flowered out of season. The small bunch fitted easily into the palm of her hand, but she guessed the care that had gone into making it, especially at this time of the year, when flowers were rare.

The thin bracelets were of copper, very highly polished. Savouring the feel of the cool metal against her skin, Flavia slipped them onto her wrist. She shook her arm and smiled as she heard the bracelets clash gently together, like a tiny sistrum.

She was light-headed with happiness. Agrippina's sleight of hand with a sleeping potion, the problem of Lucius Maximus, the painful mystery of her lady's death and that elusive potions buyer: these would all keep. She wanted to thank Marcus at once.

She thought of going into his room and the temptation grew stronger. He would look so beautiful asleep. Would he think her brazen? 'I hope so,' she said aloud, astonishing herself by giggling.

She touched the flowers to her cheek, then turned and lowered her head. Trying to catch their faint scent, she inhaled deeply–

She could smell smoke. Even as she stiffened, Flavia saw a coiling shadow further along the corridor and heard a faint crackle coming from the direction of Marcus' room.

The villa was on fire.

For a second Flavia was stunned, watching that insidious wisp of smoke, the thought, *It cannot be happening again* piercing her like a sliver of ice. Then she reacted.

'Wake up! Get out! Get out, there's fire!'

Even as she yelled, Flavia was moving. She

pelted down the corridor through the chok-
ing smoke, coughing but sprinting now
towards Marcus' room.

'Get out! Fire!' She thumped the nearest
wall, losing her flower posy and feeling a
frightening heat in the plaster, but finally
hearing puzzled shouts and blundering
scuffles from the kitchen, furthest from the
site of the blaze.

*The kitchen would be where you would expect
a fire to start.* The thought rose from the
bottom of Flavia's mind but she ignored it,
shouting over her shoulder, 'Hadrian – get
up! Get out!' as she burst through into
Marcus' room.

She was met by a dazzling pool of flame
and the stink of burning oil and cloth. Smoking oil dripped from the window, across the
table and down onto the floor, where bundles
of rags were burning up into skeletons of ash.
There were more burning rags on the table
under the window and the oak wood was
scorching. The window shutters themselves
were drawn together, but ajar.

Lying on the bed at the end of this ever-
closing track of spitting, flaming rags, was
Marcus. A weary Marcus, still in his travelling cloak and sandals, his face half-obscured
by the filthy fug, his rapid reactions and wits
stunned by the billowing smoke.

'Marcus! Get up!'

He snorted and rolled onto his side away

204

from her.

'Marcus!' Flavia could not reach him across the sooty, smoking pool of oil, where now one of his boots burned, casting lurid shadows across the roof. There was water in a pail, though, close to the door.

'Wake up!' Flavia tore down the door hanging, plunged it into the water, heaved it out, dripping, and flung it over the oil. The heat from the oil seared her hands, but there was a stepping place for her to reach him.

'Marcus!'

Plucking the pail off the tiles, Flavia launched herself across the bundled damp door hanging, reached the foot of the bed and threw half the contents of the pail at the prone figure on the bed. 'Get up!' she shrieked.

Red-eyed, sodden-haired, Marcus reared up cursing. 'What is happening?' he roared.

'Fire!' Flavia panted, shaking his right foot and jerking her head at the deadly pool of oil. Above the spit of the flames, she could hear Gaius marshalling the others.

'Get up, up—' she repeated, not releasing Marcus' foot until she felt him tense and heard him snarl, 'Right girl – now let go of me!'

Leaving the pail for Marcus, she turned at once and jumped back onto the still-damp door hanging and then across to the threshold. Only then did she look back.

205

'Hurry!' she urged. 'The others are safe now. We must go!'

He was coming, straight off the end of the couch, reaching the door ahead of Flavia and dragging her through it, dowsing the door with the rest of the water from the pail, slamming it after them.

As the door closed on those dancing, wicked little flames, Flavia tasted salt and soot on her lips. Her hands were beginning to sting badly, but she could move quickly enough. There was no need for Marcus to stop.

'I can walk! Go!' she rasped, breaking off to cough some more.

She felt a rush of air as Marcus shook off his cloak and wrapped it around her, saying quickly, 'Come, then.'

They hurried along the corridor, Marcus knocking a wall lantern flying as he failed to duck, but there was no time to check if the lantern was lit or not – they had to get out.

'Someone did this,' Flavia panted as they ran. 'Oil on the floor, rags, the window shutters ajar. Someone must have been watching you, saw you return tonight–'

'That will keep–' Marcus broke off as a heart-rendering scream sliced through the eerie half-light, half-smoke of the corridor.

'No!' Flavia shouted, starting after him back the way they had just fled to the study, praying as she stumbled, *Please – please.*

Please let Hadrian be unharmed, let him have cried out from shock, from fear – not from pain. Please, never from pain.

In the narrow corridor she could not see much beyond Marcus' strong running figure, only an increasing glare of light as he closed on the study that could only mean one thing. The unknown arsonist who had attacked Marcus tonight had also lit a fire in the study.

'Hadrian, where are you?' Flavia called out, her lungs feeling as if they were charring. She was finding it increasingly difficult to take a full breath and her sight was blurring. Where was the boy? She had left him in their small chamber, safe and a long way from the fire – the two fires.

'Hadrian, leave those, they are only parchment! Come on!' Marcus was shouting as he pushed the study door open to its widest, his dark head weaving this way and that as he searched desperately for the small boy. 'Hadrian!'

The study was full of burning rags and flaming scrolls of papyrus. The wolfskin rug was no more and there was the same dreadful smell of oil, but no Hadrian.

Flavia ducked and saw movement under the desk. 'There!' she shouted and dashed forward, batting a floating, sooty piece of papyrus out of her way. She reached under the desk and her straining hands found a trembling Hadrian and Nero, the boy's right leg horribly blistered.

'I found burning rags and a lamp in here … overfull … tried to put it out … oil spilled on me…' Hadrian gasped, his narrow face sweating as he wiped a grubby hand across his eyes, clearly fighting back tears. 'Take Nero–'

'We are taking both of you, my lad.' Marcus scooped him out from under the desk, scowling as Hadrian flinched and cursing in Latin, 'Mithras and the gods, we need water!'

'Water's in the stable,' Flavia mumbled, grabbing the snapping little dog and bundling him none-too-gently into her arms. From a long way off she could hear shouting and this time not just Gaius: their nearest city neighbours were awake and rushing out into the foggy darkness to help.

Still crouching, Flavia turned for the door. On his feet first, Marcus steadied her up and they moved together, out of the study, along the corridor, out past the dining room to the main entrance where Gaius and the others were already crowded onto the steps, their faces dull with shock.

'Everyone here?' Marcus was asking. 'Everyone safe?'

'Yes, master,' Agrippina sobbed, leaning hard against her elderly, whey-faced husband.

Not again, Flavia was thinking, as a crowd of neighbours with pails and jugs of water

208

ran towards them and past them. *It could not happen to me again. I was not going to let it happen. I was not going to lose anyone else that I love to a fire.*

Dimly, she sensed Nero squirming and yapping against her, felt his breath close to her ear, and heard Marcus shouting for a deep pail of water so that he could get some of the fire and heat out of Hadrian's injured leg. She braced her back against one of the entrance columns and tried to stand, then found herself sinking down ... down...

With the stench of fire still vivid and the burning in her hands now spreading its scorching pain all the way up her arms and into her head, Flavia lost consciousness.

Chapter 11

Flavia remembered only disconnected moments from the rest of that night. The first was Marcus, holding her by the shoulders, peering intently into her face, calling her name.

'Hadrian hurt,' she mumbled, closing her eyes against Marcus' scowl.

'Pina has him with that blistered foot in a pitcher of water. Sulinus has gone searching for a salve,' she heard him say. He brushed her hair off her forehead and wiped her face with a damp cloth, his touch gentle. 'You should have told me about your burned hands.'

'You had more important things to deal with.' Flavia forced her eyes open again. The glare of the fire was diminishing as a line of people passed jugs and buckets of water from one to another, from outside to within the villa. As she shook her head to clear it she saw two figures with brooms pass by her on the steps and go inside.

'By Mithras, girl! When you slumped against the column like that and Nero jumped from your arms...'

Marcus' voice faded and his fierce, harsh features blurred into the midnight fog. When Flavia came to herself again, she was laying with her head pillowed in Livia's bony lap, with Marcus' cloak bundled around her.

Her fellow Celt gave her a gentle smile. 'You are back with us again. That is good. Master Marcus will be pleased.'

'He is inside,' Livia went on, speaking slowly as if Flavia were very young. 'Checking that the roof is safe. That the fires are out. We will sleep in the stable for the rest of tonight. Master Marcus says he will stand...'

Flavia drifted away.

She woke in the stable, in the pre-dawn cold. Sulinus, Gaius, Pina and Livia were curled in sleep around her. Beside her,

Hadrian was jerking in a dream, his thin lips locked together. Outside the stable and their nest of straw she could hear Marcus' quick, firm step.

He was guarding them. Flavia took comfort from the thought as the ache in her hands grew worse.

'We are alive. We escaped,' she whispered. There was joy in that, a fierce delight in having thwarted Lucius Maximus' devious plans. Who else could it be? Flavia thought, cradling the dreaming Hadrian and stroking his shaggy, ash-flecked black hair. It was still too dark to see the wound on his leg. She shivered, pitying the boy, and her mind flashed back to the moment in Marcus' bedroom, when she had found him threatened by fire. If she had not been able to rouse him—

'I would have lost him, like my mother and father,' Flavia said aloud, her voice rasping with emotion and smoke. She felt a tear fall down her cheek. Before she could turn her head, another tear splashed onto Hadrian's dirt-smeared forehead. The child flinched and stirred.

'I am thirsty, Flavia,' he croaked. 'My throat hurts.'

'I will find you some water.' Flavia began to ease Hadrian off her side onto the straw, but felt him tremble. She bent her lips to his ear. 'Shall we go outside, just the two of us?'

He nodded, his face closed down in that hard, flinty look he had worn in the great baths, when she had first met him as the slave Rags.

Anger against Lucius Maximus gave Flavia the strength to lift Hadrian in her injured hands and carry him outside. The fact that the boy did not protest, did not even seem to notice, worried her. She was keen to see if, out under the skies, she might be able to take a look at his blistered leg.

The helpful neighbours from last night had gone. Stepping out from the stable into the courtyard, Flavia thought the place looked deserted and even more strange, untouched. There was no sign now of the fire. She could smell charred cloth and timber, though, and here and there on the gravel paths there were abandoned or broken water jugs.

She could not see Marcus and for that moment was pleased: she did not want him angry at her for moving. Forgotten after what seemed an age, she felt the slim copper bracelets on her wrist and wondered when she would be able to thank him for them.

'Not long for your drink,' she told Hadrian, swinging him to ride on her hip. In the semi-dark he did not see her flinch as that simple transfer jolted the nagging pain in her hands into raw agony. Desperate not to drop him, she straightened and tried to concentrate instead on finding a pitcher of water, walking a few unsteady steps towards the house.

Close to the ivy-clad statue of Pan, Flavia spotted an unbroken jug of water. She lifted it, held it while Hadrian drank, her own throat parched and sore from the fire. When the boy raised his head and smiled at her, Flavia smiled back, although by then her grip on the jug was turning her sick with pain. Aware that it would do Hadrian's leg no good if she fainted, she leaned against the cold stone Pan, wondering if this leering pagan god mocked her.

'Here. Take a drink before you slide down this piece of marble as well.'

Marcus caught her gently round her middle and, before Flavia could protest, he lifted Hadrian from her hip onto his.

'How is my centurion this morning?' he asked. Squeezing Flavia's waist with his free hand, he said, 'Drink. It will ease the pain.'

Flavia stared at the small leather flask in his hand. 'What is it?'

'One of cook's potions.'

'No thank you. I am not drinking anything more of hers,' said Flavia crisply.

Marcus shot her a quizzical look that had her clenching her jaws – it was plain that Pina had told him of her drugged night-time tisane. For a dizzying second she was nervous that Marcus knew the whole of what Pina and the others had been doing with their potions-making and tried to brace

213

herself for interrogation.

'I presume Sulinus' salve is acceptable?' he asked quietly, spiriting a small clay pot out of his tunic. His muddy tunic, Flavia realized, as the slowly brightening sky showed him plainly. He had been awake all night.

Flavia nodded. She was on the point of thanking Marcus for his gifts when he reached out and touched the bracelets on her wrist. 'I am glad you found these.'

'They are–' Flavia began, when Hadrian interrupted.

'Can I have more of that salve on my leg, Marcus?' He turned his head to Flavia, a pleading look.

'Would you like me to do it?' she asked.

'Yes, please.' Hadrian thrust out his bandaged right leg. 'Sulinus did it last time,' he said, as if that explained everything.

'Steady on, young man. I think we will be better sitting down.' Releasing Flavia, Marcus lowered the boy onto the grass beside the statue and straightened at once.

'You are shivering,' he told her. 'I will fetch a brazier.' He smiled. 'It will be like that first time we met.'

Turning, he strode away into the villa, re-emerging moments later with the long flat brazier he had carried out to the garden before. Flavia watched him carefully lowering the glowing charcoal into position, his face unusually solemn, almost tense, and saw how he favoured one arm over the other. Realising that he too had been injured last night, she fought down a new spasm of anger against Lucius Maximus. Because of him, she might have lost this brave, good man.

But he is not yours to lose, an unwelcome inner voice reminded her and after that she was grateful to be concentrating on unwrapping Hadrian's bandages. While she did so, using the tips of her fingers to spare the boy pain, she said, without looking at Marcus, 'I will tend that shoulder of yours, too. Where you ran into the lantern.'

She heard Marcus clap a hand onto his upper back.

'It is nothing,' he grunted.

'Then it will not matter if I look, will it?' She raised her head then, to drive home both point and riposte and found him glowering at her, his fists tapping at his belt.

'On one condition,' he said. 'I treat your hands first.'

'Maybe,' Flavia said, gently peeling back the final covering from Hadrian's foot. She heard the boy suck in a deep breath and felt him stiffen. At once, without prompting, Marcus took Hadrian's hand in his and pressed it.

'Hang on there, centurion. You are doing bravely,' he said.

Through pale lips and a narrow, pallid face, Hadrian managed a smile.

215

Hadrian's blisters and burns were undoubt-
edly painful, but not too deep. Flavia tended
them swiftly, wrapping his foot and leg in
the softest piece of linen that Marcus could
find for her. Afterward, the boy stretched
out beside the brazier and slept again.

'We should do your hands now.' Marcus
reached for the small clay pot of salve, but
Flavia held it behind her back.

'Your shoulder,' she said, and nodded
towards the rising sun. 'Soon you will have
other claims on your time.' Which was true,
but she was wary of him touching her in case
she revealed too much of her feelings and
there was also the selfish desire to touch him,
to ease his pain. 'My hands are better,' she
lied. 'I don't want you to bother about them.'

His jaw tightened, the blue-black stubble
on his chin seeming almost rigid, and then
he sighed. 'Very well, Flavia. If that is how
you want it.'

Shrugging off one shoulder of his tunic, he
sat on the grass by Hadrian, his back to her,
his body unmoving. There was a scarlet oil
burn in the shape of a half-moon on his left
shoulder blade which must have pained him,
but he allowed her to smooth salve onto the
wound without a murmur of complaint.

His back was as toned and perfectly
proportioned as a statue's and that was how
it felt to Flavia – as if she was tending a

stone man. Under her sore, raw hands his skin felt cool, as if his very flesh was determined to resist her.

But he bought me flowers and the bracelet, Flavia reminded herself and yet, when she had finished and showed him the empty clay pot, Marcus simply rearranged his clothes, nodded a silent thanks and rose to his feet.

'Take some rest,' he said, as cold and calm as if old Gaius had just tended his naked back, and then he surprised her by handing her another small flask off his belt.

'It is plain water,' he said, his blue eyes glittering with what could have been amusement – or anger. 'You can drink it safely.'

He left her then, marching away to the stable, shouting for Sulinus and Gaius.

In a more fashionable part of Aquae Sulis, close to the great bath, the Decurion Lucius Maximus was meeting one of his spies. The informer was a ratty little man after Lucius Maximus' heart. Dishonest and greedy, Cassius pretended to be a war veteran and beggar by day, parading through the streets in ragged clothes and a begging bowl before changing into fine perfumed linen at night. He took charity from others and lived well on it, but was not generous himself: Cassius' slaves lived in dread of their master.

Because of his daily transformation from war 'veteran' to rich man, Cassius had a private bath, a smaller-scale version of the great bath itself. It was there, in the hot pool, where he and Lucius Maximus were discussing the events of the previous night.

It was early in the day for bathing, but Lucius Maximus considered himself above such petty customs. Sprawled on one of the marble underwater steps that also served as seats within the bath, he wallowed in the water that had taken sweating, driven slaves all night to heat and took a swig of warm mead.

'Anything to warm oneself in this vile climate, eh?' he remarked, addressing his fellow-bather after Cassius had given his report of last night's fire. 'Although I doubt if Brucetus needs more warming. The study and his bedroom: both in ashes, you say? Excellent!'

Lucius Maximus laughed and drained off the rest of the mead, snapping his fingers at a hovering slave for a refill. 'You have done well for me last night, Cassius. And well for yourself, considering your fee,' he added sourly, his handsome face taking on a familiar look of petulance.

'There was danger,' Cassius whined, his bathing strigil poised in mid-air above his scrawny shoulder as he sought to placate his patron and employer with a stream of justifications. 'After the affair with the tribune's horse–'

'Which you bungled.'

'No, my lord! I was watching the villa of Marcus Brucetus – as you had instructed – and waiting for a moment to act against him – as you had instructed. I saw the chance to do the tribune an injury that would look like an accident and took it. Any other man would have ridden off and noticed nothing amiss with the harness, but the girl, my lord – that little blonde slave – she noticed and warned him.'

So much the worse for her, thought Lucius Maximus, but he said nothing, allowing himself to be amused by Cassius' endless excuses.

'The tribune is no fool, my lord, and fire-setting is a dangerous business, especially if the whole building is not to be destroyed – those were your instructions. For me to remain undetected and ensure that Marcus Brucetus was there, and that he, a soldier, neither saw me nor suspected what I was doing–'

'You were well paid for your trouble.'

Ignoring the rest of the arsonist-spy's complaint, Lucius Maximus stroked his newly-washed beard. Cassius had indeed performed better than expected. Although he longed to be revenged on that apology for a Roman, that half-breed Brucetus who'd had the insolence to publicly disarm and then humiliate him, the man was a citizen. If he had been killed in last night's fire, there would have been questions, an investigation. No, better that the fool suspected nothing, and put it down to slaves' carelessness. Any papers belonging to his old adversary Valeria would have gone up in smoke. As for the rest of his plans, especially for the slave girl: they were well in hand.

Lucius Maximus smiled as he considered the small, blonde, slave. If all went to plan, then before the festival of the Saturnalia was over, she would be his. And then the girl would learn what it was to serve a true Roman master.

For the rest of the day after the fire, Flavia saw little of Marcus. He was busy clearing out the charred furniture and hangings, instructing the others in cleaning, explaining to those who came to see him that he and the rest of his household were safe and well. As for the sooty villa itself, he made a joke of it, saying that he had lived in more ruined forts and survived. The builders were coming after the mid-winter festival of the Saturnalia to extend the servants' quarters: they could attend then to any fire-damage.

Later, Marcus went out into the city and returned with food for everyone. He also brought the rangy, one-eyed legionary Otho back with him, and several more tough-looking war veterans, to act as guards in future.

Whether from shock, or from the wearying pain in her hands, Flavia slept a lot, and so did Hadrian. Waking briefly during the first night after the fire, she found herself still in the open air, beside the statue of Pan and the glowing charcoal brazier. Hadrian was sleeping on one side of her and Marcus was standing guard above them, talking softly to Otho. She was shy of interrupting their conversation and so closed her eyes and pretended to still be asleep.

When she opened her eyes again, it was full day. A bright, mild day with cloudless blue skies. She felt much more alive and her hands were far less painful, but strangely enough she still felt dizzy. Somehow the sky above her seemed to be moving.

Flavia turned her head and realized that her instinct was not wrong. The sky was moving, because she was. She was lying on a narrow cart – Lady Valeria's antique mule-cart – now floored and padded with pillows and cushions and what seemed to be half the bedding from the villa.

'What?' she murmured, and tried to sit up in the trundling cart.

'Flavia! You are awake!' From the end of the cart, where he had been riding dangling his uninjured leg over the side, Hadrian limped across to her. The pale child of two nights ago had become a bright, high-colored boy again, proudly wearing his bandages as if they were badges of office and scattering a handful of newly-made biscuits all over the floor and bedding of the cart.

'We are going on a picnic! Nero's staying with Otho to guard the villa, but we are going to pick mushrooms! We are going to the forest!'

His delighted shouts alerted everyone. Marcus stopped the cart at once, gave the reins of the old mule to Gaius, sitting in front beside him, and turned to look at her.

He smiled, the stark planes of his face softening with tenderness. Flavia, full of mingled joy and apprehension, felt as if her stomach had flipped over. This was the Marcus she had known on their visit to the great bath and the sculptor's, generous and approachable, indulgent and teasing.

He teased her a little now, saying, 'I wondered if we might travel all the way *through* the forest before you stirred. How are you?'

'I'm well. How is your shoulder – sir?' She stumbled on the question, unsure what to call him. They had been through so much together, but he could still make her feel shy. Make her blush, as she knew she was doing now.

Marcus raised a thick black eyebrow at her formality, but said nothing. Instead he turned to Gaius and the other three household servants, who had been walking beside the cart with baskets. 'Change places with

Flavia for a while, will you?' he asked pleasantly. 'Go on ahead to the ford and wait there. We will catch up.'

Speaking, he stepped from the cart, and came round to the back to help Flavia down, but she was ahead of him, sliding out of the cart as a visible sign of her independence. Marcus gave a grunt of amusement and waved on a very knowing-looking Gaius. 'Go, then.'

Flavia heard the cart roll away, accompanied by Hadrian's shouts of encouragement to the plodding old mule. Standing, she felt steadier, more herself, and stood her ground as Marcus came even closer.

'I see the warrior is back in you, Flavia – if indeed it ever left.' Stopping directly in front of her, Marcus lowered his head so their faces were level, his blue eyes lively with humour. 'The doctor suggested that a change of scene might be beneficial to you and Hadrian, but I still think it is too soon for us to resume your weapons training.'

'Especially the wrestling,' Flavia said ahead of him, delighted when Marcus gave his deep belly laugh.

'True enough, little Celt! So I must content myself with other lessons and today I hope that you will be my teacher.'

If only I could be in the way I'd like to be, Flavia thought, her mind flooding with images of Marcus and herself that would

223

probably not be out of place at one of the forthcoming revels of the Saturnalia. He was now so close to her that not even a scrap of papyrus could be slotted between them, yet he made no move to take her in his arms. She wished she were bold enough to embrace him first, but found herself saying instead, very awkwardly, 'If I can be useful to you, sir, I will.'

'In the woodland you love? Yes, Flavia, I think you will be. You can tell me the names of your native flowers and birds.'

He was smiling as he spoke and she wondered despairingly if he was mocking her. 'Of course,' she said, stiffer than ever.

She moved to walk past him but he blocked her path. He raised a hand and for a wonderful instant Flavia thought he might take her hand in his, but he merely raked stiff fingers through his own tough, straight hair. 'You have lost all your glow again,' he said quietly. 'What is it? Are you in pain? The doctor promised me you would be all right.'

'What doctor?'

'The doctor I brought back with me from Aquae Sulis to look at you and the boy. Have you forgotten?'

Now that she thought about it, Flavia discovered that she did have a hazy memory from earlier that morning of someone peering into her eyes and sniffing her hands. Whoever the doctor had been, she was relieved that Marcus had not brought the sinister apothecary from the shrine of the great bath home with him, but thought it wisest not to admit that.

'I don't really remember him,' she said.

'Well, he will remember you. When he asked if you needed help in washing and dressing you were most insistent that you could do both yourself.' Marcus brushed the sleeve of her sunshine-yellow gown, a half-smile tugging at his lips. 'And of course your determination succeeded.'

Praying that he was not laughing at her again, Flavia said, 'I probably thought he was you.'

The moment the words left her mouth, she wanted to call them back. 'I meant that I would always prefer to be independent,' she stammered, but Marcus waved aside her explanation.

'No matter,' he said curtly. 'The doctor also suggested moderate exercise – but of course you will need no help in walking to the ford.'

He turned and stalked away, leaving Flavia to catch up as best she could.

Marcus was scrupulous in allowing Flavia her independence after that and, despite her injured hands, Flavia was too humiliated and proud to ask for his help in climbing back into the cart once she and Marcus had rejoined the others at the river ford. With Marcus driving again and Hadrian scrambling out of the nest of bedding and cushions to join Marcus and Gaius in front, Flavia sat quietly with the others.

Any excitement she would normally have felt at leaving the city for only the second time in her life was subdued after her latest estrangement with Marcus. Pina and Livia's giggling chatter across their gathering baskets made her feel lonelier than ever. Hoping that no one would notice her silence, Flavia made a play of studying the passing countryside.

They were across the river and climbing out of the city suburbs now, leaving behind the earth ramparts and ditch that surrounded Aquae Sulis along with its crowds and smoke and building noise. While her fingers distractedly tugged at the sleeve of the yellow gown she did not remember changing into, Flavia spotted a grand tomb set close to the road they were on: a woman's tomb, with painted and moulded plasterwork and a detailed inscription that she was too far away to read. Kneeling up in the cart, her arms resting against the top of one side, she watched the tomb for a long time after they passed, remembering Lady Valeria and her own visit to the sculptor's workshop in Aquae Sulis, when she and Marcus had been speaking to each other.

'Hello!' Marcus greeted a group of women vegetable-sellers returning to their country homes, their produce sold in town, as the cart rumbled past them on the cobbled road. One of the women waved her empty basket in greeting: she wore a fur-lined hood that might have been the twin of the hood belonging to the mystery potions buyer whom Gaius and the others were secretly working for, but Flavia felt too dispirited to worry about their subterfuge now. It was easier to watch the landscape and those travelling within it: the narrow corn fields lying fallow close to the city; the grassed-over ruins of an ancient hill fort on one of the steeper hills; a shepherd driving his bleating sheep to another part of the downs; a Roman dispatch rider, pounding past them along the highway.

This was the Roman peace Marcus had alluded to but, looking out from the cart, Flavia did not feel peaceful. Her body was tense as she struggled to maintain her outward composure and her ears were pricked, waiting to hear Marcus, waiting for him to speak to her. Surely he would speak to her?

For now, he was answering Hadrian's questions. 'Yes, I know it is late in the day to be gathering mushrooms, but does that matter? This is a holiday.'

'And will there be wolves and boars in the woods?' Hadrian asked, his lean face shining with expectation. The boy was sitting between Marcus' legs now, snapping the reins in his skinny arms and 'driving' the cart with him. Flavia envied him his closeness to Marcus and was ashamed of her feeling. Her stomach contracted with a painful lurch as she heard Marcus' ringing laughter and easy answer, as if he had no cares in the world.

'Hardly, my lad, with your leg in the state it is in! No, there will be no rough hunting today. Otho tells me nobody remembers boars in those woods, and certainly no wolves.'

'That is a blessing,' Agrippina chimed in, but Hadrian was already asking more.

'Otho – the solider with one eye? How did that happen? How did he lose it?'

'Hadrian!' Livia and Agrippina scolded as one, making his name a remonstration, but Marcus only laughed again and said that the boy had a right to be curious.

'It is no secret how my friend lost his eye and Otho does not mind anyone knowing,' Marcus went on. 'It was while we were serving in Germania, when little Aurelia and her mother were alive.'

His voice faded a moment, then continued in a flat, rapid monotone. 'A new tribune had joined our legion, a man fresh from Rome who had never seen a real battle. He was sent out from the fort into enemy territory on a foraging party – I told him he was taking too few scouts, too few men, too many raw recruits, but the fellow simply quoted texts back at me, some rubbish about the excellence of the Roman legionary against the barbarian. He dismissed my advice and set out with a pitifully small escort.'

'He ignored you?' Hadrian seemed torn between astonishment and anger, and Marcus said quickly, 'Not so hard on the reins, the mule is doing as well as he can.'

'But this man ignored you? What happened?'

'His unit was attacked, of course: it was too tempting for the tribes to ignore. I heard the news, summoned experienced infantry men plus a cavalry unit of auxiliaries, all locals, and we marched and rode out into the forest to stop a massacre. Otho was with me, riding at my side. We rescued the fool commander, though not before several of his own men had been killed.'

Flavia watched his strong profile and yearned to comfort him. Was it in that ambush that he had been scarred? she wondered, staring at the small ragged war-wound close to his lower lip. My poor love, she thought as a shudder ran through her that had nothing to do with the uneven cobbles of the road.

'Otho was knocked off his horse by a sling shot – when I got him over my own horse, I thought he was sure to be dead; his face was a mass of blood. But he has a thick head.'

Marcus gave a harsh laugh and called to the trotting mule to hurry.

'What did the man say when you rescued him?' Hadrian asked eagerly, while Flavia felt her stomach plummet for the second time.

'I do not remember. He probably quoted something. He was your typical—'

Marcus broke off, leaving Flavia to supply the fatal term *desk-man* in her own mind. The cart ran into a hollow and lurched suddenly, flinging her off-balance so that her chin struck the top of the cart side. Refusing to rub her sore face, she stared out over the lush green downs, thinking about desk-men. When they had first met, Marcus had been scornful of her being a scribe. Now she understood why.

Lost in her gloomy thoughts, Flavia took little notice of the rest of the journey until Marcus turned the cart off the road and guided the mule down a seemingly endless track criss-crossed with tiny streams and bordered with clumps of alders. The alder was once sacred to her people, she recalled, though she could not remember why. Many forests that had once been holy were now only hunting places, frequented by men carrying nets and spears or by small groups of charcoal-burners, their limbs and clothes and faces blackened by their trade. There were several charcoal-burners working on the edge of the wood to which Marcus finally brought them, a small, dense grove of tall limes and oaks and hazel trees bursting with ripe nuts.

He spoke with the charcoal-burners for several moments, asking directions. Beside him Hadrian stared open-mouthed at the black-faced men, with their camp of rough tents built around a smouldering, soil-covered 'stack' of new charcoal.

Finally, Marcus turned to Flavia and the others.

'We need to go on foot from here. We can leave the cart here and walk down there–' He pointed past a holly tree to a narrow trackway of sunken logs, weaving through the trees. 'There is a clearing ahead, where we can stop and do our gathering. And other things,' he added mysteriously.

He swung a war-whooping Hadrian down onto the forest floor and then helped Livia and Agrippina from the back of the cart. Still shy and tense with him, not sure now what he thought of her, Flavia jumped down immediately after Marcus had taken the cook in his arms, thankful that her long slim legs did not give way under her.

'Still making your point about independence?' Marcus quietly remarked, handing Livia and Pina their baskets. Reaching past Flavia into the cart, he burrowed under the

231

cushions and brought out sticks and two cloth-wrapped bundles. Both clinked with the unmistakable sound of pottery.

'Food, in case we do not find enough in the wood,' he said. For the first time in what seemed an age to Flavia, he looked her up and down, but without smiling, so that she was uncertain if his apparent softening towards her was just her own wishful thinking. He flicked one end of her thick shawl with approval, then glowered at her light sandals.

'Watch where you put your feet in here.' Turning away, he tossed aside another cushion and brought out four javelins, their iron tips wrapped in sacking, from the bottom of the cart.

'Here.' Laconic even for him, Marcus stripped off the sacking and planted one, point first, at her feet. He took up the two clinking bundles and marched off to give an ecstatic Hadrian the shortest javelin, keeping two for himself.

'I thought we were looking for mushrooms,' Flavia called after him, but it was Gaius who smiled at her, fingering his long, wispy moustache.

They moved off into the woodland along the sunken log track way, Marcus and Hadrian leading, with Hadrian running ahead and off the path to scramble under the low-branched hazel and elders. As the trees closed round them and the sounds and smoke of the charcoal-burners' camp re-ceded, Hadrian picked a fallen crab apple out of a tumble of acorns and took a huge bite out of the peach-colored apple.

'Yuck! Sour!' he exclaimed, tossing the apple away. Undeterred, he launched him-self at a heap of fallen leaves, kicking through them with obvious glee and, to Flavia's relief, seemingly no pain in his wounded leg.

'Don't wander ahead too far!' she and Marcus called out together, but Marcus did not look at her then, or acknowledge the moment in any way. Instead, striding easily along the mossy track, he was asking Livia – Livia, not her – the name of the brightly-colored bird roosting on a bare elm tree.

'It's a jay,' Flavia murmured, telling herself that Marcus had asked Livia because the tall, slender Livia and squat, weather-beaten Sulinus were walking beside him.

Falling behind, Flavia gave herself a talk-ing-to. She had no right to inflict her anxiety or unhappiness on anyone else. It was a glorious sunny day and the woods she missed so much in the city and had always wanted to spend time in were as vivid as a fresh wall painting. Bright in their autumn splendour, light sparkled on the gold leaves of the birch and on the bronze of the oak canopy, while here and there a rich green and flash of ruby revealed another holly or yew, both with berries. Outside the wood, this section of forest had seemed small, but weaving along the track way deeper and deeper into the close-grouped trees, she felt as if the woodland had expanded to shelter and embrace them all. The air was still and warm and everywhere she sensed life. In the flutter of birds' wings through the wild roses, in the vanishing flick of a bushy red tail as a squirrel scrambled along the branch of a pine tree, in the wholesome scent of leaf-mould and crushed acorns.

'Come on, Flavia!' Hadrian yelled at her, a small, straddle-legged figure standing hands on hips further along the track way. 'I can see the clearing! There are blackberries and other berries... Marcus says juniper and mushrooms! Lots of mushrooms, white and yellow ones!'

He whirled round and ran off again, a little more slowly than before and with a slight limp.

'Don't worry.' As Marcus also broke into a run to race Hadrian into the clearing, Gaius walked back towards Flavia so that he could speak to her. 'Marcus will carry the boy on his back soon enough.'

'I am sure he will,' Flavia said. 'Are you enjoying this outing?' she asked.

'Are you?' the old slave responded. 'Marcus was most concerned that you and the boy be content.'

Had Gaius been indulging more than

usual in his favourite warm mead? Flavia wondered. His delicate features were unusually red and he looked altogether pleased with himself. That was the second time he had called Marcus by name.

'You cannot work it out?' Gaius looked round, waving at his wife who ignored him. As Flavia and Gaius watched, Agrippina stepped off the track into the brightness of the clearing where Marcus and Hadrian had already gone.

'You know, Pina says it's supposed to be a secret, but I don't see why,' old Gaius continued. He was standing beside Flavia by this time, breathing a heady mixture of mead and wine over her. He must have been drinking from earlier, but why? And why had Marcus made no comment?

'You are going to know soon enough, anyway.' Gaius beamed at her, as if the sight of her carrying a javelin and no gathering basket gave him immense pleasure. 'The boy, too. He is free as well. Marcus is to adopt him.'

Flavia found herself gripping the shaft of the javelin so hard that it hurt her burnt hand. 'What do you mean? What are you saying?' she whispered.

'We are free! Marcus has freed us this morning! Livia and Sulinus, Agrippina and myself! What is more, he approves of our business venture: he is going to use some of his own money to help us do more!'

'What?' Flavia felt as if one of the oak trees had just toppled on top of her. Gaius and the others free... Hadrian adopted ... business ventures...

Red-faced with excitement, Gaius was gabbling.

'Marcus approves of what we are doing! He says we can carry on living in the villa as his tenants and *paid* servants and Sulinus can carry on growing the lavender and herbs we need in the gardens and Pina can still use the kitchen things...'

Gaius, clearly befuddled with a mixture of wine and liberty, was swaying gently on the track in front of her. He and the others were in business, free and with plans for their futures.

'I – I congratulate you,' Flavia stammered. It was, after all, what she had hoped for and now that they were free, Gaius and the others would be forever safe from any consequences of her own deadly secret, from her own crime of forgery.

'I am pleased for you.' Flavia knew her voice sounded flat, but better that than the rising hysteria she could feel beating in her throat. Her eyes were swimming now with tears of rage as shock was replaced with indignation.

Marcus. Master Marcus. *Her master.* He had freed everyone but herself!

Chapter 12

After her shock and anger came dis-illusionment. Whatever interest Marcus had shown her meant nothing in the end. She was nothing to him: a slave to be fed and watered like a hunting dog, well-treated to ensure loyalty. Less than a hunting dog. One of the despised desk-men.

Scarcely aware of doing so, Flavia began to walk back along the track, her fingers tense around the javelin. She had no place here, among people who were free. She was a tool like a stylus.

'Where are you going?' Gaius called after her. A stooping, wrinkled, homely man, slightly tipsy because he was celebrating, he stood on the track with his gathering basket at his feet, no doubt staring after her.

'Need to take a break – amongst the trees!' Flavia panted. 'I will not be long!'

She flipped her fingers at him over her shoulder without looking at him, so that Gaius would not see her white lips and star-ing eyes. 'Go back to the others!' she called.

Had Gaius, whom she had once thought of as being like a father, even pleaded with Marcus for her freedom? Had his wife? Or were they, and Livia and Sulinus, content with how things were? Why not? They were free, and approved. Even before today, she had already fallen out of favour with Marcus – if favour it had been. Perhaps his seeming concern had only ever been for the novelty of owning a female scribe.

She would tell the charcoal-burners when she reached them that she was going to walk back to the city along the Roman road. They would be able to inform Marcus that the slave-scribe was returning to her proper place: the study of the town villa. No doubt there was correspondence to answer, letters to put in order even after the recent fire. Her longing for freedom, her plans to save whatever little money she was given in order to buy her freedom, had turned to nothing.

Behind her she sensed no alarm, heard no more shouts. No one was going to miss her. She walked faster, closer to the edge of the track, her shawl catching against the thorny stems of a wild rose bush. She ripped the shawl free and hurried on.

There were soft grasses and ferns beside the track now, a good place for her to make her escape into the trees, although why she was troubling to maintain that particular piece of fiction for an uninterested Gaius was something she did not want to consider. Taking a deep breath, Flavia stepped off the track and plunged into the undergrowth.

Weaving among the hazel and bramble and the blazing scarlet splashes of the guelder rose bushes, she moved rapidly away from the track. She would return to it later, when she could be sure that she would not break down when she spoke to the charcoal-burners.

Flavia began to run. Wherever possible she sprinted between the trees, skidding down grassy banks, leaping over fallen logs, her legs shearing wildly beneath her, cutting away the distance between herself and the city. Her shawl floated out behind her, catching again on a low oak branch and she angrily shrugged it off and left it hanging, only to return to it moments later.

'This is not mine. Nothing belongs to me,' she muttered, plucking the shawl from the branch and tying it round her middle. The air was so warm and she felt so stuffy, that it didn't matter how she wore the thing. Nothing mattered.

Dimly and already it seemed from a great distance, she heard new shouts, one voice louder and more urgent than the rest. Marcus himself, she thought grimly, choosing a new direction, away from his bellowing voice. She splashed across a small stream, thinking savagely that her master would not be pleased because she had soiled her sandals. His sandals. These were his limbs that she was driving forward, running as she had not done for years, since she was a little girl.

Her lungs were burning more than her hands and she had a stitch in her side that jabbed like a hot needle. Defying her body, Flavia climbed out of the stream basin through a tangle of ancient and decaying birches, red-capped mushrooms and dead grass, to the top of a jutting limestone escarpment, where only a few wind-twisted juniper bushes had taken root. Scrambling on her hands and knees, she moved off the summit and down the other side. Forcing herself to her feet again, she stumbled along a narrow track, a badger or deer run, between spreading oaks and massive hollies.

Deeper and lower still she went into the forest – for it seemed a forest now, rather than a wood: much larger and more silent than before. As she stopped and leaned over, rubbing the stitch in her side, the idea drifted into Flavia's hurting mind that perhaps she was lost.

She thrust the thought aside, or rather the idea was lost under a renewed tumult of emotion. 'Why must it hurt so much?' she burst out. She felt betrayed and even resentful, knowing that she was shackled to Marcus by more than the chains of slavery. He had been kind to her, he had seemed to care for her, and he had made her love him. He had changed her life forever. Even here, in this forest, surrounded by bare branches and bushes draped with the long straggling seed heads of wild clematis, where the faint trickle of running water somewhere further along this track was deadened by the moss-covered trunks of trees, where her side hurt and her burned hands ached and her right foot was torn by an unseen bramble, Marcus was with her, inside her head. Always present in her thoughts. She could picture him so easily: the shining, straight dark brown hair, forbidding black brows, watchful eyes that missed nothing. That small ragged scar by his lower lip. His tanned, muscular arms. His shoulder blade, burned in the shape of a crescent moon, the skin puckering by the wound and yet so smooth and hard everywhere else. So tempting to touch.

'But not by me,' Flavia said. 'He does not want that,' and she began to cry.

She wept into her burnt hands, torn between hurt at still being a slave and longing to remain with Marcus, even if that meant being owned by him.

Ashamed of this dark wish, Flavia was also aware that she should be seeking another path, another way back to the track before the swift winter sunset came. Listening through her own sobbing, she thought the silence of the forest mocked her. She regretted her angry impulse in storming off the track and was sorry for not shouting back when Marcus had roared out her name. Yes, she was merely his slave, but he had shouted for her. Had he been angry then, or anxious, or both?

'I don't want him to be angry with me anymore,' she told a blackbird who sang out an alarm call at her through the undergrowth. She tried to smile at the childish thought, wiping a weary arm across her streaming eyes.

She was lost. It was time she admitted it. She must find the stream she could hear gurgling in this treescape of trunks and branches and fallen leaves, and follow its course. That would guide her back.

Flavia set off again along the grassy animal run. The turf became wetter and she could hear the running water more distinctly. She walked past an elder bush – the elder was lucky, a healing tree: how she knew that, she did not remember, but the sight of the small bushy tree with its hanging jewel-like sprays of fruit would have given a tiny lift to her spirits, had she not been so unhappy.

Some of the elder branches had broken, sheared off by the passage of a heavy body. Pausing on the animal track, Flavia spotted the standing stump of a lightning-blasted black poplar, its remaining bark scraped and scored heavily down one side, close to the path. A creature had used the stump as a scratching post.

What creature? Flavia thought, as she glanced about the still, silent forest. Through the trees she could see the glisten of the stream now and more: closer to herself, a muddy, water-filled hollow between two slender young oak trees, one growing leaning over the rich ooze of dark mud. An animal had come here to wallow, browsed on some of the fallen scatter of acorns, then clambered out up that shallow bank where the grass was flattened and muddied.

She knew of only one forest beast that wallowed in mud, ate acorns and used trees as scratching posts. She did not need to go closer into its den or see its cloven tracks in the mud. Marcus' friend from Germania was wrong: this woodland did have wild boar in it, one at least, and she was in its territory.

Wild pigs do not eat people, she told herself, but she was not sure. Lady Valeria had never ventured into the forest and Marcus had never taken her with him on his hunts. The habits of a boar were unknown to her. She had never seen one alive, only eviscerated and hanging from the butchers' shops in the city, the powerful heads and tusks malevolent even in death. They were dangerous, she knew.

'Let it not be a mother with piglets,' she whispered. Scraps of older knowledge, gleaned from her fellow Celts, were rising into the front of her mind. Of all wild things, a nursing mother with young was the most dangerous. She had no wish to hurt anything and in any encounter her wish would be granted – armed with her light javelin and with no hunting experience, she was no match for a five foot long boar.

Never be too proud or too overconfident to withdraw. Marcus' voice in her head, impressing one of his battle lessons on Hadrian and herself, especially the boy. *If you can walk away from a battle, do so.*

In any retreat, try to be calm. Try not to turn your back on the enemy at once: withdraw a step at a time, shielding yourself and your companions.

'Good advice, sir,' Flavia said, amused even in her dread at addressing someone who was not there. She did not want him here in this section of forest. She did not want him or the others in danger.

Marcus might have denied her freedom, but talking to Marcus in her head had calmed her. She could move her feet again.

Walk backwards steadily, she told herself, and did so, listening and watching for any sign of the wild boar. There were no blackbird calls of alarm, no new shadows, and no rushes of movement. She must look foolish, glancing about, walking backwards, but that did not matter.

You need to get off the path, it is a path made by the boar, she warned, but leaving the clear animal track was hard. It would be slower going in the forest.

At least she could no longer see the patch of muddy water where the boar had its wallowing place. Taking a deep grateful breath, Flavia gagged at her own rank scent.

'Please, Lord Jesus, let the wind blow this away from the boar,' she prayed aloud, striding sideways up the steep slope she had slid down. Here, where the land rose sharply was a good place to leave the boar-path.

Quickly, before she froze, Flavia ducked off the grassy path and made for a wild apple tree, snatching some of the sour fruits off a lower branch. If nothing else, they would quench her thirst later. Telling herself she must do it, she turned her back and attacked the tree-filled slope, climbing as rapidly as she could. Slowing as the ground levelled off, she began to walk towards the sun.

How long she wandered in the woods Flavia did not know, but at some point, spotting two huge holly trees topping several young birch and oaks, she realized that these were the same hollies she had walked past earlier that day. She had walked for hours, but only in a circle.

Dazed and horrified, Flavia sat down heavily on a heap of leaves, shivering. Untying her shawl, she drew it back across her shoulders. It was growing colder. Squinting up through the tree canopy she saw glimpses of a red sky: already sunset and soon it would be dark. She longed to curse her own stupidity, but felt too weary and sick at heart to bother. Where was she? Where was Marcus? Was he safe? Had he already left the forest? What about the others?

She did not want to spend the night in the forest, but it looked as if she might have no choice. Plucking wizened blackberries from a bramble bush, Flavia ate the fruit and broke her fast for the first time in hours, trying to fight down an inner panic. She had her javelin. She had no fire-flints, but if she could find a suitable stone she could strike sparks off the iron tip of the javelin. She would be able to make a fire. She would drink at the next hollow tree – the trunks of such trees usually had water. She would survive the night.

'You are not alone,' she said aloud. 'God is–'

Flavia could not go on. It was Marcus she thought of, but he had clearly tired of her; he had not even stayed to look for her.

She wanted to sink her head in her arms and weep, but a stubborn pride stopped her. She was a Celt. Her people belonged in this land and she wouldn't be beaten down. Marcus had not freed her, but she would give him no cause to despise her.

Get up! she told herself.

Clinging onto the pale, shredding trunk of

a mature silver birch, she rose to her feet – and then she saw it.

A long javelin cast ahead of her and some way off its own track was a browsing boar. Its snout was buried deep in the soft earth as it rooted for food. It looked sleek and powerful, its long body steaming and glossy in the dim, leaf-patterned light of the woods, and at the same time curiously disarming, with its constantly pricked-up ears and dainty trotters.

Scampering round those incongruously tiny feet were several squeaking piglets, each no bigger than Nero and all tumbling like puppies, pretty with their brown and cream striped fur. They were also turning over leaves but making a game of it, jostling and chasing each other. If she could have watched them in safety, Flavia would have considered them adorable.

'Ahh,' she whispered, somewhere between admiration, awe and alarm. Do not be angry with me, mother, she thought. I wish your babies no harm.

Cautiously, sliding her feet, she took the first of many slow, backward steps, stiffening as she caught a new movement from the corner of her eye.

At the other side of the boar, at a distance greater than the height of two men, a tall shadow stepped out from behind a tree. It was Marcus, and he had seen her, but she did not know if he had seen the boar – there was a dip in the forest floor between them, where the beast was foraging, and he might not have realized that the mother was there.

'Go back!' she yelled, stamping her feet at the boar and brandishing the javelin.

As Flavia had known she would, the mother reacted at once, charging at her with ear-splitting squeals of rage. She could hear Marcus shouting as she threw the javelin wildly – not at the mother or her babies but anywhere – and then tried to climb the birch.

She could not do it. Dropping onto her knees, winded, her hands in agony, she saw Marcus draw back his arm in what seemed to be slow-motion. Even the charging boar seemed to be slowing.

'Don't hurt her!' she shouted, and screamed as he released the javelin. It landed at the base of a tree ahead of the oncoming boar, its length juddering like a plucked harp-string.

Confused, the boar skidded off and returned to her piglets, head down and shoulders hunched as she watched the man and woman through small, maddened eyes. Not daring even to breathe, Flavia remained perfectly still.

A tree's length across from her, as red-eyed as the boar, Marcus did the same.

'Touch her, pig, and you are meat,' he growled.

The setting sun flashed on the long steel blade of his hunting knife. He looked ready to advance, and Flavia sent up a desperate prayer that he would not move.

The moment seemed to go on forever while the beast faced them down. Finally, its tail whisking furiously, the snorting boar turned away from both of them and trotted further into the forest, her piglets streaking after her.

Flavia looked up at Marcus. Although there were several trees still separating them, he was approaching rapidly and she understood one thing already. He had risked himself for her and he had saved her, as she had saved him.

Renewed hope that perhaps he did care for her blazed in Flavia, but what she said was, 'I didn't want you to hit her. The boar, I mean. She has young.'

'I gathered that.' He sounded drained, but there was a kink of humour there, and also that well-remembered kindness. 'I aimed to miss.'

Her eyes did not seem to be focusing properly. She thought Marcus had split into two for a moment, both of them as sweaty and dishevelled as she felt. 'I could not let you blunder into her,' she said, keen to explain.

'I understood that, too, little Celt.'

'I thought you might be killed—' Beneath

her, Flavia felt as if the earth was rolling. She could feel herself starting to slide away, although she was not standing, she was still on her knees. She wet her dry lips with her tongue, determined to add one last thing before the rolling darkness took her.

'I could not bear to see you hurt.'

The ground rose up to claim her and for the second time in as many days she blacked out.

Marcus caught her before she fell face-down amongst the tree roots and grass. 'Flavia!'

His heart thumping painfully, he turned her in his arms, dismayed at what he might find. 'Flavia!'

There was no blood on her anywhere, no mark or wound on her except for her hands. The boar had not touched her – and how like the girl to be concerned for the beast.

It had been one of the hardest things he had ever done, to cast the javelin beyond the boar, to startle and confuse it and drive it away. The risk of merely wounding such a creature, of it goring Flavia, trampling her in its pain, made his stomach turn over.

'Flavia.'

Her lips moved and her head rolled into the crook of his shoulder. She was still unconscious, but as he gathered her closer she gave a little sigh and turned towards him, as if in a true sleep. Her hand rested and then pressed closer against his waist, snuggling against him like a small animal, and her fingers relaxed and opened.

Four small apples rolled out of her burned hand to lie against his belt. His clever, stubborn, brave little Celt had been collecting food.

'Flavia.' He could not stop saying her name over and over, to convince himself that he had found her, that she was safe. When he considered the alternative, the last few desperate hours that he had spent searching for her, terrified that she might be injured or worse, he was horrified.

Squealing and snorting, the boar burst back into his memory. He could not stop thinking about the way Flavia had stood against it, shouted to it, and drawn it on. Her courage appalled him. Again and again, he saw the boar charge. If it had not been turned by his javelin, if it had kept going–

Marcus discovered that even in a crouch, his legs would no longer hold him up. He sank into an untidy seated sprawl on the woodland floor, his back against the birch tree, Flavia in his arms on his lap. He turned his head away so that his tears would not fall on her, but he could not stop the tremors shuddering through his body.

He had thought himself strong enough, tough enough, but seeing her match herself against the boar while being helpless to stop her, and these last few hours when he thought he had lost her, had stretched him to the limit of his endurance. Today had been the longest, vilest day of his life.

The not knowing – where Flavia was, and then whether she would even survive the boar – had almost been worse than watching his wife and little Aurelia on their final sickbeds, when he had prayed to every god and spirit that he knew of to save them. Here in these woods, in this bewildering maze of trees and half-paths and bushes that closed you in and muffled your ragged shouts and pleadings into less than the squeak of a mouse – here was real terror. He had searched wildly, run until he had thrown up and then run some more. His guts dry-heaved now and his throat was hoarse with yelling, but he had found her. His Flavia.

Poor, battered little Flavia. Poor chick. He wanted to hug her tighter, but dreaded hurting her. She was breathing steadily now, all strain smoothed from her face. She was beautiful to him awake, alive and ardent, graceful in all that she did, but it gave Marcus a sharp, sweet pleasure, a poignancy mingled with fear, to see her asleep. As she was now, she was hidden to him, a mystery. But still so pretty.

Provoking and tempting awake. Innocent and secret asleep.

He wished he knew what their current quarrel was about: she had been guarded with him for days, since before the departure of Pompey and Julia Sura. And she had certainly rebuffed his help with clothing herself. Yet only a few weeks earlier, when they had been together in the study, she had seemed to revel in his embrace. Had her responses then been merely the effect of the wine? Or had she since changed towards him?

Marcus scowled and tried to relax his grip on the small, supple body in his arms. He respected her too much to kiss her when she did not know it and it was never his style to force himself on any woman, especially one in his care. He saw too much of that with men like Lucius Maximus.

Yet, he was sure Flavia still liked him. She wore the bracelets he had given her: she seemed pleased with those. He remembered her arguing fearlessly with him at the sculptor's, remembered teasing her in the great bath. She had smiled at him, then. Was it his imagination, or did her smile come less readily now? Had he done something to offend her? Had he gone against a local custom in some way?

But at this moment, these things did not matter. Flavia was alive and unharmed, and that was everything. She was already beginning to stir and that in itself was another cause for celebration: that she was not stunned or hurt in any unseen way. For the moment, though, while she was so still and quiet in his arms, her eyelashes flickering slightly as she woke, he could not help staring.

Feeling a mixture of guilt and delight, as if he was a small boy stealing away a plate of sweets, Marcus indulged himself in looking at her. How had he ever thought her skinny? She was as lithe as a water goddess. The golden apples she had laid by his belt were not as glossy or as delicate as her hair. It pooled by his elbow, an astonishing golden tangle, still secured in its single plait but already escaping in tiny curls around her ears and forehead. Her lashes and narrow eyebrows were slightly darker, giving definition to her slender face and sharp little chin.

Her forehead was dusted with tree bark, her cheekbones tinged with the same pale rose as her mouth – but then today, her mouth was unusually pale. She had a long scratch running in a diagonal gash down her left cheek and the side of her neck. The briar that had scratched her had left a thorn in her throat. Gently, so as not to alarm her, Marcus brushed it away.

Gray and changeable as the northern sea but far kinder, her large eyes opened wide.

'Thank you for my bracelets and the flowers,' she said drowsily, lifting her arm with the bracelets and looking straight at

254

him, coming more and more awake. To Marcus it was like being caught in a dazzling spot of sunlight through clouds. It was an instant before he recollected what she had just said.

'What?' He had not expected that.

She bit her lower lip; a habit of hers when nervous. 'I wanted to tell you before you ask me–' She broke off and swallowed, but continued to look into his eyes. 'Ask me why I left.'

So that was it, he thought. She was expecting a reckoning. Did she fear him so much, know him so little? He cursed himself for a fool – he had done this so badly. 'Flavia, I am not here to scold you. I–'

'Are the others safe?'

That question and the interruption was more like her, he thought, nodding. 'They are fine.'

'Hadrian?'

'The boy is doing well; no bad memories of the fire and his leg is healing. Tomorrow he will be limping less.'

'Good. That is good.'

He could feel her relax, and a shock of pleasure tingled his nerves as she rested her head against his chest, her warm breath close to his heart. That small, unconscious gesture of hers, her turning to him willingly, gave him renewed hope. Surely she still liked him?

I am nervous, he thought, amazed. I have fought men in battle with more ease than this. Her courage, her determination, her intelligence all made him feel wary, in case he did not measure up – an idea a man like Lucius Maximus would find absurd.

He was so aware, too, of the distracting touch of her, the feel of her, her skin, her scent. He wanted to touch her more, have her touch him.

First he wanted there to be no more misunderstandings between them, beginning with the events of this afternoon.

He had lost his cloak somewhere in his wild search in the forest and had to make do with tucking her shawl closer around her. Once his hand brushed her thigh and the contact glowed in her eyes.

'Are you warm enough?' he asked softly. He wanted her to be comfortable.

'Yes.'

'I have a flask of water. Would you like a drink?'

'Later, please.' Her clear eyes narrowed, as if she had suddenly remembered something, and she became very still. 'Later, sir.'

The sir was a warning that he had work to do in winning her trust. Marcus fought down a strong wish to box old Gaius' ears and told himself to be patient. Thinking of his own mother, he reminded himself that Flavia had been subject to other people's whims and wishes for all of her life. This would take time.

They had time tonight, for the sunset had already bled away in the western sky and twilight was turning the trees to columns of silver and steel. Moving in strange woodlands at night was folly and Flavia was already spent. They would rest here tonight: he would find them shelter. He would need to light a fire soon – boars and other creatures such as wolves were also active at night – but he would not say just yet that they would have to stay here. He wanted to explain something far more important.

'When you could not be found, I sent the others off home with the cart,' he began. 'Including freedman Gaius.'

He knew then, when her eyes never wavered, that the house steward had talked.

'Gaius told you that he is now a free man,' he said, with a calm he did not feel. The old busy-body had no right, no business to speak. He had forewarned Gaius, but not so the fellow could go blabbing.

'He said you had freed him,' Flavia said slowly. 'Him and the others. He was so excited.'

And drunk, thought Marcus harshly, remembering the steward tottering in the forest, even more bandy-legged than usual.

'And when he told you, you assumed that I would not free you also?' he asked quietly.

She tried to rear up, but he tightened his hold, lowering his head so that she would see his face clearly in the dim light, and continued quickly, 'I am not so unjust. Gaius spoke out of turn. As I told you when I met you, loyalty cuts both ways.'

Looking down into her rapidly paling face, Marcus almost confessed his secret thought that slavery was wrong, certainly life-time slavery, but then he knew that would mean explanations about his past, and his mother. Much as he trusted Flavia's sense of honor, and her kindness, dare he trust her with that particular knowledge?

More even than that, he feared that she would think him mad: everyone owned slaves, even freedmen. 'It was always my intention to free all of you,' he went on, hoping she would believe him, hoping she knew he was being sincere. 'Beginning with you, Flavia.'

She was silent, rigid in his arms. Desperate to convince her, Marcus raised his head, motioning with his eyes at the surrounding forest. 'I remembered how you said that you loved woodland. I was going to free you formally here, in a place you loved best. You and then the others.'

He had hoped to please her by that, make the moment of her liberation even more special by announcing it here, with her companions around her. He had wanted to prove that he cared for her, not as master for slave, but as a man for a woman. Instead, with a few ill-chosen words, Gaius had shattered his plans and driven a new wedge between Flavia and himself.

'Gaius knew this because he is my steward, and conscientious to a fault.' Feeling increasingly foolish and futile, blushing as he had not done since he was a boy, Marcus laboured on with his explanation. 'Until I explained, he was protesting about leaving the city; he did not want to go away from the villa so soon after the fire. I did impress upon him, however, that the change in your status was supposed to be a surprise. We must thank the drink for his loosened tongue,' he added grimly.

She was staring at him, her face very pale. 'But I thought...' Her voice faded.

'That is why you ran away, was it not? You thought I was not going to free you. That you were still my property and slave.'

Even to himself, Marcus sounded accusing. He could appreciate why she had thought what she had, why she had reacted as she did, and yet it still pained him. Brutally squashing the rising question *How could you believe that of me?*, he said gently, 'I am sorry. I should have told you earlier.' What did it matter where he freed her? The act was the important thing, not the setting.

'I am sorry,' he said again, pierced anew as

259

he felt her shiver. It was growing cold and the long winter night was drawing on. 'I need to find us a place of safety.'

He could do that, at least. It would be good to do something right.

Flavia raised her hand and touched his shoulder, sensing the slight recoil in the strong body shielding hers. It was altogether part of the miracle of the past hour that he was unsure of her, when for so many of these last few days she had thought him cold and angry.

She could not stand the thought of him so tense and unhappy. 'Marcus.' He was looking fixedly at the palm of her hand: quickly she hid the burn-wound there from him. 'Marcus. I am glad you have told me now.'

She was not sure in the semi-darkness, but when he raised his face to hers she thought he was blushing. She had heard him out with astonishment, then wonder, then joy. He had come looking for her, not as his property, but because he cared. She could see spikes in his hair, scratches on the arms enfolding her, and a large mud-stain over most of his body, blackening his tunic from his hip to his right ear where he had clearly stumbled into the dirt, scrambled up again and kept going, careless of his own appearance.

Surely he must love her, if only a little?

'I was so afraid I had lost you,' he said, almost a groan. He kissed her forehead, resting his chin briefly on top of her head, drawing her closer still.

Half-sitting, half-lying on him, her side against his chest and flank and belly, her bottom pressed into his lap, one foot resting against his braced left leg and her other leg resting against the length of his hard right leg, Flavia fought against a wave of contentment.

'We must move, Marcus. We must find more shelter.'

'We should.' He nuzzled her neck. 'You smell so good.'

Flavia struggled to sit up straighter. 'Marcus, don't tease! I am sweaty, my clothes are dirty, my shawl feels to be in tatters.'

She felt his deep rumble of laughter. 'Typical female, always fussing.' He stroked a hand down her arm. 'You look wonderfully messy, like a half-fledged eagle.'

'What!'

She could see his open grin at her indignation. 'Steady there!' He playfully touched her nose with a thumb. 'Don't let freedom go to your head.'

Flavia's eyes filled up at his words. It seemed so real, and yet at the same moment, so madly improbable. The thing she had yearned for was now hers. 'Am I really?' she whispered. 'Truly free? Is there not a ceremony to perform, words for you and me to say?'

'You are right.' Marcus rose to his feet with her still in his arms. He kissed her on the mouth, a swift, sweet kiss. 'The legal niceties will have to wait until we are back in Aquae Sulis, but here is what I want to say to you.

'I, Marcus Brucetus, now free you, Flavia, to be whatever you wish. In the hope that you will remain as part of my household as my scribe and bathing attendant, in return for a generous salary.'

He smiled at her, his eyes very blue, the ragged scar close to his chin scarcely showing below his full lower lip.

'What do I say?' Flavia murmured, overwhelmed by his tenderness, by the realisation of a dream.

'Whatever you want to say. Whatever you feel is appropriate.'

She was free! Free, and he still wanted her to stay with him. It was more than she had dared hope for – in a moment, Flavia knew she would start crying.

Trying to prevent herself melting away into salt water when they were still far from home and in possible danger, she crooked a finger and beckoned him to lower his head again. As he did so, she caught both arms around his neck, boosted herself in his embrace and hissed against his grubby ear, 'I agree to everything, Marcus Brucetus, and now you must let me down, because there is shelter to find and in my experience, no man knows how to put together a good fire.'

'Provoking little wench!' Marcus grumbled, but he lowered her to her feet.

Chapter 13

The blue-black of twilight had given way to complete darkness. Side by side, she and Marcus walked through the forest, moving and breathing almost as one, testing each step they took. Stopping frequently to listen for predators, they steered clear of places where there might be animal trails or water courses. Marcus explained that even a dry stream bed could be a danger if there was a sudden flood, and that deep valleys were also to be avoided, because of the tendency of overnight frost to settle in low areas.

'Did you learn these things in Germania?' Flavia asked him, as he paused again to listen and she to gather up more wood for their eventual fire.

'There and here in Britannia, especially on the long northern wall. The local soldiers taught me a lot in both places.'

And Marcus had been willing to learn, the lesson, Flavia acknowledged, guessing that other Roman tribunes would be very different.

They made a night-camp in the lee of a small hill, out of the direction of the prevailing wind, in the prickly shelter of another huge holly tree. The holly's branches grew in an almost perfect circle around its central trunk, shutting out the rest of the woodland except for a small gap bordered by a jutting piece of rock and an ancient level, smooth boulder that lay close to the tree.

Following Marcus into the living heart of the holly, Flavia found a natural space large enough for even Marcus to stand up in, and the ground beneath bone-dry, with no animal dung or tracks. The gap in the tree made by the rock gave them a place for a fire and the small low boulder a perfect hearthstone.

While Marcus checked the holly overhead to ensure that no dead branches came crashing down on them overnight, Flavia laid out the twigs and kindling she had collected on their impromptu hearthstone, saying a prayer of thanks to the old Gods and to Christ as she worked to make a fire.

Nodding approval, Marcus stalked into the empty space of their holly tree-shelter. Dropping a wide flat stone onto the dry earth from one hand and a small, roughly-tied bundle from the other, he said, 'We will need to be warmer than this to last the night. I will hollow out a sleeping place for us first.'

Speaking, he unfastened the water-flask and a small leather pouch from his belt and untied the belt. Shrugging off his belt and tunic, he allowed both to drop to the ground.

Except for his sandals and a loin cloth, Marcus was now naked, but he took no notice of that. He began working again at once, digging with the wide flat stone into the loose soil, heaping the earth alongside.

Exasperated at herself for feeling shy of him even though he had simply stripped off for hard, manual labor, Flavia tried to match his matter-of-fact attitude, concentrating on coaxing the fire into a clear leaping mass of flames, then gathering heaps of dry leaves and grass in her shawl from the ground close to their camp. Only an arm-stretch away from her, while she removed spiders and the odd damp leaf from their bedding, Marcus continued to dig.

Soon he had cleared a large rectangle of soil near to the trunk of the holly and beside their fire to a depth greater than the length of one of Flavia's feet. When she knelt beside the growing hole to push away more earth, she was smartly rebuffed.

'Not with those burned fingers,' Marcus told her, then, when she daringly thrust her tongue out at him, 'I saw that. You can help pack in the dry grass and leaves in a moment. May I have some water, please?'

She had little choice but to look at him

fully. Quickly, she recovered the water flask and held it out to him. He thanked her and gulped down several large mouthfuls, throwing back his head.

'Oh!' The soft exclamation escaped before she could stop it. The surrounding darkness seemed to flow off him like water. She could see the reined-in energy of him, see it almost shimmer as he moved. In spite of it being a winter's night, a faint sheen of sweat covered him like a second skin and, for a dreadful moment, she wished that she was still his slave. To help undress him utterly, even the final barrier of the loin cloth ... what would that be like? What would it be like to run her hands down those long runner's legs? That flat, hard stomach? His neck and arm tendons looked as rugged as tree roots and the sight of the long sweep of his shoulders and flanks, ending with that small potent hollow in the small of his back, seemed to send tingles down her spine.

'Flavia?' Marcus shook the water flask in front of her eyes. 'Would you like some?'

'Thank you.' She took the flask and wet her parched mouth, forcing herself to turn away and pretend interest in the fire.

He slipped past her a moment later, murmuring, 'I will just clean myself off. I noticed a hollow tree with water in one of the branch stumps just a little way back; I can find my way easily, even now. If you wish,' – he gave her a piercing glance – 'you can make us somewhere to sleep.' He nodded at the brightly burning fire. 'You can leave that now. You are free to make us a bed.'

Free. She was truly free. Hugging that miraculous knowledge to herself as Marcus' swift footsteps were submerged under the competing long, mournful cries of two different wild cats, Flavia dragged the dry leaves and grass into the hollowed-out space. When she had finished, she was surprised at how snug it was, with the earth walls around them and the heat from the fire reflected back from the jutting boulder.

But where should she place her shawl and Marcus' tunic? Side by side or apart? Walking up and down in the narrow space between their 'bed' and the fire, Flavia was torn between fear and desire. What should she do? What?

'Flavia?'

The soft question stilled her rising panic as she raised her head to look into her former master's face. His smile gleamed at her, bright in the remaining light from the sky. 'Orion the hunter is rising,' he said. 'Can you see his belt: the three bright stars? And how do you do down there? How are your hands?'

Flavia had forgotten her injured fingers, but she was relieved to break off her too-intimate stare with Marcus and glower at her thumbs instead. 'Well enough, I think,' she mumbled. Relieved to be moving away from that soft, springy bed space, she padded towards the fire and Marcus.

'Up you come.' Carefully avoiding her hands, he scooped her up, lifting her out of the hollow, setting her down beside him. 'Look at the pole star. How bright!'

Flavia nodded, wondering how it was that freedom had robbed her of speech. What should she say to him? How should she act?

'These northern stars have a special place in my heart,' he said.

Because of Drusilla, Flavia thought treacherously, blushing at her own envy.

'Listen, the cats are seeking each other. They are getting closer.'

'Not to fight?' Flavia asked, glad that her tongue was working again.

'No, little Celt, they have other matters in mind tonight.'

Was it possible for her blush to deepen? Feeling as if her face must be glowing like a winter sunset, Flavia cast around for something intelligent to say.

Marcus was looking at her; she could sense his gaze. 'You are enough,' he said cryptically. 'I wonder if you will purr like a cat, my little wild, free cat?'

'I may scratch instead,' Flavia countered, feeling at once peevish and flattered. He had acknowledged she was free – but did she want to be free of him?

She flinched as the two cats yowled again, their falling cry suddenly cutting short in the still night air.

'They have found each other,' Marcus said, and now he gently lifted her hands in one of his. 'You are sure your fingers are not painful? I have a salve I can make, one an old centurion taught me.'

'I am very well, thank you,' she answered, still shy of this beautiful, half-naked man, still partly astonished that she was alone with him.

'Then I shall prepare our evening meal – such as it is,' he replied, 'And no, you cannot help. For your first meal in freedom I shall serve you.'

He smiled and Flavia found herself too stunned to answer.

So Marcus untied the rough bundle he had carried with him all that day since leaving the villa and laid out the food he had brought with him on the cloth.

'I want you to sample the flavors of my country,' he explained, careful to not stare at her. He had earlier drawn the rough bedding and her shawl and his tunic together and suggested that she lie down. When he looked up from his setting out he found her sitting primly upright on the thin layer of dry vegetation and clothes, her back resting against the earth wall he had made. She was not scared any more; she did not tense each time he approached, but she was nervous.

'Walnuts, raisins, figs, pine nuts and cheese.' He pointed to each in turn. 'We have olives, too, and bread.'

She nodded, her golden hair silver in the fire-light. 'Thank you,' she said. 'There are the apples, too: food from my land that we can share.' She stopped as if she had said too much and changed the subject. 'How is your shoulder?'

'Healing,' Marcus responded, with a brusqueness he did not feel. It was mid-winter, but although he was half-naked he was far from cold. Instead, he was back to thinking of tedious military maneuvers, re-lieved that his loincloth disguised his current state. 'Are you hungry?' he asked, wishing she would answer something like, 'Yes – for you.'

'A little,' came back her discreet reply. Then she surprised him by adding, 'will you tell me more of your homeland? I like to hear you talk.'

Beneath the bright belt of Orion, with the holly and the fire protecting them from the wild wood, and the homely scents of smoke and cheese reminding them of the villa in Aquae Sulis, they began to eat.

'Antique bread.' Marcus smacked his lips. To him it tasted as good as one of Clodius' feasts. 'Would you like a piece?'

Flavia pulled a face and reached for their water-flask. 'This cheese is so salty!' she exclaimed.

'Not if you eat it with the raisins,' Marcus replied. 'That is what we do at home.'

'Home across the sea?' Flavia asked quietly.

Marcus cursed inwardly as he saw her slightly withdraw from him, the glow in her delicate face lessening as she tried not to frown. He had said the wrong thing, speaking of home, where he only wanted her to feel at ease, his equal. I have to be sure she wants me, he thought. He remembered his mother, what she had told him. He did not want to make the mistake his father had made.

'Do you miss your home, Marcus?'

'Sometimes,' he answered, then, afraid of how that might sound, he added hastily, 'Not very often these days.' Aware of the heat of the fire on his bare chest and a greater, aching heat in his loins, he was tempted to roll into his cloak and feign sleep. But that was cowardly, no way to win this proud, brave, free little Celt. He wondered if the spirits of his wife and daughter could see him. His wife would approve, he knew. Drusilla had told him many times that if ever he were widowed, he should find another woman, another wife.

'Here, try a raisin with the cheese,' he

271

coaxed, pinching up a few plump raisins and stretching his hand towards her. Slowly, her fingers reached for him in return: he was tempted to seized her hand, catch her tight and pull her towards him, but he must wait. This must be her choice.

'Mmm, yes, they do work together.' She plucked another raisin from his palm and nibbled it with the cheese, her face showing nothing but relaxation and simple enjoyment. Or so he assumed. Her next question startled him.

'How did you come by that scar beneath your ribs? I saw it by the firelight when you moved,' she went on. 'But I am sorry. If you do not wish to speak of it–'

'No, no. I had forgotten it, that was all.' Her bright, curious eyes on his body made him think of anything but war. Telling himself yet again that he must be patient, he began to explain.

'It happened when I rescued Otho from that skirmish I told you and Hadrian about. A skinny young painted warrior slashed at me with a long sword and I got a glancing blow down my rib. It didn't go through to the lung, thank the gods. It looks far worse than it was.'

She was listening closely, her hand poised in mid-air above the cloth and their food. Marcus touched her hovering fingers with his own hand, encouraged when she did not draw away. 'One thing I do remember was that I didn't hit back – of course, I was too busy hauling Otho over my horse. And besides, I have never been sure if it was a woman. I do not hold with killing women.'

'I know you do not.' Respect and – pray Mithras! – more than respect flared in her face.

'I am glad you know this, especially since at times – Too often! I know I have been brusque with you. You need not deny it, Flavia.' *Generous little water goddess,* he thought in his heart, hoping his intent, if not his silent words, would reach her. 'But it has been hard.'

'Yes.'

That brief admission on her part gave him great hope: surely she felt the same to him as he did to her? Even if she did not, now he had a chance to explain. 'Ever since that night in the study, when Hadrian burst in on us, it has been impossible. Other people are...'

'Always around,' she finished for him. 'I know.' She squeezed his fingers, her voice very soft. 'Lately, I was afraid that you were angry with me.'

'For what?' he asked, astonished, and now shock spurred a confession from his own mouth. 'I was afraid you were no longer interested in me!'

She looked at him a moment, then

273

lowered her head. At a distance, Marcus thought he heard a faint purring, but then told himself that was impossible: the wild cats would be far away by now. He listened to the crackling fire and the creak of the holly boughs above them. 'How is it that we have misunderstood each other?' he asked, astonished afresh.

'Fear, perhaps. Or too much feeling. A dread of losing what we have...'

He was amazed by her speech: it directly echoed his thoughts.

'A keenness mingled with shyness.' Her voice fell, cracking like the fire. She looked at him again, her gray eyes as wide and open as the night sky above them.

'In my land, here, we hold the apple sacred,' she suddenly burst out. 'We gift apples to our friends.'

They moved together, but Marcus' reach was longer: he lifted one of the small crab apples off the cloth before Flavia could touch it and leaned towards her, presenting the golden apple with a cluster of raisins and figs.

'Please accept this, then, as a sign of my friendship.'

She blushed but took it readily, devouring the bitter-sweet crab in a series of dainty bites. Marcus imagined her lips and teeth touching him and wished there was a way...

Flavia was pointing at his navel. 'You have dropped a pine nut.'

She leaned closer and deftly sucked the pine nut off his middle, her lips soft against his skin. Abruptly she sat back on her heels, her expression shifting from delight to horror.

'I am so sorry,' she whispered. 'I don't know what came over me. What must you think?'

He could say she was a delight, that she moved him in ways no other woman had ever done, but he wanted to comfort her at once. His eyes never leaving hers, he took a handful of raisins and dropped them over her, finally closing the gap between them as he lowered his head to tongue the fruits off her. Even through the yellow haze of her gown her skin was luscious, tasty.

With her eyes clamped tightly closed, Flavia felt his tongue slipping between the folds of her gown, darting across her stomach, stealing between her breasts. 'My delicious Flavia,' she heard him whisper, and now her eyes were stunned open as he lifted her, straight over the cloth scattered with fruits and bread, into his space.

'Marcus–' She clutched at him, wanting more of his love-play while at the same time being wary of it.

'All is well, little one.' He ran his palm over her lower ribs, his blue eyes smiling into hers as he glanced up into her face. 'My free girl.'

'Free Celt,' Flavia amended, blushing as she wondered why that distinction should be important.

'Bold little warrior.' He gobbled a raisin from a ruck in her gown, offering her a second with his mouth, gripping the dried fruit between his teeth. When she accepted it without thought, warmed by his open smile, he laughed and hugged her close.

'I would have us know more of each other, and all of each other,' he said, stroking her hair, 'but only if it please you, my free Celt.'

'Yes, Marcus. Yes.'

His handsome face was fire-bright, his blue eyes glittering yet gentle. 'Are you sure?'

Without regret, without another thought, Flavia answered, 'I love you.' It was enough, because it was everything.

With a low hiss of released breath Marcus gathered her closer, kissing her cheeks and eyes and lips. 'By Mithras, I am glad! So glad, little water goddess, to be under your spell.'

He lay down on their rough bedding with her draped across him, running his fingers through her hair, feeding her walnuts and raisins, asking if she wanted another drink of water. When she shook her head, he smiled.

'I have not told you much of my homeland after all, and this small feast of ours was to honor it,' he said. 'But no matter, we shall

276

have time enough, later.'

Later than what, Flavia wanted to ask, but he was caressing her again, unfastening the shoulder brooch of her gown, easing the loosened garment and her white under-tunic past her pert waist and trim hips, hanging both over a nearby branch while he kissed her.

'Am I learning right?' she asked, when his lips broke reluctantly from hers. 'You will say if I do something wrong?'

'Easy, there, Flavia!' He ruffled her hair, cunningly untying her plait at the same time. 'This is no writing test. I understand well that this is new to you, but there is no wrong. Believe me!'

She did, because she trusted him, and now, when he blew teasingly in her ear and called her a delightful desk-man, she felt too agreeable and content even to correct his 'man' to 'woman'.

'Your fingers, they do not pain you?' he whispered, lifting her hands from his chest and kissing them.

She shook her head, proving her silent assertion by beginning her own exploration of his body with her fingers, tentatively at first and then with an increasing excitement and sureness. She felt him tense and shiver under her hands, his breath coming quicker. Suddenly he groaned, tugging off his loin cloth and flinging it into the darkness beyond the fire, embracing her afresh.

'You are a true child of Venus,' he growled, rocking her to and fro on his long, muscular body, letting her feel his hard manhood. 'No man could resist your touch.' He wound a loose streamer of her hair about his thumb, grinning at her puzzled look. 'I know you do not understand me quite, but you will.'

Cupping both her wrists between the thumb and index finger of one hand, he brushed his other hand about her breasts and flanks, revealing and evoking a pleasure in Flavia that she had never known before. As she moaned softly, he kissed her.

'Pink and cream, like roses,' he mouthed against her ear, 'and a dark red heart.' His hand moved lower, parting the folds of her loin cloth, shimmering through her intimate golden curls, lower to the moist, silken place between her thighs no other man had touched. She whimpered, alive with new sensation, wanting more, wanting him.

'Marcus!'

Her strangled call of his name seemed to be a signal. He lowered himself onto her, easing them both slightly to the side so he did not smother her.

'Put your arms about me, little one,' he coaxed, smiling down into her eyes. 'All is well, believe me.'

'I do, Marcus. I–' Flavia forgot the rest of what she was saying, surrounded as she was by melting walls of gold: the flickering fire; the moving bronze of her lover; the feeling deep within herself of a pulsing, rising tide of sweetness. The wave caught her up, urging her to move her hips as Marcus smoothly eased himself within her, whispering her name as he did so.

They were together, united. Flavia knew a freezing moment of happiness, of a time utterly new, and then he began to move within her again. Her body lifted to his, enfolding and welcoming him, moving as he did.

Free Roman and free Celt, their need and desire equal, sharing their delight in each other, they melded joyously into one.

Chapter 14

Alight with happiness, Flavia woke in the dawn chill, instantly reassured that the events of the previous night had really happened when she found herself locked into the crook of Marcus' arm. She kissed his shoulder and, although he slept, his strong hands tightened briefly around her. Proud and content, she breathed in his scent and listened to the waking forest, watching the night shadows give way to the colors and contours of daylight. She felt at peace with everything.

Was this the holy marriage the traveling Christian teacher had told her about? The teacher had mentioned letters, a letter to the Corinthians, where marriage had been discussed. He had not told her much, because she had been a slave then and unlikely to marry. But the teacher had stressed that if they wished, men and women should love and marry.

There were different forms of marriage, Flavia knew. In the simplest kind, a man and woman lived together in mutual respect for a year and were then considered to be husband and wife.

Was that not what she and Marcus were doing?

She blushed, recalling her confession of love to him from last night. Marcus cared for her deeply: the way he treated her proved it. He had spoken, too, of weeks and months, suggesting a time spent between them, time they would be together.

But he has not said that he loves you, Lucius Maximus hissed in her mind. *If he cares so much, then why not?*

'Silence,' Flavia muttered, something she could order Lucius Maximus to do, now she was a free-woman. *Marcus freed me,* she told herself.

Did that mean she was no longer his?

She shivered and clung closer to her former master, taking this chance of his sleeping beside her to study him. Gold and shadowed in the burgeoning light, his face was youthful in sleep. How long and thick were his lashes, she considered admiringly. She delighted in how his dark hair curled at its tips across his forehead, like a wave clipped by the breeze. She longed to wind a curl about her fingers and plant a soft teasing kiss into his ear. Most of all, she wanted him to wake and smile at her.

Stirring as if in answer to her wish, Marcus yawned and stretched, kissed her on both cheeks and smacked his lips. 'How are you this morning, Flavia? I trust you're happy.'

'More than I ever thought it possible to be,' Flavia answered, her heart racing in response to his smile. 'And you, my--?' She stopped herself before she said 'master', suddenly aware again of her naked state, as if she had been rolled in the icy morning dew.

'You are getting cold. Let me warm you.' He pulled her onto himself, wrapping one leg about her, leaving her in no doubt as to his erect state. 'Or are you in a hurry to leave for some reason?'

'The others will be worried--' She broke off as Marcus' fingers drew up and down her back, tracing the letters of his name, then hers.

'They will still be asleep,' he drawled. 'As we can be again.' He kissed her mouth and began to draw the same letters across her breasts. 'Is this acceptable, I trust?'

Again that word trust. Already disconcerted by what Marcus was implying and what her body seemed only too eager to share, Flavia felt a new scalding blush of shame beginning close to her breast-bone. Trust. Marcus had unconsciously shown it last night, leaving his javelin and long hunting knife within her reach. She had trusted him not to hurt her in their joining. But how far could she trust him? Dare she trust him with her deadly secret? But what was care if there were secrets between them?

'Marcus, I need to ask you something.'

Coward, Flavia berated herself, but in the end she could not bring herself to speak of what she had done after Lady Valeria's death. *Let me have a little longer with him in peace,* she pleaded with her conscience. She was afraid of tarnishing what was between them.

This morning, with Marcus smiling at her with bemused tenderness, yawning and scratching the stubble close to his jaw, it was all new and incredible. She wanted to remain with him in this private world for just a few hours longer.

'Yes, my free-woman?' he prompted, flicking her bottom with a hand in a way that was half a caress, half playful pat.

'I have two questions.' Nervous of more distraction, Flavia stared at his chin, which was surely less erotic than his mouth.

'Only two? You looked thoughtful enough for a thousand.'

She longed to kiss that small ragged scar, Flavia thought, hastily scrambling her mind together and giving herself a stern warning not to be sentimental.

'When Gaius told you about their potions-making business,' she doggedly continued, 'Did he say when they had started it?'

'Not only when – just before Lady Valeria's death – but why: to buy themselves out of their slavery. They were going to petition me at the start of the mid-winter Saturnalia for their freedom. Yours, too, although Gaius was most insistent that you knew nothing of their scheme.'

Marcus frowned at the few remaining glowing logs of their fire. 'My steward seemed to think I would be angry at their enterprise; he kept repeating to me, "Flavia has nothing to do with it. She is not in-volved." I had quite a time convincing him that I was not angry and that he and the others were free without payment. You too, of course,' he added, his eyes flicking back to her, and lingering.

'Gaius. My freedom.' Flavia could hardly take it in. She remembered Gaius saying to her, 'We are not doing anything wrong. Just give us until the end of the month, then we will explain everything. I promise.' Here was the reason why: Gaius had been planning to ask for their freedom at the start of the Saturnalia. Why not? It was a time when, by tradition, slaves could do almost anything they liked, without fear of the consequences.

Her former fellow slaves had been concerned for her. Not only that, they had been as busy protecting her as she had ever been in defending them. 'I never suspected anything like that,' she murmured, humbled by their actions.

'I can help them to win a wider market for their potions,' Marcus went on. 'In the past, I have worked in trade – something Lucius Maximus would consider appalling, but then, as he pointed out, he has lands to spare. Lands and ambitions I do not share – especially not on a fine winter's morning, when I have a fiery little Celt in my bed.'

Fiery. The word stung Flavia. Fiery was the opposite of serene, and everyone who had known her said that Marcus' much-missed wife had been serene. Beautiful, auburn-haired, serene and a perfect spinner and brewer of cordials.

How can I ever match such a woman? she thought, her new free confidence crashing round her ears.

'Your second question?' Marcus kissed her ear. He must have realized the impact his caresses had on her because he held himself quite still, making Flavia ashamed of her own desire.

She wanted to ask, Can you love me as you loved Drusilla your wife? She wanted to know if she was normal, longing to make love when the day was dawning. Surely only toga girls did that and only because they had to?

She shivered and he said, 'You are still cold: why didn't you say?'

Carrying her as easily as a doll, he climbed casually off their bed, and whirled her about, plucking her white under-tunic off the branch and draping it round her neck between her breasts.

'I don't know where your loin-cloth's got to,' he observed, nuzzling her left breast and making the ache between her legs grow sharper. He slightly raised his arm that was cradling under her knees. 'Did you know you still have your sandals on?'

'So have you,' Flavia said, put out by Marcus' seemingly easy dismissal of his own arousal. Perhaps it was different for men, she thought, aggrieved.

'I can warm you, you know.' Marcus' breath was hot against her neck as he gathered her closer, tickling her. He laughed as she squirmed a little. 'As I mentioned earlier, we could warm each other in very … appealing ways.'

Now he was laughing at her, she thought, trying and failing to push herself away from the warm buttress of his chest.

'Are you going to put me down?' she demanded.

He stopped laughing. 'That's your second question, is it? Here is my answer.' He deposited her on the ground and stalked off, snatching up his own loin cloth.

'Marcus–' Flavia wanted to explain but he kept his back to her.

'We should move before the she-boar brings her piglets along the forest trails for their morning wallow,' he said, in a voice that brooked no argument.

'You are not being fair!' Flavia protested.

'And I am not made of stone, girl. One thing you should learn is not to tease.'

'I wasn't!' Hurt by his use of 'girl', Flavia stepped towards him. She could hardly believe how the morning had changed so quickly. 'You know I do not tease!'

Putting on his loin cloth and still without looking at her, Marcus began to stamp out the remains of the fire.

Somehow Flavia dressed, reordered her hair into some kind of plait and set out after Marcus, who, already clothed and carrying both javelins, strode through the woods at a fearful pace. They burst out of the forest close to some narrow strip fields but no one was working there to see them as they hurried along the fallow earth.

Too proud and annoyed to ask Marcus to slow down, Flavia fell behind. She was passing a sacred elder tree, left standing in the deep field ridges, when Marcus turned and came back to her.

In spite of their earlier quarrel, Flavia felt her heart lifting as he approached. His fingers were tapping a steady rhythm against his belt.

'I am sorry for what I said.'

He was glowering but, Flavia realized, not at her. He kicked a loose pebble into the field ridge separating them, looking down, and then his face lightened. He crouched and gently plucked a tiny flower, growing in the bottom of the ridge.

'I should have been named after a bear,' he said, and held out the flower. 'May I?'

Under his tan he was blushing. Even he could sometimes still be shy, Flavia realized. Her heart full, she nodded, holding her breath as he carefully tucked the tiny blue speedwell into her hair, touching the side of her head afterwards.

'I have never known it be like this,' he said cryptically. 'My temper got the better of me. It will not happen again.'

'I know,' Flavia said. 'I trust you.'

She did trust Marcus, and it pained her to think that he still did not know everything about her. Now, as they walked along the field ridges across the gently curving downland towards the distant glitter of the Roman road known by some as Corinium Street, he took her hand and told her, in a quiet, almost sombre voice, that he had yet to thank her for saving his life on the night the villa caught fire.

'That's twice you have saved me,' he said. 'I am deeply in your debt.'

'Not at all.' Flavia sensed that here was a moment when she could introduce her own debt: that of the truth about what happened after she had found Lady Valeria in her study, calm and peaceful but no longer living.

'Marcus, I need to talk to you.'

'About who may have set the villa on fire? Yes, you are right, it is time.'

This was not what Flavia had expected, but she went along with the change of subject because it was important.

Striding beside her, Marcus was looking grim again. 'The fire-setters did not care. I think they were after me, and maybe legal papers, but to them it obviously didn't matter who else was hurt. Whoever did it, they are going to suffer. I am going to find out how Lucius Maximus arranged it and then–'

Marcus struck his thigh with his free fist. 'I vow it,' he said.

Alarmed by his promise, Flavia said swiftly, 'It may not be the Decurion.'

'Who else? Who else has the motive? Or

the means.'

Marcus quickened his pace, attacking a steep slope leading off the downland as if Lucius Maximus was waiting ahead for him on the paved road. It was all Flavia could do to keep up, but she was determined to speak.

'Lucius Maximus is a dangerous enemy,' she panted. 'Powerful, with powerful allies. Even your own commander thinks well of him. He could wreck your career.'

'Shall I tell you something?' Marcus whirled about, stopping in front of Flavia so quickly that she stumbled against him. He caught her before she fell, his hands gentle on her but his voice implacable.

'This proud Roman career my family think I should pursue – tribune and higher – it usually means the killing of others, of anyone who stands in the way of the Empire. Yes, Roman law brings peace in the end, but at what cost? I find myself asking that question more and more, and when I see men in place like Lucius Maximus... If I do not stand against him, who will?'

Why does it have to be you, Marcus? Flavia ached to say, but she knew he was that kind of man, and that she loved him for his integrity – so how could she complain?

Soon, he would also make the connections between the sudden death of Lady Valeria and the ambition and greed of Lucius

Maximus. Afraid that Marcus might strike out at the Decurion in anger, without planning, if he even suspected Maximus of murdering Valeria, Flavia did the only thing she could think of at that moment. Torn between pride and anxiety, she stood on tiptoe, took his head between her healing hands and kissed him.

He kissed her fiercely in return, his arms clamping round her. He would not release her even when a raucous catcall from nearby Corinium Street alerted them to a passing carter.

Later, on the road to Aquae Sulis, Marcus bought them a ride from another carter; a pewter merchant with a bony gray pony even slower than Lady Valeria's old mule.

On the way into the stirring city, Flavia was even more thoughtful than usual, Marcus decided. She listened to his plans to talk to the sculptor Dexter and toga girl Messalina again to try to persuade them to be witnesses with him against Lucius Maximus and observed quietly, 'You have no proof that Lucius Maximus had the villa fired. But someone must have been watching the villa – they struck only when you had returned from seeing off Commander Pompey, and not before. They struck when you and the rest of us were already too weary to notice anything suspicious.'

Marcus allowed himself a grim smile. 'I have already asked Otho and his veterans to keep watch for lingering strangers. Otho knows how to hide: the villa will seem deserted.'

Flavia nodded, her eyes fixed straight ahead between the slogging pony's ears on the earth ramparts surrounding the city. They were inexorably closing on civilisation. Marcus could not yet properly see or smell Aquae Sulis, but he could hear it in the faint shouts of the chestnut sellers and the quack doctors peddling their cures for pain relief and immortality. Usually, he enjoyed the hurly burly of towns, but today he wanted to spend longer with Flavia. He began to calculate how long it would be before it was likely that they could be alone again.

He wondered if he should tell her about his mother, about his ancestry, but again put it off. He had grown so accustomed to the snobbish reactions of people like Lucius Maximus that he was wary of admitting anything.

Once they returned to the villa, Marcus decided, he would complete the formal ceremony to free Flavia. He should do so, he thought, before they became more entangled. Perhaps he should have spoken last night. He wondered if she would stay with him, like Gaius and the others: he had asked her to, but it would be her choice. He

291

did not want to do as his father had done with his mother.

Looking at Flavia, sitting on her haunches beside him, her chin resting on her knees, Marcus ached at the thought of losing her.

She glanced at him, her eyes very bright. 'Back to the villa soon.'

'Yes. I wish we were not.' He clasped her hand, looking into her face while around them the crates of pewter cups and plates rattled and clashed and up ahead, the carter sang a tuneless ditty. 'I would like another day with you in the woods – without the she-boar.'

Flavia laughed heartily, and then her free hand suddenly flew to her mouth. 'Of course,' she breathed. 'Why didn't I think of it earlier?'

She knelt up on her knees, close to where he dangled his own legs over the end of the cart, and spoke quickly and quietly. 'I know of a place where we can be private in the city, and safe. It is a place slaves – I mean people like me – know. I can take you there, only you must swear to keep it a secret. Please?' she added, her golden fringe dropping into her eyes as she ducked her head anxiously towards him.

Was this her secret? 'I swear,' Marcus said, raising his hand palm up. 'I will not betray your trust, Flavia.'

Her eyes clouded a little as he spoke, but

she said steadily, 'Then I will guide us.'

Leaving the carter in one of the side alleys close to the Great Bath, Flavia darted ahead through the ever-increasing crowds and took Marcus off in the direction of the small hot spring sacred to the healing god Aesculapius, a part of the city he had rarely been in. She sped past the tall, oval, roofless walls of the small healing spring, her bright hair visible to Marcus even among the throngs of visitors and worshippers who gathered to make offerings and offer prayers to Aesculapius. Coming to a cross-roads, she glanced back to check that he was still following and walked quickly down a narrow, unpaved side street.

'Not far,' she said as he caught up. She slowed as they reached the high boundary wall of a private house. The back boundary wall, Marcus registered, as Flavia looked up and down the street.

She stepped close to him and muttered, 'When no one is close we climb over the wall. The house is deserted,' she added.

Marcus stifled amazement and questions and waited for Flavia's tense, 'Go!' before launching himself at the high wall.

There were jutting stones and easy hand-holds in the weathered stone and Flavia climbed as swiftly as he did, nimbly reaching the flat top of the wall and rolling over the other side. He did the same, dropping afterwards into the garden of the deserted house.

Flavia came beside him. 'Will you wait here? Just for a moment. I don't think there will be any of my people here at this time, not so early in the morning when there are many tasks to be done, but even so I need to make sure we are alone.' She gave him a considering look. 'You would alarm them.'

'I will wait.' Folding his arms, Marcus leaned back against the boundary wall.

It was hard for him to watch her leave, darting between the bushes and trees of the overgrown garden, but he knew that he must. She had to know that she could trust him.

Her footsteps were soon lost in the clamour of the unseen streets around them and in the fallen leaves and bare earth paths of this strange, deserted place.

The garden was wildly overgrown, full of straggling rose bushes with wizened red hips and unclipped rosemary and lavender bushes. The little of the house he could see through the bushes and the spreading branches of an oak tree growing in the centre of the garden looked very old. He could just make out some sagging timber walls with peeling paint and a broken-tiled roof.

'What is this place?' he asked when Flavia returned, skirting round a rosemary almost as tall as she was.

'It is supposed to be haunted by the last owner, who was rumoured to be a sorcerer,' she answered calmly. 'I think that is why it is still deserted. That, or the man's family cannot agree what to do with it. A slave showed me how to come here many years ago, soon after I had lost my parents and before Lady Valeria bought me. I think he was sorry for me. He said it was a place of safety and peace for slaves, that if the owner did haunt the house and grounds, he gave no trouble to slaves. The slave told me that we could be ourselves here and no one would see.'

She tilted up her chin, the rising sun lighting her red lips and rose complexion, making her look prettier than ever. Marcus forced himself to attend to what she was saying.

'The slave made me promise never to tell anyone else about this place – except for one person, who must also swear the same.'

'And that's me?' Marcus asked, astonished and amazed afresh, honored and touched by her confidence.

She smiled at him: an old smile, a secretive smile that he had sometimes seen on his mother's face. 'It is safe to go on: no one else is here,' she said. 'I will show you round.'

Walking quickly, to show that she did not regret her decision to share this place with him, Flavia returned along the twisting beaten-earth path between the rampant rosemary and lavender bushes. One more twist of the path and they reached the heart of the garden and its startling secret – a private outdoor pool, its shimmering waters steaming in the sun.

'By Mithras, what a place.' Looking around, Marcus halted beside her, dropping onto his knees to test the waters of the deep, lead-lined pool. 'It's hot!' he exclaimed, shaking moisture from his hand.

Flavia pointed to a large lead pipe leading away from the pool in the direction of the deserted house before it was lost in the luxuriant undergrowth.

'We think the owner fixed a conduit some-where off the spring waters of the Aescul-apius spring and directed some of the thermal water here,' she explained. 'The pool drains somewhere, too, but we do not know where.'

Marcus sat back on his heels. 'We?'

'Those of us who come here, when we can.'

'Your own private bathing place.' Marcus jumped to his feet again and walked around the marbled perimeter of the pool. 'I am surprised nobody has tried to make money with it.'

'We are careful who we tell,' Flavia said, squashing disappointment at Marcus' mer-cenary approach, but he was staring across the sun-gilded water at the leaf-strewn

296

timber portico leading to the deserted house.

'I am not surprised at that,' he said quietly. 'It is beautiful.'

He watched a small breeze tumble a bronze oak leaf along a small marble walkway leading from the semi-derelict portico to the edge of the pool. 'Mysterious, quite eerie, but also ... comforting. As if you are in an entirely different world.' He turned about, pointing to the sparkling spiders' webs on the lavender bushes, rimed with heavy dew. 'Somewhere forgotten by the rest of the city. A place where magical things become possible.'

'You understand,' Flavia whispered, breathing out in relief.

He smiled. 'It is more than likely that the old owner saw an easy chance to grab some free hot water, but what he has made here, what time has made ... I am not surprised he was thought to be a sorcerer.'

Marcus held out both hands to her. 'Thank you for sharing this, and be assured – your secret will be safe in my keeping.'

Flavia walked to the edge of the secret pool and joined him in studying the waters.

'It has hardly changed,' she murmured. As if from far off, she caught a faint whiff of incense wafting from the altars close to the spring shrine to Aesculapius. Listening, she could hear nothing of the city outside the high boundary walls, only her own breathing and the creak of the bare-branched oak tree. A raven was perched in its branches, preening itself. She and Marcus were standing away from the shade of the empty house, in a clear patch of warm flagstones where the bushes had not yet encroached. The sun was warm on her skin and Marcus' hand around hers warmer still.

'Go on.' He encouraged her memories.

'After the old slave showed me this place, I returned only once.' Still haunted by the remembrance, Flavia chewed on her lower lip. 'It must have been two or three years later; I know I had been a while in Lady Valeria's service and learned that she was as kind as she was formidable.'

'She was,' Marcus agreed, squeezing her fingers.

'Lady Valeria had sent me to buy some new sweet wine. She loved wine.' Flavia's gentle smile faded. 'Before I reached the wine shop, I was chased in the streets by two youths. Two well-fleshed sons of centurions, in rich black and red tunics. They pointed at my hair and said something about blonde hair in other places and yelled, "Let's get her!" I thought they were going to kill me. It was only when I was older that I realized what they were after.'

Aware of the stiffened figure beside her, Flavia suppressed a shudder. 'No one stopped them,' she went on. 'A few by-standers cheered: it was a good joke. Two hearty boys having sport with a little slave girl – no one saw the harm. I was running between stalls, trying to lose them, trying to keep in mind which streets were dead-ends. I was terrified that someone would grab me and hold me for them.

'I ran along the street past the healing spring of Aesculapius – I thought that perhaps among the worshippers I would be safe. And then it was as if I remembered for the first time in an age; as if the memory came just as I could run no more.

'I thought: the deserted villa, and set out for it. I knew where to go, as if my feet remembered. I climbed over the wall as if I had wings on my back helping me. I heard the two youths go blundering past in the street and I laughed, because I knew I was safe. I had remembered the place in time.'

Flavia pointed to a bare patch of earth close to one end of the rectangular pool. 'It was early summer, and there were peonies growing and flowering there. I had never seen such vibrant, opulent flowers before – they don't grow naturally here. I didn't even know what they were called until I saw a drawing of one, years later, on a medical papyrus scroll my lady had me read.'

'It is a healing plant,' Marcus agreed. 'My mother grows it in the garden at home. I think she has also used it in magic, so I suppose a sorcerer–' He shook his head.

'But I have never seen it growing here.'

'The scent of those blood-red flowers made me drowsy.' Releasing Marcus' hand, Flavia walked to the patch of bare earth, sat down on her heels and trickled a handful of dirt through her fingers. 'I stretched out by the pool and slept. Then I bathed in the waters. I felt as if I was washing those chasing youths off me; I felt cleansed.

'I was very late, returning with the wine, but my lady never scolded. After that, I started to dress in cook's cast-offs, which were baggy.'

'Shapeless,' Marcus said.

Flavia nodded, trickling another fistful of dry soil through her hand. Her fingers and palms were healing quickly: she felt no pain at all. 'Isn't it strange, though, how I forgot this place for so long and then thought of it in that way, exactly when I needed a safe haven.'

Marcus lowered himself onto the marble edge of the pool. 'And why did you need to remember it today?' he asked softly, sculling the water again with his hand.

Flavia knew why, but the thought of admitting it made her heart race harder than when she had been chased through the streets. 'After that, I never returned here,' she said, putting off the moment. 'I supposed I didn't need to.' She raised her head and looked at Marcus. 'I remembered it when Lady Valeria died, but then–' she stopped and swallowed. 'Then you came, and the memory slipped away again.'

'Until now.'

'Yes.'

Marcus unlaced his sandals. 'Is this your secret?' he asked gently without looking at her. 'Is this what you have been hiding from me?'

Her throat felt was if it was swelling painfully, blocking her breath. Swallowing again, Flavia shook her head. 'No,' she managed, conscious that Marcus deserved an answer. 'No,' she said again.

'Do you want to talk about it?'

Flavia nodded for a second time and Marcus must have seen the slight movement out of the corner of his eye. He beckoned to her. 'Come and sit with me. Dangle your feet with mine in the water. Trust me, Flavia, as you have before. I will listen to whatever you say.'

Chapter 15

Are you a free Celt or a coward? Flavia thought. She forced herself to rise and walk across to him. He was smiling, seemingly easy as he dangled his feet in the water, and he hugged her as she sat beside him.

'Give me your foot,' he whispered, and when she complied, he began to untie the tangled knots of her sandals.

'You must understand I acted alone,' she began. 'What I did, I did because I was afraid. I knew that as slaves we could all be under suspicion and then we might be tortured to compel us to speak. Roman law allows the torture of slaves.'

Marcus' fingers became still on her left foot.

'Gaius especially was terrified. He had heard of a Roman family where the master had died suddenly, leaving no will or final word, and the entire household of slaves had been crucified. Gaius learned this only a few days before Lady Valeria died. He was very shocked.'

Flavia wanted to stop. She thought of discarding her shawl, slithering out of her dress, distracting Marcus with love-making. She knew she could do it. But what then? How would he trust her afterwards, with this difficult truth half-told between them?

'I understand, Flavia.' Marcus softly drew her left sandal away from her foot and put it on the pool side next to his; an ordinary, everyday action that linked her to the real world. His next words calmed her further. 'I am beginning to understand what you probably did and why. Had I been where you were standing then, I would have done the same.'

Flavia thought: How far do I trust Marcus? And the answer came to her at once: I trust him with my life. Supported by this, she found she could continue.

'You asked me how Lady Valeria died, and I told you the truth then. I did find her, sitting in her chair in the study, an empty wine cup by her hand. She looked as if she was asleep. There was no stress in her, no sign of fear. I didn't realize for a moment what she had done – I thought she had died in her sleep. Then I caught a whiff of the dregs in the cup. They smelt strange, spices and something else.'

She shook her head. 'Lady Valeria did not have a particularly good sense of smell, or taste, and she had forgotten that I have. I realized that she had–' Flavia's voice began to falter – 'had probably taken her own life. That she had done what she said she always would do, one winter, and had crossed over into the after-life to join her husband. But she had forgotten to leave a note.'

'You wrote that final message to protect Gaius and the others,' Marcus said. 'Easy for a scribe, to copy another's hand.'

'Yes.' Flavia felt exhausted, sitting with one foot in Marcus' lap and one end of her shawl trailing into the hot water of the pool. But she had one thing more to say.

'There's something else you must know

about me. I don't want there to be any more secrets between us. I want you to know who I am. All that I am.'

She withdrew her foot and knelt up on the hard marble. Marcus was sitting watching her, his feet and hands quite still. She wondered how she would feel if she saw disgust on his handsome face.

I trust him, she thought, and said, 'I am a follower of Jesus Christ. I am a Christian.' She gulped in a fresh breath of air. 'I don't know what you think about Christians, what you have been told about us. I know some pagans think we are evil trouble-makers. I believe in loving and helping others. I believe in a heaven for everyone.'

'I know,' Marcus said. 'That shows in everything you do.'

Flavia tried to look at him but found she could not: her eyes were swimming with tears and she was sobbing, crying harder as he gathered her to him, embracing her.

'Hush, little one, it is over,' he said, rocking her stiff kneeling body to and fro in his arms. 'If all Christians are like you, then they are wholly excellent to me. You have acted as you always do, with courage and honor and love. Hush!'

He tried to wipe the tears away, but more spilled from her eyes. 'My sweet Flavia,' he said, taking her head between his hands, waiting as she raised bleary eyes and a blotched face to his own. 'It is no wonder that Lady Valeria loved you so much. You knew that, of course? Because she did. *My youngest daughter*, she called you.'

'But you said she called me mettlesome!' Flavia wailed, her hands beating against Marcus' shoulders.

'So she did, sweet, that too. She knew you well, I would say– Ouch! Watch those flying fists! You don't know your own strength.' He trapped both her hands in one of his and, as her mouth opened in another sob, his lips closed on hers in a kiss.

Deep within her, Flavia felt a familiar spiral of desire.

'We mustn't! Not here!' she cried, trying to break free. 'Someone may come.'

'But you have already said no one does at this time of day,' Marcus murmured against the side of her mouth. His tongue lightly flicked the edge of her lips and when she gasped, he neatly recaptured her mouth afresh.

Flavia tried to fight the feelings of delicious bonelessness and fire that were coiling through her hands, breasts, and most disturbing, through her intimate parts. 'No!' She twisted her head away from Marcus' searching mouth.

He laughed and lifted her easily off her knees and onto his lap, brushing her flyaway hair away from her flushed face. 'Is this not the best way, little Celt, for me to prove to you that I believe and respect all that you have told me?'

What about love? Flavia thought, refusing to look at him. Why do you not say you love me? Quick and poisonous as the attack of an adder, she recalled Pompey's words about Marcus' wife and daughter: *I was sure he would grieve forever for them.* A flare of jealousy burst in her.

Using the strength of anger, she successfully pushed herself away from Marcus' broad, warm chest and to the full stretch of his encircling arms. 'If you respect me as you say, then you should respect my wishes!'

'But I do respect you.' With an almost lazy strength, Marcus would not allow her to struggle off his lap. 'I respect and honor you, and certainly I heed your wishes.' He cupped her breast and gave a knowing, irritating smile as Flavia's own body betrayed her, as her limbs stopped squirming and trying to escape and were frozen instead in delight.

'See what I mean?' he said, his fingers slowly circling her breasts.

Flavia felt her nipples peaking, becoming hard. Torn between indignation and desire, she was having difficulty finding her voice.

'This is the comfort and attention you need right now.' Marcus gave her a hard, swift kiss. 'You see I do respect your wishes,' he said, chuckling as Flavia lifted her head to be kissed again.

Goaded by his amusement, she bit him on his lower lip and when he flinched and drew back a little, said through gritted teeth, 'This pool is a place of tranquillity! Are we animals, to give in to our every moment of need?'

'Not an animal,' Marcus rumbled, licking his lips. 'More an angry, pecking bird. But I know how to clip your wings.' He shot her a look from his deep blue eyes that both stirred and alarmed her. 'You are still a fledging when it comes to the arts of love-making.'

Damn him for being amused, Flavia thought resentfully. 'We cannot! Not at this hour!'

Deliberately taking his time while she was firmly pinioned and fast in his embrace, Marcus lowered his head. 'This moment of comfort seems to be turning into a contest,' he said, slowly kissing her throat. 'You should know that I am very competitive. I always respond to a challenge.'

He removed her shawl, dropping it casually and untidily to one side. Unable to stop him without a fight that she would surely lose, Flavia tried another tactic, forcing herself to go limp. 'We cannot,' she repeated. 'It is too early.'

'For a long, languorous swim in this astonishing pool? Why else show this to me, Flavia, unless some part of you didn't wish us to bathe here? It is true, isn't it?' he added softly.

Flavia tried to roll off him, but quick as she was, Marcus was just as fast. Seizing her arms, he rolled her right over onto her stomach and pressed his weight against the middle of her back.

Breathless, Flavia felt as if she had just been felled by a falling anvil. 'Let me up!' she yelled, kicking and lashing out where she could with her arms.

'You will get more dirt on that pretty dress,' Marcus warned, as he grabbed her bucking right leg and calmly proceeded to untie and remove her remaining sandal. 'But then again, it is a warm day for winter. I think our clothes will dry quickly.'

'No!' Flavia shrieked as she realized his intent. She kicked out but Marcus had already slipped into the pool and now strong arms were locking around her, scooping her off the marble.

'To bathe now is a scandal!' she exclaimed. 'Really, Marcus, please. We mustn't. It's wrong and it is the middle of winter!'

He stopped with her hanging in his arms above the sun-dappled water. 'If you truly believe that–' He turned with her back to the edge of the pool.

Against her own conscious thought or wishes, Flavia heard a low moan of disappointment escape her lips. Her eyes widened and she stared in horror at her grinning captor.

'Pax, little Celt, I will not let you deny yourself again.' He brought his arms down into the limpid water and released her legs so that she floated against him. 'Have you ever been bathed by a man?'

'Of course not!' Flavia found her feet on the warm leads of the pool floor. Deeply relieved that she could stand and not have the swirling water close over her head, she added, 'I am quite capable of washing myself, thank you.'

'Is that so?' Marcus' easy smile foretold trouble and Flavia's stomach gave an alarming lurch. 'Not in the way I will do it,' he said.

Marcus felt her relax slightly as the warm water flowed about her. Her eyes were tightly shut now, her face colouring rapidly to a shade deeper than the early morning sun. That was all right. She could be angry with him and shy of him. He wanted her to have no regrets or terror, especially after the profound and moving revelations that she had shared with him.

Flavia's secret, he thought, marvelling afresh at her ingenuity and courage. Such burdens she had carried on her narrow shoulders. Such love for Lady Valeria and the others. He could sense the truth in her every word.

And another surprise: Flavia a Christian. He knew little of this new, exotic faith, but if she was a convert there must be good in it.

'You can open your eyes,' he reminded her, taking a certain wicked satisfaction in her scandalised responses. But he must remember that everything was new to her, including what he planned to do next.

Talk to her about your mother, about Drusilla, his conscience pricked, but Marcus thought that talking later would do just as well as sooner. She was gorgeous, her sunshine-coloured hair haloing her pretty face and those sweet familiar escaping tendrils and curls plastered against her forehead and by her ears. Her softly-parted, freshly kissed mouth was as red and lush as a pomegranate seed and her warm, smooth skin voluptuous as a lily. With her wet gown sculptured to her body and her gray eyes engaging his with their appealing mixture of apprehension, curiosity and emerging sensuality, she intoxicated him.

'Marcus, our clothes,' she said, in almost a whisper, as he touched her waist and then her breast through the clinging wet linen.

'We will change at home. Tell Hadrian and the others we were caught in a local storm.' Marcus was already caught. More than the finest painting he had ever seen or hoped to produce, more than the most evocative of

310

scents or music, Flavia stirred him, but at present it was his own earthier desire that was the problem. If she touched him at all, he wasn't sure if he would be able to hold back.

'Is this a dream?' she murmured, capturing his mood exactly as she rested her head against his shoulder, giving in a moment to temptation, Marcus guessed. 'Dreams can be dangerous.'

'Not this one,' Marcus reassured. He was determined it wouldn't be. She was locked in his arms, standing with him in the middle of this amazing pool, with the steam from the waters releasing the perfume of the enclosing rosemary and lavender bushes. Their own private, secret bathing place.

'I have wanted to do this for so long,' he said, drawing off her belt, feeling her gown billowing around his legs.

'Did you bathe Drusilla?'

Her face was burrowed against his chest, so Marcus couldn't see her expression. 'Little Aurelia used to join me in the barracks bath house in Germania,' he answered truthfully. 'She and the other youngsters used to play games in the baths.'

'Did–'

'No more talk.' Marcus raised her chin with his thumb and kissed her, tumbling her clothes off with swift, sure hands. I have you now, little water goddess, and in your own element, he thought, his voice abandoned in the heat of the moment. She made his very skin crackle.

He wanted her to revel in every instant. The desire to honor and promote her enjoyment helped Marcus to control his own aching need as he gathered her back to himself with undisguised delight.

She had her eyes tightly closed again and he scooped water and lightly washed her face, smiling as her lips quivered and almost kissed his fingers. He sensed the conflict within her between pleasure and propriety and longed to prove to her what a sexy little creature she was, but he did not want her to feel ashamed afterwards by anything they did.

He stopped her hand as he felt her fingers on his belt. 'Next time you can bathe me,' he said, with a lightness he did not feel. He found her caresses far too erotic. 'That is a promise.'

Her throaty giggle almost drove him over the edge. He felt her stand on tip-toe and then, using the water itself as an added support, bounce lightly off her toes to snatch a kiss as light as the beat of a moth's wing from his mouth.

'Flavia!' He lowered his head and kissed her back. The provoking wench was playing with fire.

'We have no bathing oil,' he said, keeping to the practical. 'But I am sure we will manage.'

It was easy to begin with her hair, which fascinated him, and hard, too, when he really wanted to share so much more with her than bathing. But they were learning each other, he sensed, and he wanted her to trust him. That mattered above everything.

He released her plait, hearing her muttered apology that she was wearing none of the combs he had bought her and responding with a hand-ruffle of her loosened hair, saying, 'Those are probably gone with the fire, but I will buy you more.'

'I will buy my own,' she shot back instantly. 'From my wages.'

'Well said!' Marcus grunted, teasing her in return by tickling her under her arms until Flavia was giggling and thrashing against him, water splashing everywhere.

'Stop, stop!' she cried, almost hiccupping with laughter.

He spun her round, the water making her virtually weightless, and tucked an arm around her waist. 'Now for your back,' he said.

He stroked the water over her, gently kneading the muscles on either side of her spine, hearing her breath quicken each time his hand approached her waist. Thinking about the faint sprinkling of freckles by her right shoulder blade and how taut and fine her skin was, he washed her arms. She seemed to shimmer in his arms, the rising steam wreathing her face so that she almost appeared to be wearing a veil made of mist.

Torn between passion and a strange sense of mystery, Marcus again reminded himself what he was supposed to be doing. Although he had not yet touched certain areas, he could not resist kissing the back of her freshly-bathed neck.

'And your legs.'

With her damp head pillowed against his middle ribs, he lifted her quickly so that her feet flipped off the pool bottom. He caught her right leg and brought it closer to the surface, the warm water adding a further dimension of sensation as he ran his hand slowly over her sleek calf and thigh. He was equally scrupulous in his attention to her left leg.

'And the rest.'

Flavia shivered as he turned her round to face him, his legs threading through hers. She felt increasingly strange in this soft, mobile, warm medium of water, and not only because she was an indifferent swimmer.

'Marcus.' She tried to think of the words to express concern and found she had forgotten them. She was rapidly forgetting any sense of decorum. The secret pool itself added to her confusion, the scents of its lavender and rosemary bushes perfuming the air and its steam condensing and sparkling on Marcus' long black eyelashes, dampening the ends of his tough, dark brown hair.

'Close your eyes a moment,' he said.

To show her trust in him, she did so, feeling the water rise and fall in a subtle lingering embrace against her breasts. Everything here was voluptuous; she could imagine losing track of time and place.

'You can open them now,' Marcus said against her ear.

He was naked – his tunic, belt and loin cloth mere shadows on the bottom of the pool. 'I will fetch them up later.' He smiled. 'With your own.'

'Oh!' Flavia had forgotten that her gown and under-tunic languished under this flood of gently swirling, gray-green water. Above the water, his upper torso glistened in the spray and sun, the harsh contours of his face softened by the rising steam.

And by love, perhaps? Flavia hoped it was love, although when she recalled her jealous question about his bathing habits with his wife she was ashamed.

She gasped afresh as he took her hand and laid it against the middle of his chest. She could feel his strongly beating heart, the pulse increasing as her fingers moved, almost of her own volition, touching his bronzed skin below and above the water. She found herself smiling at her own exploration.

He touched her in return. Gathering water and allowing it to run through his fingers, he bathed her breasts and her trim, flat stomach. The water trickled between her breasts like the gentlest and warmest of rain-showers as his hand followed, defining every curve.

'Marcus!' She felt to be splitting in two between shock and delight. She twisted in his arms, shy and at the same time proud, because he made her feel beautiful, desirable.

There was no disputing the last. He would not allow her to touch him intimately, saying with a quiet laugh, 'You don't know your own effect.'

To her own inward horror, Flavia pouted. 'That is not fair,' she began.

'Maybe not, but it is my choice.'

'Bully. Brute—'

She could go no further in her catalogue of insults because Marcus lifted her high in his arms out of the water, as if she were an acrobat on display in a Roman circus.

'Let me down!' Flavia struck out at him with her feet, stiffening as she suddenly wondered what he could see of her.

'Your wish is my command, lady.' Her brute and bully was gradually letting her down with one arm back into the pool, while his other hand slicked more of the warm, silken stream across her hips, and lower.

'Should I show you another lesson in love-making, little Celt?' he said, running his lips across her damp breasts. 'Should I bear you away to the edge of this pool and have my way with you in the manner shown on Greek vases? We could watch our own reflections.

'But no,' he continued. 'I believe it is far better this way, face to face.'

He entered her, sliding into her more smoothly than the water itself, kissing and holding her close until she was ready for more. Then he began to move, joining with her ever more deeply, more intensely.

They finished clamped along each other, with Flavia's back against the pool side, her hands drumming against Marcus' shoulders as they took and gave to each other, embracing and saying each other's names until a final blinding tide of pleasure engulfed them both.

Afterwards, Flavia had never felt more seductive. Marcus had never felt more alive. Jubilant, they dressed each other, laughing when Marcus tried to tie Flavia's belt on his waist and when Flavia absent-mindedly donned one of his sandals. The morning sun shone on them brighter than ever and they were in holiday mood.

Flavia felt as if nothing bad could happen today. Hand in hand, she walked back with Marcus through the deserted overgrown garden, aware of his glancing eyes on her. Energised by their love-making, she was confident that today he would put into words what he felt about her.

Reaching the boundary wall that would lead them back into Aquae Sulis, Marcus insisted on going first and then on reaching an arm down to pull her up lightly after him with a speed and sureness that left her giddy. No one saw their descent from the wall top as Marcus swung her down and jumped into the narrow alleyway, his feet padding on the unpaved street.

They darted through the city hand in hand in their soaking clothes, warm where really they should have been chilled and careless of any stares. A farrier on one street pointed his metal-working hammer at Flavia and shouted in good humour, 'Here is a pair who think the Saturnalia's come early, when it's only the first of the new month!' while Marcus gave the bearded man a ribald response.

Distance flowed under their rapid feet almost as fast as the pool water had drained off their bodies. Flavia's loosened hair began to curl as it dried and her wet gown slapped against her. It would be good, she thought, to finally reach the villa, to change and dress her hair, and to help Marcus to comb his mop into some kind of order. And then there would be reunions, all the delights of a homecoming. She would see Hadrian again, and Gaius and the others. Marcus would perform the ceremony that would formally free them.

Once free, she could accuse Lucius Maximus of murder and not be questioned under torture.

'I can hardly wait,' she said aloud.

The sun was high when Flavia and Marcus walked through the gated entrance to the villa, Marcus flinching slightly as he saw the patient lines of men and women standing under the portico, waiting to speak to him in the tablinium.

'Word must have gone round the city of our return. I had best change and begin seeing those people at once,' he said.

Flavia nodded. She understood his obligations as patron to these people and knew that he took them seriously. 'I will bring you some wine,' she promised, gently disengaging her fingers from his.

It was time for them to re-enter the real world.

As she and Marcus drew closer to the house, Hadrian pelted down the main entrance steps and across the paths. Clearly recovered from his leg injury, he bellowed greetings and sprayed gravel in his wake.

'Marcus! Flavia! Why are you wet? There is a messenger for you, Marcus, a dispatch rider from your former commander Pompeius Gellius. He is waiting for you in the tablinium. You are to set out at once to

319

Eboracum! Why are you staring at Flavia, Marcus? She isn't going. Come on!'

The wiry, shaggy-haired boy who was already growing out of his russet tunic dragged Marcus back up the stone steps with him.

Numb and dazed by the swiftness of events, Flavia entered the villa by the small kitchen door, the joy of her homecoming extinguished.

Chapter 16

There was no time for long farewells. Marcus had been ordered to the northern garrison city of Eboracum to discuss matters of 'grave state importance.' It was imperative that he leave at once, on an urgent summons.

Flavia's hands shook as she read the orders aloud to Marcus in the shuttered, dusty tablinium where the travel-stained messenger was lolling on a couch beside a low table with a spilled measure of wine. After delivering his letter, the messenger had suddenly dropped asleep in an almost comical manner, his pewter wine cup slipping from his hand and rolling on the floor tiles under the couch as he flopped back on the cushions and began to snore.

'Let him rest, since he is going back with me,' Marcus said, grabbing Hadrian's reaching arm to prevent the boy from prodding the hapless rider awake. 'Has his mount been attended to?'

'I did that,' said Hadrian, puffing out his thin chest. 'Anyway, the rider's going to pick up a new horse on the way back. He told me that himself.' His face glowed as he was pleased to remember.

Crowded in the doorway, Gaius and the other newly-freed servants looked uncertain and uneasy, unsure what to make of this. Standing behind them, his rangy figure topping them by half a head, Otho nodded to his fellow warrior.

'I will stay close and watch this place while you are gone,' he promised.

Marcus raised a hand in acknowledgement, then turned to Gaius.

'I am sorry, freedman, but I must beg a favour of you. Could you let the people waiting to see me know that I cannot see them today and that I don't know when I will be back?'

'Of course, Mas – Sir – Marcus.' Gaius stopped as his wife Agrippina jabbed him in the stomach.

'We hope you have a safe journey, Marcus,' she said, her fine Egyptian eyes sparkling with unshed tears. As Marcus looked at her, she muttered about leaving the kitchen unattended and disappeared.

One by one, Gaius, Sulinus and Livia also bade Marcus a safe journey and melted back into the shadows of the narrow corridor between tablinium and kitchen.

'Want me to show you more sword-play?' Otho asked Hadrian.

'Yes!' Hadrian raised a whoop that would surely have woken the rider, had he been less exhausted, and trooped out happily with the grinning one-eyed solider.

'By Mithras, what a morning.' Marcus opened his arms and Flavia flew into them, anxiously touching him all over. 'I am all here,' he said, giving her flowing hair a gentle tug.

'Just make sure you are when you return,' Flavia said.

He smiled, and kissed her forehead. 'You will write to me, scribe?'

'Every day! Any rider travelling north will find himself carrying them.'

'And I will send letters back. I swear it.'

They both started as the rider slipped lower on the couch, his mud-stained mouth open in another rasping snore.

'Poor man,' said Flavia, wondering if she could suggest a small delay.

'I cannot stay.' Marcus almost seemed to read her mind. He cuddled her closer, as if to take the sting from his next words. 'The letter said it was urgent. Pompey would not have written that if it wasn't.'

'That is his seal?' Flavia pointed to a wax impression at the base of the tablet.

Marcus nodded. 'I checked that first.' He sighed. 'Things seem to keep conspiring against us. Pompey and Julia Sura were bound for Londinium on a family visit. There must have been serious trouble for them to return so early to Eboracum instead.'

'And for him to recall you,' Flavia said in a small voice. Had the northern tribes come raiding again from Caledonia? Was there war in the north? Would Marcus be safe?

'Hey! No glum face! It will not be forever.' Marcus picked her up and whirled her round, saying, as he set her down, 'You will have to get used to us parting.'

No doubt the perfect Drusilla saw him off with a bland smile. Flavia smothered the fiery pit of jealousy in her stomach and kept her face straight as Marcus gave her a final instruction.

'Gaius wants a formal freeing ceremony – he seems convinced otherwise that it won't be real – but will you draw up some simple letters for me while I'm away? Saying that I grant freedom to so-and-so. That should cover most of the legal niceties.'

Flavia nodded, determined not to cry as every passing moment brought his departure closer. She wanted to scream out her frustration at fate, yell and stamp like a child that it wasn't fair, but she had to be calm for Marcus. For him, she maintained a mask of serenity.

Marcus looked round to check that none of the others were in earshot. 'I will need to do more to adopt Hadrian, but that will keep for now. The lad doesn't know of that yet, by the way. He almost broke down when I told him he was free, so I thought I would leave the matter of my adopting him as my son until he is more used to the idea.'

'Of course,' Flavia said, adding quietly as she furtively brushed away a betraying tear, 'May I pray for you? To my God? Or would that not be fitting?' she ended in a rush.

'Pray hard, little Celt.' Hooking her off her feet again, Marcus kissed her properly on the lips, his mouth searing against hers, his arms wrapped tightly about her and then Flavia found herself standing back on the floor tiles.

'Let's get this over.' Stepping slowly away from her, Marcus stood glowering at the sleeping dispatch rider, then turned on his heel to go change into riding clothes.

For the first few days after Marcus had gone, Flavia missed him dreadfully, but told herself not to worry. She told herself that the dispatch rider had not mentioned war or rebellion, which he surely would have done if there was any urgent trouble or danger in the north. She told herself to keep busy. In addition to her work as scribe, her tasks of wheat grinding, cleaning, sweeping and such had not changed, but they felt different because she was free.

On the second day after Marcus left, she was finally introduced by a blustering and rather embarrassed Gaius to the mysterious potions buyer with the heavily-stained finger-nails: a reserved young Greek woman called Xanthippe. Given their rather strained dealings in the past, Xanthippe and Flavia exchanged a few careful words of mutual good wishes, Flavia again deeply relieved that the puzzle had been solved.

As Marcus had requested, she wrote the letters that he would sign on his return, stating that the owner of the letter was now free. She wrote them on the scraps of papyrus that had been recovered, along with a few wax tablets, from the almost burnt-out study. The study table was now firewood and ashes and while she worked, she sat on Marcus' surprisingly intact bed amidst the charred remains of his bedroom, pleased to be in a place where he had been.

Sometimes, Hadrian sat with her and copied the letters out on a wax tablet, his tongue sticking out from the corner of his mouth as he laboured. Afterwards, as a reward for the boy and as another sweet reminder of Marcus, Flavia would dash with

Hadrian into the stable. There they would practice more parrying and attack methods with the wooden swords Marcus had given them, often staying outside until after dark.

As if to echo Flavia's bleaker mood, the weather turned colder again. Outside in the city the streets were icy and within the villa they lived in the kitchen, the only really warm room.

Now that Marcus had gone, no one except Xanthippe visited them. Flavia knew that Otho had kept his promise and was watching the house, but he kept mainly to the stable, scrupulously moving out of there whenever Flavia and Hadrian appeared for their sword practice. Flavia wondered if the man from Germania was avoiding her, then decided that was a foolish idea.

The sun grew fainter and the nights longer. Livia's toothache flared up afresh. Sulinus' rheumatism made the sallow gardener hobble and list from side to side like a sinking ship. It was a slow, gray time of waiting, almost a time of mourning. Flavia was not surprised when, only six days after Marcus had ridden away, she woke to find almost a finger's length of snow covering the garden. Muffled by the snow-fall, she could hear the city streets beyond packed with people buying or selling charcoal and firewood. The usual scents of incense and tanning had been bleached away by the snow. Overhead the sky looked as dark and heavy as iron.

'Let us go the baths,' Gaius suggested, when his motley group of fellow servants gathered around the kitchen table for a warming blackberry tisane after clearing their garden growing patch and the formal paths of snow.

'What about Hadrian?' Flavia asked anxiously. The boy had surely seen enough of the great bath to last a life-time.

'No worries there,' said Gaius. 'Hadrian says he will stay here with Otho. Otho is happy for the boy to remain with him.'

Gaius tugged thoughtfully on his wispy moustache. 'Have you noticed how that big one-eyed German never seems to feel the cold?'

The same was true of Marcus, Flavia thought, with a pang, as the others fell into a discussion of Gaius' suggestion. She had already written Marcus several letters and on the day before, waiting with Hadrian and a bounding Nero by the river ford, she had found a merchant going to Eboracum who had promised to deliver them. Soon, she hoped, she would have Marcus' news in return. To learn that he had reached the end of his journey safely would be a blessing.

Around her, meanwhile, the talk seemed to be reaching a conclusion.

'I don't see why not,' Sulinus was remarking, scratching a thick finger under his conical weather-worn hat.

'It will be good to buy a few snacks there, and save me having to cook later,' Agrippina said, draining off the last of her tisane.

'I have the money Mas – Marcus gave me when he told us we were free, so payment is no problem.' Gaius ostentatiously shook a small pouch of coins hanging from his belt.

Livia was also nodding. 'It will soon be the Saturnalia,' she said, in her quiet way. 'This can be our own early holiday. A way of marking our freedom.'

Flavia felt compelled to mention a warning. 'But that's it, we are not yet officially free. We need to be careful.' She glanced at each of the carefree faces in turn.

'We will be, we will be,' Pina said, with an airy twist of her fingers. 'Honestly, you are only fretting because Marcus isn't here.'

Missing Marcus, Flavia seemed to find him everywhere. She recognised his bright gaze in a rainbow puddle of melting ice. She saw his beloved shape in the retreating figure of a metalworker, kicking disconsolately through snow. His black brows glinted out for a moment on the brooch of a passing stranger and a statue mirrored his height, though not his grace.

It was a perverse pleasure, Flavia knew, her heart lifting each time she spotted these bitter-sweet reminders. And Gaius had been

328

right: it was good to be out of the villa and battling with purpose through the ever-busy streets towards the great bath. Wearing a pair of Marcus' socks on her sandaled feet, in her brown gown and woollen shawl, Flavia felt her spirits unaccountably lifting as she helped Livia to carry a bundle of towels in a dry covered pail, both of them keen to avoid the snow-covered pot-holes. She thought of the last time she had bathed, with Marcus, and was further warmed by the memory. Soon, she knew, she would have a letter from him, something more of his to treasure.

It was still early for bathing, a long while before the fashionable hour when men like Lucius Maximus might be present. Flavia entered the great bathing complex without any sense of foreboding. She watched with tender understanding as Gaius proudly counted out coins in the changing room where Hadrian had once worked to buy each of them a locker space.

'There you go.' Gaius insisted on pressing a small number of coins into her hand, too. 'For a snack, or a drink. No point in starving yourself until he returns.'

'Thank you, Gaius.' Flavia smiled, keen to show the elderly steward the respect and gratitude he deserved. She realized that here was one of the few times in Gaius' long life when he would have been able to be generous. She flipped a sparkling silver coin with finger and thumb, catching it deftly and holding it aloft like atrophy. 'Thank you!'

Gaius' thin red moustache quivered with pleasure.

After undressing swiftly under one of the towels she and Livia had carried in with them, Flavia neatly folded her clothes and sandals into her locker and set off for the great bath itself while the others were still debating whether to go to the cold plunge pool first, or one of the hot sweat rooms.

Agreeing to meet them back at the changing room when the brief daylight had begun to fade and the lamps lit, she set out on a tour of remembrance, deliberately retracing the steps that she and Marcus had taken on their visit to the bath.

She stopped where Marcus had kissed her, where she had sat on his knee for the first time. Leaning against one of the massive pillars that supported the barrel vault of the great bath, she crouched on the top step, the last of four wide steps running all the way round the bath, and closed her eyes, urgently reliving every moment that she and Marcus had spent here.

When she finally reopened her eyes, checking that her towel was still modestly draped about her, Flavia was startled to find the bath full of people and ringing with the calls of a chestnut seller plying his trade inside. Bewildered for an instant, she had to remind herself that Marcus was far away in the north.

'Flavia! Darling, how lovely to see you again!'

The flame-haired toga girl Messalina detached herself from the bony arm of a balding man with an angry boil on the side of his neck and hurried along the aisled walkway of the great bath to join the younger woman.

'Darling, you must meet my divine Titus, a pearl among men.' Messalina grabbed Flavia's arm in a needle-sharp grip and added in a soft voice, 'Stupid and rich, the best combination. Why have you draped your towel like that? You will never attract the customers that way.'

Shock at Messalina's assumption brought Flavia straight to her feet. 'I am not here for that!' she snapped, but Messalina simply tutted and turned her to face Titus and his entourage of perfume and oil carriers.

'Smile, Flavia, you are pretty enough,' Messalina encouraged in the same low undertone. 'I know it's hard when the man who bought you tires of your charms and makes you come here to earn him money, but there are worse ways to survive.'

'Marcus would never do that! He is not—'

'No, I didn't think he was the type, either.' Messalina gave Flavia's arm a companionable squeeze. 'But then he has gone off, hasn't he? And you are here, lurking with intent as we say – Titus! Come and say hello to Flavia. She is new, so be kind. Or you will answer to me.' She gave Titus a brilliant smile.

Horrified that the rumour mill was already working over Marcus' departure and that Messalina considered her not only as a toga girl but as her possible protégée, Flavia almost choked on the woman's rose perfume.

'I am sorry, some other time.' She backed away, aware of the beautiful Messalina's pitying look, and fled from the great bath into the nearest corridor.

Flustered, Flavia remained in the corridor until she realized that the light had changed and the sun moved behind its gray veil of cloud. Still she hung on, ashamed of her cowardice but not wanting to encounter Messalina's helpful pity again.

'She was bought and then betrayed by Lucius Maximus. Her experience has made Messalina suspicious of men. Who can blame her?' Flavia's whispered reasons seemed to echo in the narrow, clammy corridor and she shivered. She wanted to be warm again, to feel cleaner than this. She would go back and take a swim.

She acted on the idea before she lost her nerve, hurrying down the aisled walkway and turning by one of the statues towards that pale green water. Part of her shrank from it, because this was not an act of joy but a self-conscious wading into the great bath amongst others. She had done it before, with Lady Valeria, but today, hastily discarding her towel at the base of a marble bench as she stalked down the wide bath steps until the water reached her neck, she felt as if there was a sign inscribed across her breasts, reading in capitals, DIS-CARDED BY MARCUS BRUCETUS.

She could imagine Messalina's response if she told the woman that she and Marcus had made love. Closing her eyes and washing her face, Flavia could almost hear that soft, pitying voice.

And you believed his words, his promise of your freedom? Then why didn't he declare it before witnesses, some of his friends? That would have been enough to make it legal. He did not have to wait for papers to be drawn up. Darling, that is just the kind of things men tell you. Now that he's had you, you are no longer a novelty.

'Marcus wanted papers and formality to reassure Gaius. That is what he told me and that is what I believe. I trust him,' Flavia said, clenching her teeth and wanting very much to hit out at something as she bobbed away from the edge of the bath. Not her fellow-swimmers, who were mostly elderly or infirm: the early bathers, who came to soothe their aching limbs in the warm, healing spring waters before the younger, fast-living set took over the complex.

Staring up at the huge windows above the pillars, Flavia saw them looking gray, reflecting the gray skies outside. There would be more snow soon, she thought. A few flakes had already blown into the bath from the open ends of the barrel roof. Below the falling snowflakes, only the bathers and the pale green water itself had any color.

'We must talk.'

Messalina had returned from wherever she had been with Titus. Now she slipped into the water to join Flavia.

'Listen!' she said, her voice low and a touch spiteful, 'I know you do not want to hear this, but you are deluding yourself. Marcus has gone and left you – don't deny it! Dexter had a letter from him today, sent from Eboracum! Something about a funerary monument and "other matters", whatever they are.'

Marcus was safe. For a glorious moment, Flavia did not care about anything else. He was all right!

'Flavia! Are you listening to me?' Messalina gave her shoulder a sharp jab. 'Your master Marcus didn't mention you anywhere in that letter.'

'Why should he?' Flavia responded, swimming out of the indignant toga girl's reach. She almost added, 'Is there no other Titus waiting?' but thought that would be too cruel.

'Flavia, don't be blind. He is the same as all men...'

Flavia ducked underwater and blocked out the rest, swimming in her careful way to where she had left her towel at the foot of the marble bench and surfaced there.

'Must go!' she called across to Messalina, hurrying up the wide steps to retrieve her towel. If the master sculptor, Dexter, had received a letter from Marcus, perhaps there would be one waiting for her at home, she thought, her heart quickening in happy anticipation.

There was no letter, no message at all from Marcus when Flavia and the others returned from the baths. That evening she wrote again to Marcus, and a letter to Julia Sura, the commander's wife, telling her about the fire at the villa. Remembering what Julia Sura had told her, Flavia also confessed all her suspicions about Lucius Maximus, including those of murder.

Dexter had also said that Lucius Maximus knew everything that was going on in Aquae Sulis. Flavia thought of a way that the Decurion could do this, a method she decided to share in her letter to Julia.

She longed to tell Julia about her freedom, and about Marcus and herself, but in the end felt too shy and too unsure. She kept thinking about Marcus' beloved wife and child, both lost to him but never forgotten. It was shaming, but she felt jealous of them: they had been certain of where they stood in Marcus' affections. And Pompey, his old commander, had said that he had thought Marcus would grieve forever for his wife and daughter. Did he perhaps still long for his lost wife, even when he was in her arms? Flavia wondered. He had said that he liked her, and it was clear from how he dealt with her that he found her appealing, but, even though she was now free and his equal, he had not offered her marriage.

He loves you, she told herself, as she went about her work in the following days. But the same nagging question haunted her: If Marcus loved her, why had he never told her? She had told him – she had said the words, 'I love you', on their night together in the forest, when they had made love for the first time. Now when she remembered her face burned with mortification, as she thought of herself confessing feelings that perhaps he did not share. Desire and affection, yes, but love?

Every day that passed in the darkest month of the year brought silence from Marcus. Flavia told the bewildered and disappointed Hadrian that letters were often delayed or even lost, but these logical explanations did not really satisfy her. At night she dreamed of Marcus, of running to him and embracing his strong, handsome body. In the day, she searched for daisies and other flowers to place in small dishes of water in his room: a welcome in case he returned home. She rehearsed what she would say if he came striding into the kitchen, his face glowing from the bright cold of a long ride. Hadrian meanwhile polished Marcus' hunting javelins until they sparkled.

A second week began and ended. The following day, the seventeenth of the month, would see the start of the midwinter festival of the Saturnalia, a time of feasting and revelry.

Flavia had never felt less like celebrating. A new doubt had begun to grow in her mind. She had admitted her secret forgery and her Christian faith to Marcus and perhaps he now no longer trusted her. Had her confessions changed his attitude, or worse his feelings, toward her?

That night Flavia wept, sobbing quietly with her bedding drawn over her head so that she did not disturb the sleeping Hadrian. In the morning Agrippina scolded her for looking pale and skinny, 'like a plucked chicken,' and suggested that Flavia might walk into the city and bring back something special to be prepared ahead, ready for Marcus' return.

'Venison, if you can get a decent piece. You know what I like,' the cook continued, grinding more potion herbs with her mortar and pestle. 'Oh, and Marcus' favourite parsnips. Dates if you can find any, good plump ones. The sacrifice of a suckling pig will have to wait until we have our head of the house back with us again, but you can bring ginger and pepper.'

With Pina's instructions ringing in her mind, Flavia took a basket and set out. She was stopped a few moments later at the villa gate by Otho.

'You go alone to market?' he asked, in strongly-accented Latin. 'Take the boy and dog with you.'

He turned to call to Hadrian and Nero. There had been a fresh fall of snow in the night, blanketing everything. A moving russet blur, Hadrian was tumbling in the garden like an overgrown robin with the leaping terrier beside him almost lost against the backdrop of white. Watching their gleeful play, Flavia begged, 'Let them be. I will not be long.'

Stamping his booted feet, his one concession to the cold, Otho stared down his long nose at her, his single remaining eye as piercing as a thousand. 'Marcus is right. You are too pretty to go out by yourself.'

Flavia laughed outright at this absurd idea, but Otho planted his javelin in the snow and folded his bare arms across his leather-clad chest.

'Do you not know this, even now?' he demanded sharply as she was about to argue. 'I tell you, Flavia, were you not Marcus' girl, I would have had you myself. Why do you think I keep away from you? Little witch.'

'I am sorry,' Flavia stammered, truly sorry and startled by Otho's frankness, but holding her ground as the tall German unclasped his arms and stepped closer.

'Never let it trouble you,' he said. 'He found you first and I see the way you look at him.' He flicked one of her plaits and said gruffly, 'Go! Go quick while the city is quiet and the Saturnalia not yet begun. Go before I change my mind!'

With her mind in a new turmoil, Flavia hurried away.

Cassius, the professional beggar and spy, shivered. It was blisteringly hot in his private bath house, but his present company chilled him through.

'I do not accept that answer!' Lucius Maximus was saying, striking his palms on the surface of the water where he and Cassius were bathing. 'It should be a simple matter to snatch one small blonde slave. You have done it before for me. No pathetic excuses!'

Angered by the man's whining, Cassius spoke the truth for once. 'It is not simple, Decurion. Marcus Brucetus is a most protective master. He looks out for her and he has men and friends – ex-soldiers – to help him. I cannot have my people prowling too close to Brucetus' house or the veterans will spot them and capture them. Then the whole plot could be discovered.'

'Only if the fools talk,' Lucius Maximus snapped. 'I want her now!'

He must have been a sulky child, thought Cassius, glad that the rising steam would hide his expression.

'My men are watching the villa where she lives.' He repeated what he had told Lucius Maximus earlier. 'The instant she steps out alone, we shall make our move.'

'Bring her to me, Cassius. Straight to me.'

'Why does this girl haunt you?' Cassius asked, genuinely puzzled by Maximus' passion. 'Do you think she knows what happened to her mistress?'

'What do I care if she does?' Lucius Maximus replied at once. 'She is a slave! Her knowledge is worthless! Besides, I am Decurion. No one can touch me! No one dare!'

This fellow is drunk on power and self-importance, Cassius realized, with mounting disquiet but no real surprise. He had marked the growing change in Lucius Maximus over the previous months and now he was careful to agree with the man. Whether Maximus was vulnerable or not did not really concern him, as long as the Decurion kept paying him.

'We shall continue to keep watch for her,' he promised.

'Do that, Cassius. I want her.'

Flavia was as quick as she could be, but there were queues everywhere in the food shops and spice and trinket stalls as slaves and even citizens shopped for last minute items for the Saturnalia. It was the first time she had been in the city this close to the festival. In other years, Lady Valeria had given her people small gifts of pickled fish and nuts, but had otherwise ignored the Saturnalia, insisting that her servants remain indoors and serve her, rather than follow the tradition that at the Saturnalia the household slaves for one day at least were waited on by their masters.

'The Saturnalia is a rowdy, vulgar, drunken festival, little more than an orgy,' Lady Valeria had complained. 'I will have no part of it in my house.'

Her words may have been true, but as the morning progressed, Flavia saw little to alarm her. The people in these snowy streets were intent on their money or goods. A few roughly-dressed men were crouched over gaming tables and she passed a group of giggling young slave girls, all waving napkins given to them as presents, but there was no sign of drunkenness or of wild orgies. Many

341

workshops were shuttered and closed and houses the same. There was a distant grumble of noise coming from the theatre, close to the great bathing complex, but no raised voices.

Unsure whether to be glad or disappointed, Flavia swapped her basket from one arm to the other and sped on through the slushy snow. She longed to stay and find some gifts for Gaius and the others – especially for Marcus, her heart whispered – but she still had not enough money of her own. With a sigh, her final purchase haggled for and bought, she turned to make her way home, avoiding the wine shops and taverns and drawing her shawl over her blonde hair each time she crossed a busy street.

She was close to the blank front entrance of the deserted villa where she had taken Marcus to see the secret garden and pool when she heard the sounds of flutes and drums approaching from a narrow, snow-filled alleyway.

'Ow!' She put a hand to her ear, which had just begun to sting. A small apple lay at her feet in the snow and as she stared at it, she realized that it must have been thrown down at her from the upper living quarters over one of the shuttered shops.

'To Saturnalia!' roared a good-natured male voice overhead. More small apples and nuts and then a cluster of sweetmeats rained down on Flavia and others in the street. People scrambled on hands and knees to pick up the fruit and other foods, while the racket of the flutes and drums drew nearer.

Then she spotted them, at the back of the parade. Three beggars, in rags, slinking along the alley. They carried walking sticks and their cloaks were torn but they moved too smoothly for men wracked by pain or ill health. Now that she looked more closely, she thought she recognised the small, skinny one. She had seen him before, walking past the villa, twice, no three times. But he had never called with his begging bowl.

A prickle of alarm, cold as an icicle, shot down the length of Flavia's back. Trusting her instincts, honed by years of slavery, she flattened herself into the nearest shadowy doorway, glad of her inconspicuous brown gown as she veiled her face with one end of the shawl. Scarcely breathing, she waited for this parade to go by.

They were all men. At least a score of brightly-dressed young men, several puffing cheerfully on long flutes or banging on drums and all with the rich, sleek look of Roman aristocrats and the free-born. These were revellers: quite a few clutched jugs of beer or wine which they carelessly drank from. Flavia prayed they would not notice her.

The last stragglers swayed past her hiding

343

place. One, stumbling in the snow with heavy deliberateness, dropped to his knees close to where she was. He did not see her, but his two friends, slithering over the slush and ice to haul him up, spotted the small, wary figure in the shadows and shouted.

'Hey, girl, join us!'

'Let me give you something,' the second leered, making a crude gesture with his hand.

Flavia darted away before the two men trapped her in the doorway.

'Hey, come back!'

'Party time!'

'We have the wine and you are the orgy!'

Backing along the street, Flavia heard an ominous silence descend among the flute players and drummers. Walking as rapidly as she could in a clumsy, sideways fashion, she did not speak, or run. She did not want to provoke them.

From the corner of her eyes, she saw the three beggars echoing her own movements, clearly following her. Who were they?

Under her fear, her mind was still working. If she could only reach the crossroads, she would take the short-cut down the street of the fullers and make for the shrine of the goddess Sulis at the Roman baths. She was Christian, but these men were pagans. Surely they would respect their own sacred place? Surely the goddess would protect her?

None of the other bystanders or shoppers raised a word against the rich, spoilt Romans or these creeping, silent beggars. Flavia knew she was alone and would have to deal with them herself. She thought of Marcus, going into battle, facing down his enemies. He had not turned and run, and she would not.

Cassius blessed his lucky *lares:* the blond was alone and he did not even have to grab her. Lucius Maximus was at the great bath today: all he and his men need to do was to drive her there. He signalled to the other two and they moved in closer.

One step after another, Flavia edged along the twisting, foul-smelling street of the fullers, who today at least were not labouring over their vats of washing.

'Hey, she is leaving us!'

'Going away, the stuck-up—'

Flavia closed her ears and tightened her grip on her basket. She could see the flute players and drummers returning to join their more drunk companions, see them pointing at her, muttering among themselves.

But I am going to make it, she thought desperately, just as the hue and cry began:

'Get her!'

'Run her down!'

'We need no toga girls if we grab her!'

345

'Why pay for pleasure when we can have it for free?'

'Get her!'

Flavia was already running, pelting along the street as if there was no snow underfoot, losing things out of her basket and not caring what they were. She swung into a side-alley, realized that two of those beggars-who-were-not-beggars were already there, and rapidly retreated back into the main street, towards the yowling mob. Panting, her vision beginning to double as she sprinted at the very limit of her speed, she fixed on the temple of the goddess Sulis and fled her leaden-footed, cursing pursers.

'Come here, you–'

Behind her, a coarse hand grabbed at her shawl. She tore it away, escaping again, and passed bare-headed into the temple precinct of the shrine and bathing complex where she collapsed, sobbing but safe, against one of the many smoking altars.

Chapter 17

Gradually, Flavia became aware that the worshippers at the shrine and visitors to the baths were staring at her. Afraid to leave the complex until she was certain that the rowdy and dangerous crowd of pagan revellers had moved on, she limped to her feet. Still breathless, she forced herself to move as one of the temple fortune-tellers, severe and haggard in his ceremonial clothes, bore down on her.

Hurrying away from him, Flavia found herself going toward the baths rather than the shrine. Hoping the goddess would understand, she entered the baths, handing a few coins to one of the attendants.

'Are there any ladies in today?' she asked the yawning youth. If so, she could join the women, or at least linger close to where they were and hopefully deter any more unwanted attention.

'There is a party in the laconicum,' came back the answer, with another yawn. 'You want me to look after your basket?'

'Please.' Flavia handed it across, then hesitated. The laconicum, or hot sweat-room, was where she had had a disastrous encounter with Lucius Maximus. Remembering that, especially after what had just happened in the street, she did not want to be naked: she felt too on edge. 'May I go and see them?'

'Go ahead.' The young attendant crouched with the basket between his scraggy legs as Flavia was already threading along the corridor.

Flavia did not intend to enter the hot room, but as she approached, the door to the laconicum opened and she heard voices. Women and men's voices – but then the attendant had said it was a party, and not a ladies' group.

She hid behind a statue of the god Bacchus holding aloft a bunch of grapes as a laughing man draped in a towel ran along the corridor. Seconds later, she heard splashing as he launched himself into a plunge pool.

Time to go, Flavia thought, but then she heard the man returning and recognised him by his laughter as he dragged open the laconicum door and yelled, 'You should try it, Lucius!'

He added more, provoking new laughter from the party within the room, but Flavia missed what he said amidst her own alarm and the general clamour of the baths.

Please do not let it be Lucius Maximus, she thought, when she saw the small, skinny beggar step briskly past her into the hot room. Moments later, the beggar exited, hefting a small, clinking purse. The door to the hot room remained open and she heard Maximus' drawling voice.

'Yes, I told Marcus Brucetus I would buy the girl-scribe: he was keen to sell. His whole family's in massive debt. They have to do something or go into servitude and while

348

in his mother's case that probably would not be so different, any money is welcome. I received a letter from him this morning, confirming the girl's price.'

Flavia almost cried out, 'That's impossible! I am free! Marcus would not sell me! He would never sell me to you!' Rigid in horror, she watched the door to the laconicum close again amidst laughter and a sound of clinking goblets.

Marcus had sold her?

'No,' Flavia whispered. She could not move, could not breathe for panic.

Marcus selling her to save his family?

Her mind rebelled at the thought while her heart felt to be both bleeding and shrivelling within her. Perhaps he'd had to choose: her freedom or that of his family's. Perhaps Lucius Maximus had offered such a sum that it would clear his family's debt.

'What a choice. What a terrible choice.' She could see him clearly in her mind's eye, white-lipped, his face tormented with guilt and grief. 'My poor love,' Flavia murmured.

'I will go quietly,' she said, bracing an arm against the statue of Bacchus for support. 'I will not run away or cause you any trouble.' Around her the corridor seemed to be moving, its floor-tiles shifting. Nothing was certain any more.

You could never take the place of his wife.

'I didn't want to. I understand that he

loved her. I only wanted him to love me, too, maybe in a different way.' Who am I talking to? Flavia thought. Who am I trying to convince? She brushed her aching eyes and found tears. She wanted to crawl away into a dark cave somewhere.

She would never see Marcus again. They would be parted by fate, a dreadful choice. How could he deny his family? How could she remain free at the expense of his mother and brothers?

She would never see Marcus. Flavia flinched away from the words as if from a burning brand, but they pursued her. She would never speak to Marcus, never touch him, never make him laugh again, never be in his arms. The long years without him loomed up as she pictured herself, slogging through endless days without even a distant sight of him. He would surely return to Rome, to his family.

And he would never talk to her, or call her name, or kiss her.

'I cannot bear it!' Flavia said, tears streaming down her face as the door to the steam-room crashed open and the tall, bulky form of Lucius Maximus filled the doorway. Sinking down into the shadows by the statue, she watched as he poured a brimming goblet of wine down his throat, his free hand toying with a small metal circle. A slave collar, Flavia realized with a shudder.

Hers? Would she have to wear that?

'Marcus, please, no,' she moaned, but it was too late to appeal to Marcus. If Maximus was right, then Marcus had left her behind. He had never loved her as he had loved Drusilla. He had been forced to sell her.

'Christ help me!'

The words broke from her and she shuddered anew, convinced that Lucius Maximus must hear. Instead, the man turned on the threshold.

'Wine!' He bellowed. 'Wine and a fresh towel! It is the Saturnalia and we are here to celebrate!'

A naked, sweating slave hurried to do his bidding. Flavia closed her eyes and bit hard on her lower lip to stifle her sobs. Lucius Maximus disgusted her. Marcus had not troubled to write to her, but he had written to this man, confirming her sale.

No! I cannot believe it, she thought. *I will not believe it.*

Doubt and grief welled in her again. How well did she know Marcus? She knew very little of his family circumstances, only that they were not rich like Lucius Maximus.

Is this how it ends? she wondered dully. Without even a quarrel or misunderstanding? With no harsh words between us? With no goodbye?

Still standing on the threshold, Lucius

Maximus smacked his lips.

'A good vintage, from one of my own vineyards,' he bragged. 'You know of course that I am also exchanging the toga girl Messalina with Brucetus? So he will not be entirely without companionship.'

'That is very generous of you, sweetheart,' lisped an admiring female voice from within the laconicum, a sentiment echoed loyally by several other voices.

Stricken, Flavia could only think of the toga girl's glorious auburn hair, and the way Marcus had stared at it, the way he had flirted with her at the sculptor's workshop. Messalina's pitying face flashed before her eyes and the woman's voice jeered in her head: *Marcus did not mention you anywhere in Dexter's letter. He is like all men.*

'A lush red-head for a little blonde, eh, Lucius?' another crony joked, as Flavia struggled not to cry aloud and give herself away.

'Yes, and I am going to really enjoy taming the brat,' Lucius Maximus returned, and, as Flavia's eyes flew open, he tossed the slave collar in the air and caught it.

Staring at him out of the shadows, she saw him turn again on the threshold and look straight at the statue of the god she was crouching behind.

'I am going to whip that insolent, deviant Christian until she does not know her own name,' he said, smiling.

He knew she was Christian! Marcus must have told him— How else would he know? Cast into absolute despair, Flavia knew that she would never understand this of Marcus: it was a cruel betrayal beyond her reason.

'How could you?' she burst out. 'How could you?'

Lucius Maximus laughed and pointed at her. 'Bring the little fool inside.'

Flavia was seized by two men and dragged into the laconicum before Lucius Maximus and the rest of his party. A glance through her tear-blurred eyes at the towel-draped figures lounging on the open-slatted benches of the sweat room confirmed that she was among enemies. Naked, but with her face still expertly made-up, the haughty actress who had helped Lucius Maximus to trick her before now gave Flavia a wide smile, obviously relishing her fear and distress.

'Close the door,' Lucius Maximus ordered. 'Bring the slave closer.'

Sitting on the bench in the middle of the room with his friends clustered around him, the man was flushed with the dry heat and wine, slurring his words. 'Here we are, my latest acquisition. Pretty, eh?'

Humiliated by the others' laughter and lewd calls, Flavia would not look at Lucius Maximus. Unbidden, a passage of scripture rose in her mind. The Lord is my shepherd. The words lifted the numb darkness around her a little, although she was too bereft to pray.

'Come, girl. Lift your head and acknowledge my triumph,' Lucius Maximus continued, draining another goblet of wine. 'You are mine now and you will find me very different from that interfering old woman Valeria or our less-than-noble tribune. I am well revenged on them, wouldn't you say?'

Something gold and gaudy flashed in front of her face. She jerked back, prevented from moving further by the two men who had brought her into the room. Several of the women tittered.

'Do you not recognise this, slave?' Lucius Maximus taunted, flaunting his arm in front of her. 'This was once Valeria's – it is mine now.'

Flavia blinked, shocked afresh at the sight of the wide, heavy bracelet on the man's wrist. She knew its chunky, ornate gold work and gaudy gemstones, recalled how it had gone missing from Lady Valeria's jewel box, and was appalled.

'You stole it!' she cried. 'It was you!'

'Not me personally, girl,' sneered Lucius Maximus, working his eyes around the room as he waited for his hangers-on to laugh or applaud. 'But I have an eye for quality and

354

when my agent described the piece I knew I would have it. Why not? Valeria was a relative. As a relative, she owed me rich presents.'

'Did she also owe you her life?' Flavia asked sharply, compelled by her own sense of revulsion to speak out.

Maximus said nothing, and she sensed by the sudden silence about her that she had at least surprised his hangers-on. Recalling the man's fearsome pride, she wondered if she might provoke him into a larger, more fatal indiscretion. 'Was my question too difficult for you, Decurion?'

The man's eyes flashed as he dropped the jewel onto the couch beside him and took up his wine cup. 'Who do you think you are talking to?'

'A coward,' Flavia responded, astonished at her own daring but feeling she had nothing to lose. *If Marcus really has sold me to this man I would rather be dead.* 'Someone who killed my mistress but who is not brave enough to admit it.'

'Ha!' Lucius Maximus took another drink.

'If you are as powerful as you claim, Decurion,' Flavia goaded, 'what does it matter what you confess now? Are you not among your friends?'

Lucius Maximus drained a further cup of wine, his greedy eyes never leaving her face.

'Are you afraid, Decurion?'

A muscle in her adversary's glossy, sweating face twitched as he swigged another drink.

'But then, you are not as powerful as the Emperor, who can remove whoever displeases him.'

'Ha, listen to the prattling slave!' Lucius Maximus glanced about his cronies for support.

'Of course you are powerful, darling,' cooed the actress beside him. 'You are our Emperor, here in Aquae Sulis.'

The Decurion puffed out his chest, faced Flavia and laughed.

'So what if I did do what you say?' he demanded. 'Let us agree that I did arrange for the old hag to be put out of her misery. She was going to denounce me for corruption.'

Beside him, the actress softly applauded and Lucius Maximus could not resist telling more.

'She thought it was a pain-relieving potion. A simple swap of one bottle for another, according to my agent.'

'You are drunk,' Flavia whispered, trying to back away. She could not believe what he had just said. Lucius Maximus had just admitted to murder.

Above her, the handsome, bearded face of Lucius Maximus took on a puzzled look. 'Drunk?' he repeated wonderingly. 'Maybe I am, a little. But I can tell you the name of the man I sent to dispose of old Valeria; the same one who fired Marcus Brucetus' study and bedroom.'

There was a stifled gasp that Flavia took to be one of shock, but which the tipsy Lucius Maximus clearly took to be a sign of admiration.

His voice became quicker and harsher. 'The tribune humiliated me in public, and he was asking too many questions about me around this city – *my* city. That fire singed his pride, taught the fellow a much-needed lesson.'

He laughed and straightened on his bench. 'And now there is you. When Cassius came to tell me that they had found you wandering the streets and had driven you straight to the baths, I knew that my Roman gods had defeated your piddling Christian god. I guessed where you would be skulking, like the slave you are. Not so insolent now, are we?'

Lucius Maximus had known all along that she was there. He had known before he'd had her dragged out. He had known as he was speaking to the others in the laconicum, bragging about his having bought her off Marcus Brucetus.

His claim that Marcus had sold her, Flavia thought, standing straighter, facing her oppressor down – should she really believe it?

Marcus had braved the forest and the she-boar for her. Marcus had given her the first flowers she had ever had, the first pretty gowns, the first jewellery. He had saved Hadrian from the misery of this bath-house. He had said that if all Christians were as she was, 'Then they are wholly excellent to me.'

'How dare you stare at me?' Lucius Maximus roared, but Flavia hardly heard him above the rising tumult of her own heart and feelings.

How far dare she trust her lover? To the very ends of the earth.

'I do not believe you,' she said, and then, realising that she had spoken in her own native tongue, she repeated it in Latin, 'I do not believe you!'

A shocked silence descended on the entire room. Flavia unpeeled the hand of the man who was clasping her arm and shook off the other man.

'Let me go!' she said sharply, in a tone Lady Valeria would have been proud of, 'I am a free woman. You have no right to man-handle me!'

Their faces almost comic in bewilderment, the two men looked to Lucius Maximus for new instructions. Using the tactical lessons Marcus had taught her, Flavia pressed her advantage. She stepped free of her captors and walked smartly to the door.

'Stop her!' Lucius Maximus shouted, but everyone seemed frozen. She had wrenched the door open and was actually stepping over the threshold before another of the party reached her from the benches, hauling her roughly back into the room and blocking her way.

Flavia launched herself for a second time at the open door, hoping to charge the wide-eyed Roman.

'To my own free-woman Flavia, greetings from your weary Marcus,' Lucius Maximus said aloud behind her. 'I beg you to reply quickly to this letter, so I may know that you are safe.'

He smirked as she whipped round, dangling Marcus' letter, written on a thin sheet of birch-wood and folded in two, in front of her widening eyes.

'Yes, my insolent Celt, your precious Brucetus has written to you. I lied when I said he had sold you to me, but no matter: you are mine now. I was planning to steal you away from him, but seeing that you have come here to my party and fallen so obligingly into my web, I will take you now.

'And after all,' he continued, 'Your tribune *begged* you to reply and you haven't. This letter is now over a week old. What do you think he will think of your silence?'

Draped in a cloth of the finest linen, the slave collar in one hand and Marcus' letter in the other, Lucius Maximus rose. 'What will you give me for his clumsy words?' he sneered, raising newly-plucked black eye-brows.

'How?'

'How did his scribblings come to me?' Lucius Maximus finished her question. 'By the same route that all interesting correspondence finds its way into my hands. Several of the messengers who carry the imperial mail up and down this appalling country stop off the road at my villa and allow my scribes to see the letters first. My people are careful: no one else knows.'

Flavia goggled at the bland assertion, delivered in front of over a dozen witnesses.

'Of course, your tribune was wrong to use the imperial mail for such a trivial purpose,' Lucius Maximus went on smugly, swaying slightly on his feet. 'I suppose his commander allowed him to place his personal letter among the other dispatches. Using an imperial dispatch rider as one's own letter-man.' Lucius Maximus wagged a finger. 'Rather a crime, I think, but then old Pompey was always a sentimentalist.'

'You divert the Imperial mail and that is how you keep abreast. I did have my suspicions,' Flavia said, with a calm she did not feel. She longed to snatch Marcus' precious letter from the man's thick, manicured fingers, longed to give expression to her relief and joy. He had written to her!

Marcus had written to her. He had not

sold her. Nor had he betrayed her Christian faith, Flavia realized, recalling how she had called aloud outside this very room for help from Jesus. She had thought Lucius Maximus had not heard her, but he had. He had used her outburst against her.

Marcus had written to her and this spiteful, evil man had denied her his letter, allowing the letter to the sculptor Dexter to be delivered. She wondered how drunk Lucius Maximus was and how far his friends would stand up for him. They seemed untroubled enough to watch as he freely confessed to arson and murder, as he re-enslaved and kidnapped a free-woman. Perhaps it was time to raise the stakes, make them realize that they might also be under threat, she thought.

Part of her marvelled at her own cool head. Part of her knew she could think and act because her trust had been restored. Marcus had written to her.

'Tampering with the Emperor's mail is an offence punishable by death,' she said. 'Any who profit from such interference will be severely punished.'

Out of the corner of her eye, she was gratified to notice a few lounging figures shift uncomfortably, but Lucius Maximus appeared amused.

'Do you see anyone come to arrest me?' he countered, turning this way and that in the hot, airless room. 'What do you think?' he

361

asked the room at large.

While people mumbled answers, Flavia flicked her eyes across to the open door, but the man who had pulled her back into the room was still blocking her way. His unswerving support appalled her.

'How can you still help Lucius Maximus?' she asked quietly. 'Here is a man who fired my former master's home, who murdered my mistress! Lady Valeria was a great lady of this city, cut off deliberately, before her time–'

Here was the real reason why her mistress had not written any final letter of farewell, or freed Gaius and her other faithful retainers – she truly had been murdered. Her dreadful suspicions had been correct. As for Lady Valeria being in her best clothes and jewels – why not? Such things gave a woman a lift, as Flavia had learned herself.

'Enough, girl,' said Lucius Maximus with a yawn. 'Your spirit is amusing, but your rantings grow tiresome.'

Fury and horror warred in Flavia so for an instant she could hardly speak. 'You killed her!'

Traces of white spit appeared at the corners of Lucius Maximus' bearded mouth. 'Yes, I had Valeria disposed of because she was becoming a nuisance. A lesson that you should heed, scribe!'

Flavia glared at his reddened face and cold hard eyes. He was a dangerous, drunken brute of a man, someone so used to having his own way that he thought nothing of using corruption and even murder to achieve his ends. She thought of his grotesque killing of Lady Valeria, of his obscene stealing of her jewellery, of his terrorising Dexter and Messalina and no doubt many of the silent, watchful people in this room. No one was laughing or partying or admiring him now, she noticed.

'You disgust me,' she said.

'You little–' Flinging aside Marcus letter, Lucius Maximus tried to grab her by her hair, but Flavia remembered that nasty habit of his from their first encounter in this room. Weaving away as Marcus had shown her in their 'fighting', she ducked out of his reach.

'No one touch her – this one is mine!' Lucius Maximus yelled – an unnecessary order, as none of his party moved. Flavia caught glimpses of their impassive, curiously blank faces as the man came at her again.

He charged, his features contorted with drink and rage, his tall, strapping body barging into the edge of one of the sweat-benches, causing Lucius Maximus to curse but not stop.

'Let him come to you,' Marcus' voice hissed urgently in Flavia's head. 'Then step aside. That is all you need to do.'

No sooner remembered than done. Flavia

jinked away at the last moment and Lucius Maximus blundered into a marble table set against one of the walls. He yelled instinctively as his shoulder and back rested against the hot wall-tiles of the laconicum. He roared and Flavia looked about desperately for something she could use as a shield – one of the wooden slats of the sweat-benches would have made a perfect stabbing weapon, but she had neither the time nor the strength to break one off.

Over Lucius Maximus' black head she noticed a figure on one of the benches beginning to move. Another of Marcus' lessons leapt into her mind.

'In the city, if you are ever attacked by more than one assailant and you cannot get away at once, back into a corner if you can. They will have to rush at you singly then, because they have no more fighting space than you.'

'I will flay you, Christian!'

Lucius Maximus attacked, milling at her with wild arms. Flavia darted into the nearest corner and then dropped and rolled away as he aimed punches at her stomach. Bruised but still free, she scrambled to her feet and withdrew sharply from the range of those murderous fists.

'You will not escape me again!'

Over the sounds of his frenzied breathing and the rapid slap of his sandals on the tiles,

Flavia thought she heard other running feet, outside in the corridor, but that was impossible. To her despair, Flavia realized that only a few seconds must have passed and already he was bearing down on her for the third time.

I am going to lose, she thought, as everything around her seemed to grow slower, clearer. She watched in an almost detached manner as Lucius Maximus slowly drew back the fist that was clutching the slave collar to strike out at her with the metal.

There was a whirl of movement in the doorway and Marcus, her Marcus, stormed in, placing himself as a living shield between her and her drunken attacker. Marcus' sword was at the man's throat and his voice was harder than the steel.

'Blink so much as an eyelid, and you are dead, Lucius Maximus.'

Lucius Maximus' face reddened further as he realized that none of his cronies were going to raise a finger in his defence. 'I am a Roman citizen of noble birth!' he protested. 'You and your filthy Christian are nothing!'

'That is not true of Marcus and Flavia,' said a new voice, 'but I regret that it is certainly true in your case.'

Pompeius Gellius, Marcus' former commander, stepped into the room with several men. Like Marcus, he and his soldiers were fully dressed and armed, and his thin, lively face was as grave as Flavia had ever seen it.

'Pompey, my old friend!' Lucius Maximus blustered, fading as the smaller, older man held up a hand.

'No, Lucius. You are condemned and by your own confession,' he said.

'We could hear your drunken braying all the way out to the anteroom, as soon as we entered the baths,' said Julia Sura, as she stepped through into the laconicum. Trim in a dark green travelling shawl, her glossy brown hair loose for extra warmth and her handsome, square-jawed face lined with the stress of long travel, she gave Flavia a piercing glance and a brief approving nod. 'Good. I see Marcus reached you in time. I knew he would.'

'Arrest Lucius Maximus for corruption and murder,' Pompeius Gellius ordered. 'Do not let any of these others leave, either,' he added, his eyes flashing distaste at the now huddled groups of party-goers.

Within seconds Lucius Maximus was taken into custody. Sagging between three sturdy soldiers, he was rapidly paling, his face slack with disbelief.

Silently, Marcus sheathed his sword and turned to Flavia.

'I am sorry,' he said, his lean, travel-stained features paler even than those of his defeated enemy. 'We have ridden all night. Even Julia—'

'Really, Marcus! I am not made of glass,'

exclaimed Julia Sura.

'But I was so afraid that I would not find you, that I wouldn't reach you–'

He broke off, his blue eyes brooding murder as he glared at the sullen, stumbling figure being hauled past by the soldiers.

'When you were not at the villa, I thought I would go mad. Otho would say I did go mad.'

Marcus came a step closer to her, dripping melting snow from his cloak, one finger tapping at his belt. 'What were you doing getting caught up in that rabble celebrating the Saturnalia? I could not believe it when I heard them wailing in the street: "We've lost the little blonde in the sacred precinct, when we only wanted to worship her." And when one of the temple soothsayers described you, right down to your plaits– Why were not you at home, safe?'

Flavia gasped at the unfairness. However miraculous Marcus' rescue of her, she had never expected his homecoming to begin with an accusation.

'Because we need to eat!' she snapped back. 'You freed me! I can go where I like!'

One of the soldiers muttered, 'Mithras!' but Flavia did not quail. Even as Marcus strode over to her, she loved his grim, glowering face. Why are we quarrelling? she thought. He had ridden all night and had searched frantically for her. After all that had happened, why were they apart?

Marcus shot her a glowering look. 'Leaving that aside for the moment, what about Lucius Maximus? I had my suspicions, which I could not prove, but for how long have you wondered?' he asked, tapping his belt with his fingers.

'Ah!' Flavia found herself breathing out in relief. 'So you were sensible.'

'Sensible?'

'I think Flavia rather feared your passion and your reaction if she shared her thoughts with you on the matter of Lady Valeria's murder, my dear Marcus,' remarked Julia Sura. 'Quite right, too, in my view. Men can be so hot-headed.'

'But you suspected the same thing?' Marcus demanded. 'That Maximus had killed Valeria? Why did you not tell me?'

'I could ask the same of you,' Flavia countered. 'As you said yourself, Marcus, there was no proof.'

'Until you provoked a confession from him!' Marcus growled. 'And by Mithras, you are still provoking.'

The next moment, Flavia found herself imprisoned against her lover's chest, his arms wrapped tight around her and his wide cloak covering her completely.

'I think it is time I re-defined the terms of that freedom,' he said, and he began to kiss her with a savage tenderness that brought

368

tears of sheer relief tumbling from her eyes.

'Marcus, the others!' she protested, when she could speak, but he shook his head, his lips refastening on hers, and brought her even closer, clamping her against the length of his hard, warm body.

'It is over,' he said quietly, when he finally raised his head. With a gentle hand, he wiped her streaming face. 'Come, love. Let us go home.'

Chapter 18

Once in the open air again, Flavia was astounded to discover that it was still day – so much had happened. Struggling with shock and fresh grief over Lady Valeria and dazed with relief at Marcus' return, she found herself briefly longing for peace and sleep.

She and Marcus rode back quietly towards the villa, slipping silently through little straggling groups of drummers and pipers on their way to Saturnalia parties. Pompey and the others had already gone off elsewhere to interrogate Lucius Maximus further.

'Although Pompey already knows a great deal, thanks largely to you,' Marcus said, briefly squeezing her sides with his arms as he managed the horse's reins.

369

'What do you mean?' Flavia murmured. She was riding in front of Marcus with her basket across her knees, part of her marvelling at how high she was off the ground. It was the first time she had ridden Marcus' black stallion and she felt to be floating.

Her initial feelings of shock were giving way to other, more insistent emotions. Marcus had come back to her. He had called her 'love'. In the midst of her pain and confusion over her old mistress, her anger and revulsion that Lady Valeria had indeed been murdered, she was also hopeful.

And it was so good to ride with Marcus, to feel his taut belly pressed tight against the small of her back, his arms cradling her, his thighs rubbing slightly against hers with the smooth gait of the horse. The intimate, sensual contact sent tiny prickles of delight running through her and she could tell, from Marcus' own body and from the close, snug way he held her, that he felt very much the same. *Of course he does,* said Lady Valeria briskly in her mind.

Flavia started, then laughed, as a strong, rather bristly jaw brushed her scalp close to her ear and a very masculine, indulgent voice inquired, 'Did you hear anything of what I just said? That with the open arrest of Lucius Maximus, the stone mason Dexter and others like him may now come forward to be witnesses against the man's corruption?'

370

'Er.' Flavia was glad she was sitting in front of Marcus so he could not see her blush.

He kissed the back of her neck and murmured, 'Your skin gives you away, little Celt.'

Flavia sat up straighter and flicked her plaits to hide her neck. 'I am convinced Lucius Maximus had something to do with this horse,' she announced, trying to change the subject slightly. 'Do you remember, when the harness was wrong?'

'I do, and I am sure you are right. As I was saying,' Marcus continued with a self-satisfied smile, 'It was a line in your letter to Julia Sura that gave Julia and me the idea of tracing and then proving Lucius Maximus' corruption. You wrote: *Lucius Maximus seems to know so much of what goes on in Aquae Sulis and so much of others' financial affairs that I wonder if he spies on people's personal letters. I did find him in Marcus' study, clearly going through papers.* When Julia Sura read that, she thought of the Imperial Mail and told me.'

Flavia rested her head against Marcus' chest, listening to his heart as a delicious scent of freshly-baked bread wafted from somewhere. 'I had forgotten I ever wrote that,' she said.

'Well you did, clever wench, and that set Julia and me plotting. As you know, I had been recalled by Pompey to Eboracum because of state business – which turned out to be missing dispatch letters, and strange inconsistencies in the mail that did come through. Pompey knew something was wrong with the Imperial mail, and he suspected someone in the region of Aquae Sulis – the dubious writing tablets all seemed to have a connection with the city. Of course, Pompey was convinced that it couldn't be Lucius Maximus.'

'Old family. Good breeding,' Flavia muttered.

'Exactly! But Julia Sura was more sceptical. Your letter set her thinking and together she and I set a plot. I wrote to you as I had promised and asked you to write at once in return. When you did not, I knew that you had never received the mail, especially as I had seen your earlier letters. The dispatch rider returned empty-handed.

'I told Pompey, he had the rider questioned and the rider talked. We set out from Eboracum at once – I knew I was not going to be easy until I saw you again, and I didn't want you to worry.'

Marcus' long thighs squeezed hers and Flavia felt a pulse of pleasure shimmer through her body. 'Lucius Maximus claimed you had sold me to him,' she said, when she was sure her voice would be steady.

'The evil, tormenting–' Marcus finished on a curse that almost scalded Flavia's ears.

She could feel the fury rising off him, like a wave of heat. Beneath them the black horse snorted, tossing its head and jangling its harness. She gripped his arm and Marcus turned his head to look at her, kissing her lightly on the mouth to show he wasn't angry with her.

'By all the gods, when I see you and consider what that brute might have done to you had I not found you!' he moaned, kissing her more deeply.

His hands dropped the reins and his arms tightened around her. They kissed on horseback in the middle of Aquae Sulis with a gaggle of free and slave children running past laughing and one even tossing a snowball at them. It fell short but neither of them noticed: they were lost in each other's eyes.

'Flavia, my sweet.' Marcus brushed a flake of snow away from her forehead. 'You are...' More hovered for an instant on his lips and then suddenly his dark eyes clouded and became watchful.

'Marcus, what is it?'

'I– Nothing.' His face was closed, his expression one of sadness, rather than stubbornness.

Watching him, Flavia felt she might burst with pity. Keen to cause him no more grief, she clenched her teeth together, determined not to speak until she had the words right, but equally resolute as to what she should say.

She waited a moment, until she was sure the horse had ambled to a complete stop and had lowered its glossy black head to nuzzle the snowy ground. She took a deep breath and spoke.

'Marcus, I understand that your wife and your daughter will always be first in your heart. That is natural. Drusilla was clearly perfect for you. I don't want you to feel that you cannot talk about them.'

Flavia tried to smile, although she was not sure of the result. 'I hope that I am not so jealous that I make you uncomfortable with your past. After all, I like you to be comfortable, too.'

Her joke fell flat. Her admission seemed to ring in her ears. All she could hear was distant laughter and singing as others celebrated the Saturnalia while she and Marcus seemed frozen.

Then he shook his head. 'I loved them both, yes,' he said quietly. 'Ours was a marriage arranged by our families, but I grew to love them both very much. A gentle, affectionate love, born of honor and respect.'

'Of course.' Flavia felt her eyes fill. She wished she was more noble, that this serpent of jealousy did not sit in the pit of her stomach and sting her.

'But you–'

'It is all right,' Flavia said quickly, praying that she would not cry openly. He needed and wanted her and that would have to be enough. She loved him. She wanted him to be happy. 'We can be free companions,' she said. A recurring fear struck her. 'Unless you are returning to Rome, to your family.'

'My family, yes.' Marcus was silent again.

She was going to lose him after all. Marcus was a Roman tribune. He would be returning to Italy. For a wild moment, Flavia thought of asking to go with him, his free female scribe, but then shrank from the idea of forcing herself on him.

She could taste the salt of tears in her mouth as her hope died. 'I need – I need to get down a moment,' she said, and blundered blindly off the horse, almost falling into the snow.

'Flavia, wait.'

Dropping the basket, she began to run, kicking through loose snow. She did not want him to see her crying; she did not want his homecoming spoilt.

'I need,' she called back over her shoulder but she could think of nothing.

A pounding of feet behind her, much swifter than she could run. He caught her easily and she pummelled him as he turned her. 'Let me go!'

'In a moment, maybe, my free-woman, but you are going to listen.' Marcus grabbed her hands, holding her gently but in an unbreakable grip. 'You need to know something about my family. About my mother.'

She felt a tremor pass through him and grew still. 'What is it?' she asked gently, as she had done before.

He released her hands, standing looking down at her, nervously scratching the blue-black stubble on his chin. 'My mother is like you,' he said finally. 'A Celt. She was my father's slave-housekeeper. He bought her to care for his sons, my half-brothers, when his first wife died. When she became pregnant with me, he married her.

'So you see,' he said harshly, 'I am not a pure Roman. Nor a pure Celt. I am neither.'

'You are both.' Flavia took hold of his clenched fingers and rubbed and kissed them. She could feel the pain and tension in him, see the dark sense of shame staining his tanned, hawkish face. Marcus, whom she had once thought so Roman! She had already guessed as much about his heritage but now that Marcus had admitted it, this was another bond between them. Please let him see it, Flavia prayed.

'No one who truly knows you will ever be anything less than proud and impressed,' she said softly. 'And we may be kin, your mother and I.'

Marcus straightened, staring over her head at some distant point, his blue eyes unseeing. 'My father freed my mother by the terms of his marriage to her. But he was possessive. I always thought him so. He never gave her the choice. He didn't free her first, before he married her.'

He sighed, his tense strong body stiffening further. 'I know my mother would have liked the choice. She told me so. I think she deserved to be given the choice, except my father was too afraid that he would lose her if he freed her first. I know my mother has always regretted that.'

He closed his eyes briefly, reopening them as Flavia said, 'Go on, Marcus. Tell me the rest.'

'That is all there is.' Marcus shook his head. 'I am the half-breed son of a slave. A half-Roman who has never fitted in and who does not want to climb the Imperial ladder any more. I would like to stay here, in Aquae Sulis. Be a father to Hadrian, who reminds me so much of myself at the same age. Learn to farm Lady Valeria's country estate and trade and continue to help the people here who look to me as their patron and protector.'

'Then why not stay?' Flavia whispered.

Her heart seemed to turn right over in her breast at the look of longing he gave her then.

'Because I want more.' He stared at her hands, holding one of his. 'I want my free-woman scribe as my love and true companion. I love you, Flavia. I love you as I loved Drusilla and little Aurelia, with all my heart.'

He touched her face with his free hand. 'I grew to love my wife and child, but you, little water-goddess, you enchanted me at once. Did you not see this? Each time we made love, I thought you would know.'

'You never said,' Flavia stammered, caught somewhere between wonder and jubilation.

'I wanted you to be free first, to be used to being free. I didn't want my love to be a burden, an obligation. I was not sure if you felt the same way as I do – people say "I love you," in the heat of passion. I hoped and trusted that it was more than the newness of love-making on your part, but I was not sure. Only a man like Lucius Maximus would be sure! And I wanted you to know who I was, and I wanted you to have the choice. I still do.'

Marcus knelt in the snow so that their faces were almost level and he had to look up to her. He moved his hand in hers so that her fingers rested on his palm, so that they touched but he was not grasping.

'Will you do me the honor, the great honor of becoming my wife? Will you make me the happiest man of this Saturnalia and for all festivals to come? Will you marry me, Flavia? A half-Roman youngest son with a tiny estate in provincial Britannia and a young adopted son to care for and raise?'

'Yes.' Flavia cast her arms about him, hugging his head on her breast. 'Yes to everything! Yes!'

Snow had begun falling again but Flavia and Marcus, locked in each other's embrace, were aware of nothing outside of themselves.

'I love you, Flavia, my little scribe who taught me that not all desk-people are to be mistrusted.'

'Certainly not!'

'I am so happy.'

'So am I, Marcus. I love you.'

'I love you,' Marcus said again, kissing her and drawing her up with him as he rose to his feet, lifting her high in his arms. 'I love you so much. When can we marry?'

'My choice?' Flavia asked, light-headed with delight.

'Your choice.'

'What about your family?'

'My parents and half-brothers can visit us here. As for their approval of you–' Marcus looked grim for a moment. 'They had better.' His face cleared. 'But they will adore you, as I do. I know they will.'

'Then soon, please.' Flavia felt herself blushing as she wondered if she sounded too eager. 'I would like Julia Sura to be at our wedding, and Pompey. Hadrian, of course, and the others. It can be a double cele-bration!'

'Your freedom and your marriage?' Mar-cus asked quizzically, but Flavia was too happy to care about his teasing.

'Our marriage and Hadrian's adoption as our son,' she answered promptly. She loved the boy and knew Marcus felt the same.

'The first of our many children, eh?'

Flavia nodded, thinking of dark-haired sons and daughters with blue eyes exactly like their father. 'I hope that is soon, too,' she said.

Marcus chuckled and set her back lightly on the horse, grasping the reins to lead the stallion through the streets. He glanced up at her, sitting eagerly forward, her blonde hair threatening to escape its plaits as ever and her lips and cheeks glowing against the whiteness of the snow. He thought of a daughter with her colouring, as fair as little Aurelia had been, and felt no pain, only a flood of happy memories that he would share, and a rising excitement.

'I think our lad Hadrian will have more sisters and brothers to play with,' he said, giving Flavia's left foot a playful tug. 'And as you say, soon.'

'You are sure?'

'Very sure, little Briton! Trust me.'

I do, Flavia thought. Free, proud and happy, she and her husband-to-be turned into another street and joined a throng of merry-makers celebrating the Saturnalia in the snowy, lively city of Aquae Sulis. Their home.

The publishers hope that this book has given you enjoyable reading. Large Print Books are especially designed to be as easy to see and hold as possible. If you wish a complete list of our books please ask at your local library or write directly to:

Magna Large Print Books
Magna House, Long Preston,
Skipton, North Yorkshire.
BD23 4ND

This Large Print Book, for people
who cannot read normal print,
is published under the auspices of

THE ULVERSCROFT FOUNDATION

... we hope you have enjoyed this book.
Please think for a moment about those
who have worse eyesight than you ...
and are unable to even read or enjoy
Large Print without great difficulty.

You can help them by sending a
donation, large or small, to:

**The Ulverscroft Foundation,
1, The Green, Bradgate Road,
Anstey, Leicestershire, LE7 7FU,
England.**
or request a copy of our brochure for
more details.

The Foundation will use all donations
to assist those people who are visually
impaired and need special attention
with medical research, diagnosis
and treatment.

Thank you very much for your help.